ALICE IN LA LA LAND

"What happens next?" Whistler asked after the drinks had come.

"God knows. If this was the opening round of my divorce, I'm not sure I can make the distance." Nell went into her skinny envelope purse and pulled out the inventory. "Want to see?"

"I heard some of it."

"Isn't it something what a funny man accumulates?"

"Do you expect him to stand still for you taking half of all that, and whatever else I didn't get to hear?"

"I've got him by the balls and they know it," she said. There was something not so likeable about the way she said it.

She sucked up the last drops of sweetness.

"You finished?" she asked. "Maybe we should get going, then. I've got a lot to do before tonight. I plan to knock them right on their asses."

ALICE IN LA-LA LAND

ROBERT CAMPBELL

A Mysterious Press Book published by
Arrow Books Limited
62-65 Chandos Place, London WC2N 4NW

An imprint of Century Hutchinson Limited

London Melbourne Sydney Auckland
Johannesburg and agencies throughout
the world

First published 1987 by Poseidon Press, a division of
Simon & Schuster Inc., USA.
First published in Great Britain in 1988 by
Mysterious Press/Century Publishing

Mysterious Press paperback edition published 1989

Printed and bound in Great Britain by
Anchor Press Limited, Tiptree, Essex

ISBN 0 09 958180 9

For my brother, Bill

"PRETTY SOON YOU WON'T HAVE TO BOTHER LIVING YOUR LIFE. ALL YOU'LL HAVE TO DO IS BUY THE MOVIE."

—Bosco Silverlake

ONE

THE CLUB ARMENTIÈRES squatted in a short alley the locals never used after dark. There were too many chances they didn't want to take. Chances they might see some twangie boy down on his knees doing a sailor up from San Pedro. Chances they might be sodomized with a broken beer bottle like old Mr. Sheckel, who'd once been so foolish as to take the shortcut after a double feature at the neighborhood theater on Sunset Boulevard. Chances of stumbling over a body with its entrails dragging on the old trolley tracks rusting away in the middle of the dirt and weeds and garbage.

Just blocks away, on the four corners of Hollywood Boulevard and Vine Street, along the whore's stroll, there were men and women, boys and girls, who could tell true stories as bad or worse.

La-La Land had grown old enough to have more than one cancerous wound eating at its bones. More than one boulevard along which whores, catamites, twangie boys, and transsexuals paraded. Skid rows populated by the homeless. Tenderloins strewn with winos sucking on a bottle in a bag and young dopers on the nod.

But the stroll around the four corners of Hollywood and Vine was prime jungle.

The neighborhood around the Club Armentières was almost safe.

The outside of the club was painted in Day-Glo colors like

something taken from the set of a Paris street in some old-time musical. The name was spelled out in neon above the door, and again in the stained glass of the upper half. On a rainy night people paused before stepping inside, looking up and down the alley as if hoping to see Gene Kelly come splashing through the puddles.

The rotting roadbed sometimes seemed to shriek when someone stepped on the tracks, as though the ghost of an old Red Car was booming along from Santa Monica just around the curve where the nameless alley spilled into Hawthorne Avenue from behind a man-high patch of weeds.

Long, long ago, when the apartment houses along Vista and Gardner had been new, the club had been a tailor shop, then a flower stall where you could buy a cellophane packet of green weed that, when properly dried, crumpled, and rolled, made a dreamy smoke. Back then, when actors in belted polo coats drove their doxies up to Santa Barbara in white open cars.

After that it had been a two-bed whorehouse in back and a coffeehouse in front where bad poets read bad verse to the young immigrants from Wisconsin, Ohio, and New Jersey who came south every year shortly before the snow flew, beating the migrating birds by a week or two.

Now it was a theme club for the gay trade that was losing its World War I atmosphere because some customers wanted to wear biker leathers and some wanted to wear leather like cops. There were also a few Nazis and a handful of circus performers, aerialists in tights and lion tamers in imitation leopard.

When their own clubs had closed down for lack of trade they'd gravitated to the Club Armentières, where they could continue playing dress up. They were resented but tolerated by the World War I groupies. Their presence spoiled the illusion, but without them the little club in the alley would probably have gone under, too.

Inside, the music was vintage 1917, the records scratched and blurred like fingernails scraping away at old velvet. The atmosphere was smoky, smelling strongly of Turkish tobaccos and vin ordinaire. Posters printed in the two decades that straddled the turn of the century offered nude shows at the Windmill in London, Pujol the farting virtuoso at a club in Paris.

The proprietor was a florid Latin, mustached, jovial, heavy armed, fat bellied. He liked to lean his hands on the zinc bar, his head resting between his hunched shoulders, a moving picture patron in a fake Montparnasse long since dead and buried.

His "wife," Esme, dressed in black bombazine with white ruching at the throat, which concealed a prominent Adam's apple but not a shadowed jaw, a large cameo pinned between the swell produced by heavy padding and clever straps, perched on a stool in front of an old wooden bistro cash drawer, collecting for meals and drinks and smiling beneath the shadow of a mustache, scarlet lipstick all askew.

The name of the establishment was spelled out in pink neon above the bar at the proprietor's back in case you hadn't caught the gag outside the door, which had to do with that old World War I song that went "Mademoiselle from Armentières, parlez-vous."

A small group of romantics played at being other men from another time, lounging in their uniforms beneath patriotic posters of wounded heroes whose blood had faded to mauve.

Men in uniform sat at small, round tables. French, English, Belgian, and American. There was even a Russian cavalryman, looking like Douglas Fairbanks, Jr., a karakul lamb tunic draped over one shoulder.

They sat with their heads close together, laughed with their arms around one another. A few sang along with the record when there was a singer and words to the song.

A French officer kissed a British sailor on the mouth.

A slender flying officer, wearing the insignia of the Lafayette Escadrille, blushed and turned his head away. He ran a delicate finger along the pencil-thin mustache above his lip, then ran his hand along the shape of his skull, smoothing back a cap of hair the color and sheen of patent leather. He took a dull silver case from the breast pocket of his tunic and chose a cigarette.

The French officer and the British tar didn't come up for air.

"Disgusting the way some of these twats flaunt it, ain't it?" a tough at the next table said. He was wearing a studded leather jacket. He snapped a wooden match alight with his thumbnail and held it for the young airman, who hesitated as though about to refuse, then accepted the courtesy in a carefully neutral way.

"They've got a perfect right, I suppose," the airman said.

"I wasn't trying to put them down. Just making a point, don't you know?"

"No, I don't."

"Don't what?"

"Don't know what you're talking about."

"Well, I'm just saying . . ."

"Don't *want* to know what you're talking about."

The tough's bulldog face screwed up with an effort at conciliation. "Hey, I insult a friend of yours or somethin', tell me about it. Just give me the word."

"The word is 'go away.' "

The cycler's eyes went flat. "Fucking faggot," he said, but turned around to suck on his beer, casting hard looks around the room in case anyone had been witness to his rejection.

The airman stubbed out his cigarette.

He thought of the girl he'd met a few days before. A girl named Jenny, a not-so-innocent from Atlanta, a Southern magnolia who probably had a pussy that tasted of limes. She'd asked to see the places of the city where all the strange things went on. She probably meant some six-foot transvestite squeezed into mesh stockings and shoes with spaghetti straps, a couple of curly-headed nolas swapping tongues, or a pair of Sapphites doing the same. Commonplace freaks. Small perversions.

Strange was in the head. If he revealed the truly strange, wouldn't she just run away? Didn't they all just run away?

The hero of the Lafayette Escadrille got up and went over to the counter where Esme sat to pay his bill.

"Your first time with us, Lieutenant?"

"You were recommended by someone I met in New York."

"Well, that is flattering."

"Your fame is spreading."

"Two Napoleon brandies, six dollars and five cents, including service and tax," Esme said.

"Twenty-centime *marc*," the airman corrected. "There's no genuine Napoleon to be had in this place."

Esme looked hurt. "Well, you know it's all just a game, dear. But why spoil it?"

The airman put down six dollars and a dime. "Two Napoleons," he said and waited for his nickel.

Esme pointed to a bowl of cellophane-wrapped candies on the counter. "Will you take your change in a sweet?"

The airman hesitated, then chose one.

"Don't forget to read the limerick," Esme said.

He unwrapped the candy and popped it into his mouth. He glanced at the tough and smiled. He retrieved his trench coat from the cloakroom, reaching across the counter because there was no attendant to fetch it for him. After he put it on, he took a white silk scarf from the pocket and draped it over his shoulders. He read the verse on the candy wrapper, put it into his pocket, and left the club that smelled of water paint and glue. Out of a fake world into a fake world.

He didn't see the tough with the bulldog's face hurry out behind him, but he knew he'd be there.

It was cold in the alley. The trapped air gathered up a deathly chill from the worn gravel, dead weeds, and ghostly trolley tracks. The weeds were stirred by a sudden gust of warm wind that bore the curious tang of the desert, warning that the Santa Anas were about to blow. The sounds of traffic, though not very far away, were muted, strained through layers of time. The scene was a vision painted on cheesecloth. The airman walked out to the middle of the alley and stood between the tracks.

He heard the kissing sound made by lewdly puckered lips but didn't turn around.

He didn't turn around even when he heard the crunch of boots on the gravel, or felt the heavy body of the bulldog creature filling the space at his back, or even when the sodomite spoke.

"You're a birdie and I'm going to have your ass."

The airman didn't move, just stood there with his hands in the pockets of his trench coat as though thinking about the offer.

"You wanted me to come on heavy. I could tell that," the bulldog said. "So here comes heavy."

The airman waited. He waited to feel the hand on his shoulder before he spun around.

The beast took the knife in the belly just beneath his belt buckle. A small wind burst out of his mouth. The airman tried to hold him up by grabbing the flaps of his leather jacket with one hand, but his hand was too small to get a grip and he wasn't strong enough to keep the dying man from falling.

He let go and allowed his writhing victim to flop onto the tracks.

Taking a small camera from his pocket, he pushed the button for the pop-up flash, waited thirty seconds for the "ready" light to glow, then snapped off two quick shots of the body.

TWO

THE SANTA ANA winds were blowing in from the valley through the passes, sweeping up the pulverized dog droppings, gum wrappers, old newspapers, and bleached confetti, whirling the mess down along the gutters toward yesterday. The stroll at the four corners of Hollywood and Vine was doing business, drugs and booze and flesh.

A private license everybody called Whistler sat in a booth next to the window of Gentry's coffee shop, watching the citizens of La-La Land.

A one-armed counterman, Bosco Silverlake, slid into the booth beside him, put down a copy of *The Sound of the One Hand Clapping*, and stared out the window, too. "Whattaya lookin' at?"

"For. Looking *for*. A marvel. A miracle. It doesn't have to be a big miracle. A small one will do."

"Like what?"

"Like seeing a big new car with Ohio plates come driving up in front of that skinny little ten-year-old chicken selling his tender ass for a night's bed and board, and instead of a chicken hawk flagging him inside with a twenty-dollar bill, his old mother, wrapped in furs and flashing newly capped teeth, comes rushing out, gives him a hug, and says, 'Come home with me, sonny boy, I shot your cruel stepfather with your dead daddy's army forty-five and recovered the family farm upon which we have found gold and oil.'"

"That'd be a big miracle."

Whistler nodded, frowning at the difficulty of measuring miracles, since miracles, by their very nature, are outside the ordinary scheme of things. "So I'll settle if that twangie boy in the heliotrope shirt grows a beard and starts singing bass, or that—"

"That's no twangie boy."

"What?"

"That there is not a fairy dancin' on one toe. That there is Roberta Duckweiler, otherwise known as Bobby Ducky ever since she decided to have a cutter fashion her a piccolo and a pair of castanets. A tragic case."

"Tell me everything."

"When he was a she, her taste ran to girls, and more than that, she knew for certain that she was a man trapped in a woman's body. She longed for the right equipment and went out looking for the means to acquire them. Not only the necessary cash, which was considerable, but the surgeon who would undertake the job. When one was found, Dr. Helvitian, who has an office in Beverly Hills and another in Palm Springs, the operations, of which there would be several, began. Roberta had a hysterectomy, and a pedicle flap was taken from the abdomen. The penis the doc made for her was undersized and could not achieve erection. Bobby was without a scrotum; he had difficulty taking a pee; and for a time there it was even in danger of falling off."

"How do you know all this?"

"At certain times that unhappy person has confided everything to me. It's one of the sadder stories on the street. And if things weren't sad enough, after it was over, he discovered girls were no longer attractive to him. Now he dresses in purple satin blouses and wears lace underwear, selling himself to old queens and giving his earnings away to toughs in sailor pants."

"He's into perversity," Whistler said.

"In the stock market they call such a person a contrarian."

"How did we get to finance when we were discussing miracles?"

"As the Zen master Hakuin once remarked, 'A long silence may be a meditation but a yen is a yen.' "

"Christ, the things you fill your head with from those books."

Bosco grinned into his armpit, pleased to have irritated Whistler once again.

"What else do you know?"

"I know that nuns don't really shave their heads and there's always one day less to Christmas than you think there is. What do you know?"

"I know that gonifs love their cats and there's no such thing as a whore with a heart of gold."

"Dogs sometimes eat their own vomit."

"You win."

Just then a whore in string shorts that ran up her crack and framed her ass cheeks tottered across the boulevard against the light. The driver of a Mercedes, cruising the block and having his eyes elsewhere, was about to give her a free trip to the moon when Sam Bagley, the corner's prime grifter, gave a yell. The hooker jumped straight up and landed three feet closer to the curb, the fender of the Mercedes missing her . . .

". . . by a red pussy hair," Bosco said.

"What?"

"That Benzo missed her ass by a red pussy hair."

"Why red?"

"Don't you know, it's the finest."

The whore stood on the sidewalk right there in front of the plate-glass window and cursed the disappearing car. Doing an act. Getting off on the attention she was attracting from the street freaks tuning in on her action. Then she turned around and they could see the shocked look of fear in her eyes, the paleness of her bloodless face beneath the mask of paint, the trembling of her slick body. She'd come close to injury or death and she knew it. Then she broke the spell the fear of death had on her and, tossing up her hand, splaying her red-tipped fingers, she waved a careless greeting to her admirers.

"Look, she feels special. She's a somebody," Whistler said.

"I had a gazoony tell me once," Bosco said, "he'd been sitting in a coffee shop in London one afternoon a day before an IRA bomb blew up, killing five people and injuring twelve."

"So what?"

"Just what I said to him. 'So what?' And he said, 'Don't you get it? I just missed getting killed by one stinkin' day. Twenty-four little hours.' "

"What did you say?"

"I sang him the rest of the lyric. I wasn't impressed. But I thought about it. And you know what?"

"Don't make me say 'What?'"

"I learned that people run around looking for coincidences. They hunt for evidence of luck, good or bad. They want to believe their lives are out of their hands, so they're not to blame for anything that happens to them. But it's very hard to believe in luck. A person needs fresh evidence of it all the time."

Whistler said he didn't believe in luck, good or bad. There were no coincidences. Everything was cause and effect. Everything connected. You only had to look and see. Somewhere it was all written down.

That's what he said, but still he sat in Gentry's night after night, staring out at the heart of La-La Land, waiting for a miracle, large or small.

Bosco smiled a secret smile and said, "You wanted a miracle, you got a miracle. A hooker's life was saved by divine intervention."

"It'll have to do."

"If one miracle ain't enough, here comes another."

A woman, tailored and turned out like a foreign marque, with a slit cut so high in her calf-length skirt that it showed a flash of Bible sin, was crossing the street as though following the trail the whore had blazed. There wasn't a car on the boulevard would have dared hit her. In spite of the heat, furs trailed and swirled behind and around her like scarves, bringing memories of the thirties. A felt hat, the brim turned down to hide an eye, covered half the glory of her red hair. The other eye appreciated the effect she was making, an alien queen among the savages. She made a beeline for Gentry's and was through the door before a single one of the hustlers could get a notion to pat her ass or pucker up to kiss her home.

Bosco left the booth in a hurry and walked down the tiled corridor between booths and counter to the cash register, where he took his seat on the stool and waited to be used.

When she conveyed her request to him, she leaned her head in close. Anyone watching might have thought she was going to honor Bosco with a kiss. She touched his hand instead and smiled a hard-edged smile, casually noting he had only one hand, then stepped along the aisle to the place where Whistler sat with his jawbone rusted open and about to give way.

"Are you Whistler?" she asked, leaning over and kissing him on the side of his mouth.

"If I wasn't I would be now," he said.

She slid into the booth facing him. "That was from a friend."

"What's your friend's name?"

"Mary Beth Jones."

"I don't know any Mary Beth Jones."

"Well, she recommended you all the same."

"For what?"

"I need a bodyguard."

"I never scared anybody."

"My friend says she's seen you scramble and you do okay. She also says you're more smart than silly. My name's Eleanora Twelvetrees. If you decide to work for me you can call me Nell."

"There was an old-time actress named Helen Twelvetrees."

"No relation. My name was Reinbeck. I got Twelvetrees with the marriage."

"Not Roger Twelvetrees?"

"No grass grows on you, does it? You got it. Mr. Midnight America, himself."

"He must have security coming out his . . ." Whistler stuttered to a stop.

"Asshole. You were going to say asshole." She smiled softly, making the rude word an elegant observation.

"Ears. I was going to say ears," Whistler said.

She laughed. "Either way, his friends aren't my friends anymore."

"How come?"

"I'm divorcing him and he doesn't like the joke."

"What joke's that?"

"What I'm going to take away with me."

"So you think he'll try to persuade you to give divorce another thought?"

"No. I think he'll try to have me killed."

In the trunk of the wine-red BMW 633CSi was a flat aluminum camera case containing two cameras, a palm-sized auto focus and another, fancier one with motor drive, flash, and several lenses. The bottom of the case was false and contained several cheap switchblade knives, two long-barreled .22 target pistols, a breakaway rifle with a 20X scope, and several boxes of ammunition.

There was a matching suitcase in which was kept two changes

of clothes, one suitable for a casually dressy occasion and one in black with the proper shoes for prowling.

Now he was dressed in a lightweight linen suit, white silk shirt with an unknotted tie draped under the collar, white silk socks with a tan clock, and slender Italian shoes. The uniform of the flying officer of the Lafayette Escadrille was in the suitcase in the trunk.

His hands, small and delicate, the nails well-kept, lay on the wheel like a collection of ivory sticks. They fascinated the young woman who sat beside him as they drove along Wilshire Boulevard.

"You know, Connor, you never told me what you do?"

"I take pictures."

That seemed to please her. "You one of them papawhatzis that hang out aroun' the nightclubs an' the restaurants an' take pictures of the stars?"

"No, I'm not one of them."

She lost interest and turned to look out the window. "Is this all we're gonna do?"

"There's a place called the Little Club I think you'll like. They have a piano bar."

"I want to tell you somethin', we got places called the Little Club with piano bars in Atlanta," she said.

"So what would you like to do?"

"I don' know. I want to see somethin' different. Why don' we drive down that street where all the hookers and the faggot whores hang out?"

"Have you got a taste for the low life, Jenny?"

She laughed. "High life, low life, whatever, Mr. Spinneran." She bent over, her black hair falling forward like the wings of a black bird, and beat her fists on her knees, laughing and shaking her head. There was no other way for her to say how much she wanted to bite off a chunk of life even if she didn't know exactly how big a piece she could chew.

He laughed, too, but it was as though laughing took a special effort of will and concentration. At the next crossing he turned right and headed toward Hollywood Boulevard.

It was surprising how many times Whistler had heard people say they were afraid someone was trying to kill them. Sometimes from people so scared they could hardly pick up a glass of water

without spilling it on the way to their mouths, sometimes from
people looking over their shoulders every minute and a half,
sometimes from gazoonies laughing while they said it, plainly
nuts, but no less anxiously convinced that death waited for them
just around the corner.

On the other hand, it wasn't so surprising how seldom anyone
actually was under the knife or gun, but who wanted to take the
chance that somebody was seeing ghosts or imagining things?

"What makes you think your husband's out to kill you?"

"I've been threatening divorce for nearly a year."

"How long have you been married?"

"Five."

"Not much of a run."

"It didn't take very long for Roger to let the real cat out of the
bag. Five years is a long time to live with a certifiable prick."

Isaac Canaan, the old kiddie vice cop, came through the door
and walked down the aisle. The cultured way she dropped the
word and the drama of her style caught his ear and eye, and
made him miss a stride. Whistler dropped his head. Canaan gave
it back, then walked on, shaking his head as though seeing such
a classy beauty sitting there with Whistler was all the proof he
needed for the certainty of miracles.

"Wives threaten divorce all the time, and the other way
around," Whistler said.

"I know that and so did Roger. He thought it was just another
song discontented women like to sing. But I finally consulted a
lawyer a month ago and moved out of the house a week ago, the
same day Roger got my lawyer's letter."

"Has he threatened you?"

"Roger looks like a Norman Rockwell schoolteacher, acts like
a horny high school boy, and has the morals of a devil worshiper.
Ask him to tell you his war stories some time."

"War stories?"

"He was in the army in sixty-two. A year later he was a training
advisor in Viet Nam. A specialist."

"What kind of specialist?"

"Sometimes he said he was an interrogator with Field Intelli-
gence. Sometimes he said he was in the Veterinary Corps."

"What's that supposed to mean?"

"He was making jokes. He said he turned men into mules."

"How's that?"

"He bragged about how he could measure a charge of plastic so close that when it was strapped to a man's sexual organs and detonated, the poor bastard lost his manhood and still lived to regret it."

Whistler winced.

"That should give you an idea," Nell said.

"How specific was the threat?" Whistler asked, still looking for an answer to the question.

"He said he'd see me with my guts spilled on the floor before he'd let me walk off with a dime."

Whistler nodded, looked over Nell's shoulder, and nodded again.

Danny Cortez, all dressed up in purple pants and a satin shirt like some Chicano pimp, gave Whistler one eye and Nell the other.

"Ho, Whistler," he said, leaning on his outstretched arms, hands planted on the table, looking at Nell full in the face as though Whistler wasn't even there.

Nell narrowed her eyes. Whistler could see the interest and didn't wonder why. Cortez had that effect.

His skin was polished kid leather, his eyes chips of obsidian, glittering like ancient stones behind Mongol lids and high cheekbones. He looked like a Mescalero Apache out on the hunt.

"Ho, Danny, yourself," Whistler said. "Who you murdered lately?"

"Some leather jacket lost his belly button up to the Club Armentières. I just seen him put in a body bag and carted away."

"Lover's quarrel?"

Cortez looked at Whistler. "I don't think so. The lady of the house—"

"Esme?"

"Yeah, Esme, said that this hard type tried to pick up a shirley with a Valentino hairdo wearing the uniform of a World War One flyer and got turned down and put down. It maybe was a quarrel, but they weren't lovers. But, who the hell knows? They like to play games. Where's your manners, Whistler?"

"Eleanora Twelvetrees, Detective Sergeant Daniel Cortez, Homicide," Whistler said.

Nell smiled, giving Cortez tooth for tooth.

"Danny," he said.

"Nell."

"Roger Twelvetrees your husband?"

"At the moment."

"I know your husband."

"Do you?"

"Well, I don't know him, but I knew him. Not real well, but I met him a couple of times. About five years ago the last time. Before that, maybe six, seven years, I saw him around plenty."

"I married Roger five years ago."

"That explains why I didn't see him around after that. You know him a long time before you got married?"

"Hey, Danny, is Mrs. Twelvetrees a witness or a suspect?" Whistler asked, speculating about the electric river flowing between the homicide detective and the pretty woman, prickly with the suspicion that they were working hard being strangers.

"I met him in May, we did it in August," Nell said.

Cortez smiled again. "Whirlwind romance. I've heard of them. He never mentioned my name?"

"Never."

"Fame is fleeting, Danny," Whistler said.

Cortez showed his teeth again. He had a hundred ways of smiling, each smile saying something different. "Yeah," he said, "how quick they forget."

"I think you'd be a hard man to forget, Detective," Nell said.

Cortez changed his smile, buying into that good news. "When you see your husband, you tell him you bumped into Danny Cortez. Just for fun, tell him that."

"I'm divorcing him. We won't be making much small talk."

"Well, just in case, you mention it. See what he says." Cortez smiled another smile, a sweet smile. "You're a very pretty woman, Mrs. Twelvetrees. Take care of yourself down around here."

"I've got Whistler to watch out for me," she said, lifting the end of the sentence, asking Whistler the question again.

Whistler didn't like it. She'd done a little number right in front of him. Little flirtation. Little private conversation. Closing him out. Implying intimate possibilities for the man who was brave enough to be a player, putting Whistler on notice that she was soon to be free-lancing, might already be on the prowl. Laying it out that he could be the man she was looking to for help, protection, and maybe comfort. She'd worked him, making him want to say yes to her proposition just to twist Danny's nose.

"Canaan's back there in a booth," Whistler told him.

"I see him," Cortez said, still watching Nell. "You ever need me, Nell, Whistler knows where to find me." He glided off.

"He tried it on right in front of me," Whistler said, making a big show of astonishment.

"He's something, isn't he?" Nell said, laughing.

"A killer more ways than one."

"A truly dangerous man. You want to know something? He's got eyes like Roger's."

"I never noticed Twelvetrees looked like an Indian."

"He looks like a farmer. I should have said there's something the same behind the eyes."

"You like the type?"

Nell looked at Whistler with her head cocked to one side as though wondering if he were truly jealous on such short notice.

"I like your type, Whistler. Comfortable. Dependable."

"Oh, God, I hate when women say that about me." He was only half kidding.

"Can I depend on you?"

"I think you'd be wasting your money. There are operatives in pink shirts and ice cream suits driving Mercedes and Porsches working for big agencies. Agencies with ex-contenders and ex-linebackers from the Rams on their rosters. Any one of them could do for you better than I could do for you."

"Any one of them is into the size of the fee. And the size of the fee Roger would pay them not to protect me is a lot bigger than the size of the fee I can pay someone to do so."

The Santa Ana winds gusted. The plate-glass window shivered and hummed a little song.

"I don't work for free," Whistler said.

"I didn't say I was broke. What's your retainer?"

"Five hundred dollars minimum against two-fifty a day and expenses."

She went into her purse and came out with a roll of bills. She counted off five C-notes and laid them on the Formica.

"For Christ's sake, don't go flashing that kind of money around a place like this," he whispered fiercely, putting his hand over the exposed money and nodding with his chin toward the roll in her hand.

Nell unfolded and fanned out the rest of the bundle. It was mostly fives and tens, maybe adding up to another hundred, two hundred bucks at most. "You take the five, all I've got left is a flash roll."

"That's enough for some gazoony out on the pavement to cut your throat and drink your blood," Whistler said.

"You've got a colorful way of putting things."

"But true. Now put it away."

"All of it?"

Whistler lifted his palm and glanced at the five Cs. They were new bills, clean as a young girl's hair, pure as a virgin's kiss. They hadn't been in circulation long enough to have any sins clinging to them.

"You're still hesitating, Whistler. What is it now?"

"It seems like every time I get involved with a woman as pretty as you I get into more trouble than I really need."

"That's the sweetest thing a man's said to me in a long time," Nell said. "We'll worry about that bridge if we ever come to it."

Whistler still didn't pick up the money.

"We'll do this," she said. "I've got a first meeting with Roger and the lawyers tomorrow. You stay with me until after the meeting. I'll see how it goes, how I feel afterward. Maybe he's just trying to intimidate me. Let me see how it feels. But tonight I'm very nervous and I could use someone to hold my hand." She smiled and raised a finger. "That's just a way of speaking. So pick up the five hundred. If, after the meeting, we decide I don't need a bodyguard, you can give half back and keep the other half for your time and trouble."

"I think you want to flash a hired gun," Whistler said.

"All right, so I want to show the bastard I'm not without resources. What's wrong with that?"

"I don't carry a gun. I leave it home in a flowerpot."

"Well, at least I can show him I've got a friend."

She peeled off five dollars and tossed it down before popping the roll back into her purse. "That should cover the coffee and . . ."

She slid out of the booth and got to her feet. "I'm using a friend's house in Brentwood while she's away. You'll have the

room right next to mine. You want to go to your place first to get
some pajamas, or do you sleep in the raw?"

Whistler knew that Bosco, Cortez, and Canaan were watching.
And he knew that Canaan had ears like a fox. Her last remark was
a little something they'd talk about, and somehow the conclu-
sions they might draw made him feel good. He got up, took Nell's
elbow, and gave Bosco a wave as he followed the Rolls-Royce
beauty out the door.

Out on the sidewalk, he said, "Your car or mine?"

"I didn't drive. I came in a cab."

"My car's out back," he said, and turned toward the corner.
She took a step and tucked her hand into the crook of his arm.
She had long legs. Within a step or two she was matching him
stride for stride, her thigh against his thigh, leaning against him
slightly, letting him feel the gentle pressure of her breast, stealing
his heart away.

The red BMW 633CSi was making its seventh circuit of the
stroll. Some of the whores were already speculating about just
what the blond, effeminate-looking young man and the milk-
faced, black-haired young woman were shopping for. Some said
they were just tourists, some said they wanted a child of ten to
pass between them hand to hand, some said they were into
flagellation and were looking for Donna Napoli, who was elsewhere with her whips and chains tonight, and some said they
were looking for genuine Siamese twins, a rare item even among
the freaks of La-La Land.

"Oh, there she goes," a black hooker with a silver wig
exclaimed, "making like a submarine. That blond faggot has
heated up his baby at our expense and, even as I speak, she's
copping his thing."

Jenny had ducked down in the seat so fast her skirt rode
halfway up her thighs. "There she is. There's the bitch," she
whispered fiercely, as though her normal voice could be heard
outside the car amid the roar and clatter.

"What bitch?"

"My stepmother. Soon to be not."

"Where?"

"Crossin' the street, on the arm of some ragbag. She's wearin'
a hat and furs."

"I see them."

"Oh, what I wouldn' give to know what she was up to with that man. And what wouldn' my daddy give."

"What would he give?"

"Plenty."

Spinneran turned the corner and went around the block in time to see Whistler and Nell approaching Gentry's parking lot.

Spinneran pulled up to the curb, reached across Jenny, and opened the door. "Have you got money for a cab?"

"What do you think you're doin'?"

"I'm going to make your wish come true."

"You're not gonna leave me on the street?"

"I can't take you with me. You want to know what's going on, you'll have to make up your mind in a hurry." He reached into his pocket, took out a money clip, and peeled off two twenties. "Put this in your bra, and don't show it until you're in the cab."

She still hesitated.

"Well!" he said sharply.

She took the money and got out of the car. "You call me when you find out somethin', you hear?"

Whistler and Nell went into the parking lot. The sounds of the boulevard had died away as though someone had turned down the volume. The Mazda and neon glare of a hundred signs had faded behind them. Only the lights above the parking lot spilled yellow pools like new beer along the blacktop and among the automobiles.

They reached Whistler's beat-up Chevy coupe. He opened the passenger door and handed Nell inside. The car smelled of stale popcorn and old running shoes. She tucked her skirt around her knees as though he'd handed her into a limo and they were going to a prom.

Whistler remembered a night when he'd worn a white dinner jacket.

THREE

WHISTLER'S HOUSE WAS a rackety bundle of sticks and glass built with only twenty feet on solid ground, the rest was on stilts overlooking the long drop down to Iris Terrace, which hugged the hillside above Cahuenga Boulevard and its river of automobiles.

He parked the Chevy and started around to open the door for Nell, but she was already out and standing under the jacaranda tree.

"You don't have to do the Sir Walter Raleigh bit for me, Whistler. You're not a chauffeur."

"I can't help it. You've got a way about you."

"I know. I'll keep it in check." She let him lead the way down the path to his front door. "You renting or do you own this house?"

"I own it, otherwise I'd be somewhere else."

"How's that?"

"In summer I'm afraid of brushfires charging down the hillside. In winter I'm afraid the rains will wash me down on top of the traffic. In between I'm afraid I'll walk in my sleep and take a dive off the balcony."

He opened the door and hit the light switch. The overhead light in the hall went on along with three of the four lamps in the living room. He walked in ahead of her and closed the door behind them.

"Anybody ever do a swan?" she asked.

"Once, but he was a bad guy and I didn't much give a damn."

She walked into the middle of the room and looked around. For a minute he was afraid she was going to start picking up some of the mess, but instead she sat down on the sway-backed couch, crossing her legs at the ankles and folding her hands in her lap as if she were sitting in the queen's parlor, waiting for tea to be served.

There was that about her, Whistler thought. She was the sort could be dropped down in the middle of a war-torn city and still look cool and regal, above it all, refusing to notice the blood on her alligator pumps.

"Get you a drink?"

"No, thank you."

"Cup of coffee?"

"No, thank you. Nothing. Get your socks and skivvies and let's get out of here before your worst fears come true and we end up at the bottom of the canyon smashed into the roadway by a semi."

"Give me a minute," he said, and went into his bedroom.

He got out of his stained and rumpled blue pin-striped summer-weight seersucker suit and went into the bathroom. He took two minutes to look at his face in the mirror, considered a quick shave, and then decided against it, all the while the cold water tap dripped into the sink and left a stain as rough as a deposit of calcium. He thought about the leak and how he should fix it, estimating the water he was letting go to waste and the damage he was letting happen to the basin.

Thinking about water made him thirsty. And that got him thinking about how he'd be going along, not feeling hungry, when out of the blue, he'd start thinking about what he was going to have for supper, and all of a sudden he was so goddamn hungry he could eat a shoe. Or how he could go along without a woman for three, four weeks—three, four months—when some female would lean over and show him where her breasts weren't tan or showed him her leg where it gets pale and tender, and all of a sudden he felt like he'd been deprived for a hundred years. Some women, a few, made him feel like it was a thousand.

So now he was horny, but he wasn't hungry and he wasn't thirsty.

He turned the taps on in the bathtub. The water ran brown. Everybody in the neighborhood was pumping water onto the lawn, running water through the air conditioners, taking twenty showers apiece, sucking the lines dry, churning up the rust. He turned off the taps.

He ran cold water slowly into the basin until it was pretty clear. Then he plugged it and let it fill.

He stripped down and gave himself a whore's bath, balancing on one foot with the other foot in the basin so he could work the washrag around his crotch. He dried off.

"You fall in?" Nell called from the living room.

He felt like they'd been together a dozen years.

He went into the bedroom and put on clean boxer shorts and a clean white shirt. He got into a tan-striped seersucker suit that was almost as badly creased as the blue one. He thought about putting on his one good black wool worsted, but the hot sun tomorrow would bake him, and the hot Santa Ana winds would blow his ashes out to sea.

"You have a jealous boyfriend drives a wine-red BMW?" Whistler asked after he'd tossed his duffel in the back and they were on their way to her friend's house in Brentwood.

"I have no boyfriends at all. It's not the way I play the game."

"He knows what he's doing. He's hanging back far enough so I can't read his plates."

Nell turned around and looked out the back window, showing a lot of leg in the process. "I've got prairie eyes." After a long minute, she said, "Even prairie eyes can't see after sunset." She turned around to the front and adjusted her skirt. "Now do you believe me?"

"Believe what?"

"That Twelvetrees has something in mind."

"Maybe all he's doing is checking on your friends."

"You going to lose him?"

"Well, if he's tailing you, he probably already knows where you're living. Now he knows where I'm living. But, what the hell, we might as well see what's what."

He took a long, crooked way to Brentwood. The BMW stayed well back but never lost him. It followed the Chevy like a thoroughbred chasing a mutt for miles, then it disappeared.

"Oops," Whistler said, looking into the rearview mirror.

Nell turned around. "It's gone."

"So maybe we were both wrong."

They drove up Rustic Canyon right next door to the Will Rogers State Park.

The road was lined with sprawling houses. Every one of them had a sign that warned of armed response.

"That one," she said, pointing to a Mediterranean villa that was only one of two mansions occupying one side of a stretch of road as long as a city block. There was new construction on the other side.

"My God, another house going up," Whistler said, driving along the circular drive to the entrance portico. "This neighborhood is going to the dogs."

As if on cue, two unseen animals set up a clatter of barking.

They got out of the Chevy.

"Anybody home?" he asked.

"Mary Beth let me bring my dogs with me. She knows how much I love them."

"Where is she?"

"La Costa. Working the MONY Tournament of Champions."

"She's a golfer?"

Nell grinned. It was an impish look. "Oh, Mary Beth's a hooker, but I'm not talking golf."

"Holy Christ, I didn't know hooking paid this good."

"It does if you save your pennies, watch your cash flow, and don't spend your principal." She smiled, lifted her chin a little and called, "Hey, honey, honey, honey." The dogs stopped barking and started whining eagerly.

Whistler followed her to the door, his duffel dangling across his back like a sailor home from the sea. Inside, she hit the switch and the overhead crystal chandelier went on. The entrance hall was mirrored floor to ceiling at both ends so that it looked like it went on forever. A hundred Nells walked right, a hundred Whistlers followed. A quick left and she seemed to disappear into the wall, but she was only going through a doorway into another room. Whistler shuffled along behind her feeling more and more like a stable boy, or just another dog.

Her heels made quick sharp sounds across the tiles of a kitchen out of Gourmet magazine. He followed her through glass doors onto a long side porch with windows looking out onto a service patch where two English Bull terriers with big heads, crossed eyes, silly expressions, and short legs waited for a pat.

Nell squatted down, her skirt splitting along the side, showing a lot of sleek thigh. The dogs went crazy with love, but kept wary eyes on the male stranger. Whistler bent over and extended the back of his hand, the fingers loose. They got a good smell of him as Nell crooned introductions and called Whistler a friend.

"This is Bip and this is Bongo," she said.

"I'll never remember."

"You'd better. Hearing their names settles them."

"Bip and Bongo," Whistler said, tapping his forehead, "written here in letters of fire."

"Now, would you like a drink or a cup of coffee?"

"No, thank you."

"You hungry?"

"Sure."

"I'll bet you think I can't cook."

"Well, I can't, so why should you?"

"Very egalitarian of you to say that. Sit down at the table and give me five minutes. Then you'll see."

She shucked the furs down her arms and caught them in a tangle at one elbow. She pulled off the wide-brimmed hat. The hidden eye was as stunning as the one he'd been looking at for hours. A lock of hair fell loose across her forehead banded in red by the constriction of the hat. Her shoulders slumped. Her blouse looked messy all of a sudden. There was a little line of perspiration on her upper lip. Most of the lipstick on the lower one was bitten off. She was on home turf and letting down. She cocked one leg and removed the shoe, then cocked the other.

Flat-footed and walking like a duck, she shuffled out of the kitchen, just a tired lady with a little spread to her ass and her shirttail falling out.

Spinneran turned the BMW around at the top of the road; with the motor cut he drifted back to the building site and brought it to a stop alongside a stack of lumber. He got out and closed the door until it rested on the latch. He opened the trunk and changed out of his linen suit into his stalking gear: black shoes with rubber soles, black pin cords, black socks, and a thin black wraparound three-quarter sleeve belted smock made of silk. He looked even slimmer than he had in his disguise as a flyer in the Lafayette Escadrille.

There were thin crusts of spilled concrete and rutted gravel underfoot, but he hardly made any sound as he crept toward the skeleton of the house that reared up like a child's stick construction set against the sky bright with city-shine. In places he drifted sideways, enjoying the feel of it, a cat softly gliding through the dark.

He sat down and waited, elbows resting on knees, hands dangling free, head down. His hair was pale brass with the dye washed out. It fell forward like a blade, obscuring one side of his pale, smooth face for a moment before he covered it with a black watch cap.

Nell stood at the black iron-and-chrome restaurant stove and flipped omelets in two copper pans and English sausages in a third. She served them up with a dish of powdered sugar and pots of liquored jams. Whistler poured the coffee, brewed from freshly ground water-processed decaffeinated beans. There was colored castor sugar in one bowl and a dish of whipped cream from the fridge in another. One swallow and his smile spread right out to his ears.

She sat down across from him at the porcelain-topped kitchen table and dove into her plate like a trucker, looking a million in a ratty chenille bathrobe like his mother used to wear long ago and far away. "My security rag," she said when she caught the look in his eyes. "Did you expect me to lounge around in gold lamé?"

"I don't know a lot about women."

"You're joking."

"I mean, I know so much about women that I can honestly say I don't know a lot about women."

"We're full of mystery and charm."

"You're full of strategy and tactics."

"You're a pistol, you are, Whistler."

They finished their supper in silence, liking each other's company. As comfortable as an old married couple, but with a sexual edge to the silence as plain as heavy breathing.

"More coffee?" she said, touching the pot on the hot plate.

"If I do, I'll be up all night running to the john."

"That's something else women are better at than men."

"What's that?"

"Holding their water."

They did the thirty-second stare. Whistler blinked first. He got up and started stacking the dishes.

"Leave 'em." She said. She glanced up at the wall clock. "God, I'm all wrung out. You?"

"I don't need much sleep. But I won't fight it."

"Come on, I'll show you."

He picked up his duffel and trotted after her down another long corridor. Her room was at the very end. She reached in and turned on the lights. Past her shoulder he could see a bedroom all yellow and peach. Her robe seemed to take on the sheen of satin as she leaned against the doorjamb and folded her arms across her breasts. There was something magical in her moves. Whistler took a step.

"Your room's over there," she said. When she pointed the way behind him with her chin, her hair flowed back like a wave, then settled against her shoulder in new patterns. The two terriers came trotting over to the sliding doors of her bedroom. They looked at him through the glass as if they knew exactly what he had in mind, the whites of their eyes showing, tongues lolling. Grinning at him for the fool he was.

"You get hungry in the night, you know where the kitchen is," she said.

"Uh huh."

"Good night."

He walked across the hall to his room. He turned to say good night. Her door was closing. The latch snicked. He stood there waiting. The lock didn't turn. The air was electric with conflicting messages. He stepped inside his room and turned on the light.

It was well-furnished but neutral, a room in a motel. Full-sized bed, chest of drawers, chair, lamp, thirteen-inch color television with a remote control on the night table.

A small but well-appointed bathroom was through one door, a closet behind another. He put his duffel on a bench at the foot of the bed, opened it up and took out his toilet kit, a washcloth wrapped around a toothbrush, a can of shaving cream, a tube of toothpaste, and a razor.

He took a quick shower, looking at himself as he dried off,

thinking he wasn't in such awful shape. Jesus Christ, he thought, as he slipped between sheets at least three weeks cleaner than the ones on his bed at home, keep going on like this and the next thing he knew he'd be buying ladies off the stroll.

He switched on the television and rattled around the channels, finally settling on a detective series where all the women were half-naked, all the villains stupid, and the detective both good and smart. Then he watched a show about two men who lived with one woman. Then another about two women who lived with one man. He reaffirmed his reasons for not watching television. The show on the four corners was much better.

His eyes started to close on him.

At twelve o'clock, Jocko MacDoone, Twelvetrees's announcer, raised his three chins in closeup and bawled, "Are you reaaaady!" and the audience yelled, "Yeeeees!"

Whistler punched the off button and fell asleep with the hand remote cradled in his crotch.

FOUR

HUMAN BEINGS ARE provided with a mechanism that renders them unable to move if suddenly startled awake from deep sleep. Anthropologists believe it kept early man from lashing out and killing one of his bedmates in the days when man huddled together like nesting dogs. It doesn't happen all that often nowadays, but when it does it's terrifying.

Whistler thought someone had screamed, but he couldn't be sure. All he could be certain of was that something threatened. He was lying on his back unable to open his eyes. He couldn't move a finger even though he was afraid he was about to be murdered. Then the paralysis snapped and he was out of bed and running across the hall to Nell's room, scarcely aware that he was bare-ass naked. He almost went back for his pants. Then he thought, if she was inside the room under attack, a hand over her mouth muffling any more screams, modesty was a thing that would certainly go unappreciated.

On the other hand, he thought as he slammed the door back against the wall, the scream might have been born in a dream.

She wasn't dead and she wasn't dreaming. She was sitting up in bed, the whites of her eyes almost shining in the glow of a small baseboard night-light. She slept in the raw, just like Whistler. Even charged up as he was, Whistler admired the spray of freckles across her chest and upper breasts, marking her as a beautiful breed apart from ordinarily beautiful women.

She didn't try to cover herself with the sheet, but just sat there, supporting herself with her hands and arms.

"Somebody was in here," she said in a voice under surprising control.

Whistler stood in the middle of the sea of rug, sharply aware of his nakedness and the stirring at his crotch. She reached out toward the bed lamp.

"Don't . . ." Whistler started to say.

It was too late. The switch clicked on and pink light flooded part of the bed, sending reflections back from her tangled hair.

He pivoted on the balls of his bare feet, scanning the room with his nose and ears as much as with his eyes.

"The dogs."

"What about the dogs?"

"They aren't barking."

"Oh, for Christ's sake, so it was a nightmare after all."

Whistler went to the drapes at the split and pulled a panel aside. "The dogs aren't barking now either, and they should be with the light on and me in the room." He unlocked the sliding door and eased it back far enough for him to slip through.

Bip and Bongo were lying in a huddle beneath a flowering fruit tree. The blossoms trembled delicately in the hot winds that were still blowing. He padded over to the dogs and, squatting down, laid his palm flat on the ribs of one and then the other. They didn't stir but went on breathing deeply and evenly. He lifted the eyelid of one of the animals. The eyeball was rolled back, showing only a shaving of iris. He opened its mouth with both hands. The tongue lolled out. He dug inside with a forefinger and scraped out a shred of raw beef.

He stood up and turned around. Nell was out of bed and standing in the doorway, the chenille robe in her hand, still as naked as he. She was a true redhead. The triangle at her crotch shone like a burnished shield of red-gold. There were sprays of freckles as delicate as tiny autumn leaves down the front of her thighs. He took a step toward her, conscious that while he'd been examining the terriers she'd been looking at his back and buttocks, his balls hanging heavy between his legs.

"The dogs have been drugged," he said.

"Oh, my God, who'd do a thing like that to my puppies?"

"They'll be all right, they'll be all right."

She was trembling all over. She started to lift her open arms.

He kept on walking toward her but put one arm up with the palm of his hand facing her, warning her off.

She took a step toward him, welcoming him.

For Christ's sake, Whistler thought. As he came up against her breasts and belly, she parted her lips and her thighs, capturing him twice.

The flash going off was like an electric shock. Whistler heard the quick snap and whir of a motor drive. As he turned to the source, the flash went off again, stealing his sight away. He almost threw Nell aside and was through the door after the photographer, hitting the hall light switch on the wall as he ran, just in time to see a hundred small men dressed in black disappear out the front door like a hundred magician's assistants into a vanishing box.

He was too late. A shadow went through the gate and, a moment later, the characteristic thin, high whine of a revving BMW broke the silence of the night. Whistler went back to get into a pair of pants and a shirt.

The adrenaline washed along Spinneran's arms and legs. His right foot trembled on the accelerator.

He drove to the bottom of the road before slamming the door. He took his hands off the wheel and glanced at his palms, and was pleased to find them dry. There'd been the thrill but not the fear. That was the prize in the game.

Spinneran drove toward the lights of the city, shimmering as though buried deep in a lake of black water.

Nell was wrapped in the robe and sitting on the edge of the bed, clutching herself and shivering as though she was cold in spite of the sultry air.

"That sonofabitch sure knows how to ruin a take," Whistler joked weakly.

She looked up at him through her hair.

"I'll bet you're one of those characters who makes funny after an air crash."

He walked over, sat down beside her, and started to put an arm around her.

She backed away. "There was a moment there. I'm not saying otherwise. But the party's been called on account."

"On account of what?"

"On account of I'm not easy."

Whistler stood up and gave her some distance. "I never thought you were."

She looked at the sliding doors. "You think we should take Bip and Bongo to a vet?"

"They're sleeping now. It'd be something getting a vet out of bed at this hour. I'll keep my eye on them; if they don't wake up by daybreak, we'll take them to the vet."

She stared at him and started blinking her eyes. For a minute he was afraid she was going to cry, but she shook her head and hugged herself tighter.

"What the hell was that all about anyway?" she asked.

"Twelvetrees wanted evidence of infidelity."

Nell started to laugh. "That doesn't count for much nowadays."

"It counts for something when you sit down to negotiate. Everything and anything counts for something."

"Does he think all he's got to do is catch me in the raw with another man, and then he can throw me out into the snow without a cent?"

"It's an edge. Everybody's looking for an edge."

Nell reached out for the bedside phone and punched in a number.

"Be home, you rotten sonofabitch," she muttered.

"I don't know if what I think you're going to do is such a great idea."

She threw him a glance that told him to shut up, he was only the hired help.

"So you're home, Roger. Where the hell do you get off? Listen to me you sonofabitch! Why did you send some sneak around to take pictures?" Her voice was running up the scale. She was trembling and leaning over the phone as though she'd like to bite the wire and send a lethal shock across the lines to the room where Twelvetrees was sitting and listening to her. "So you got some pictures, but they don't mean what they look like they mean, and if you try to use them against me, you rotten sonofabitch, I'll do you. As quick as you'll do me, I'll do you, Roger." She took a deep breath while the receiver buzzed in her hand. Then she screamed into the mouthpiece, "I don't believe you, you bastard. Whatever you do to me, I'll do to you double!"

Then she was silent for a long minute.

"No. No. All right," she said. "For Christ's sake, I understand. Yes, I do, I understand. I'd never take it out on her. No. I'd never take it out on Jenny. I know it's her twenty-first. Of course, I'll be there."

Whistler could hardly believe his eyes. She was cooling down so fast frost was forming on her mouth. She was even smiling a little.

"I don't know. No. I don't suppose you'd do anything this foolish. But somebody did. You think so? You think some goddamn magazine would go this far? Some free-lance maybe? Miss America and Penthouse? Oh, yes, I remember that. I suppose so. I suppose some of these people would do anything for a buck nowadays. Well, yes, I'm all right, now. Yes. Yes, I believe you. I'm sorry I woke you up. Did I wake you up? That's okay then. This is going to be a painful time for both of us so we should try to make it as easy on one another as we can."

She glanced at Whistler as though asking for privacy. He left her bedroom and went into his own, slipping his bare feet into his shoes and walking down the long mirrored corridor and out of the house.

He went along the curving drive and out the gate, stood there surveying the silent street of the affluent neighborhood. The moon was bright, the world shades of blue and gray.

Across the street the new construction loomed against the sky. He walked over and shuffled through the concrete spills and gravel sprays looking for whatever. Whatever was not to be found.

When he turned around to start back to the house a house-holder was standing there in a robe and slippers, his hair tousled, his expression irritable, a little dog straining at the end of a leash.

"I couldn't sleep," Whistler said.

"Oh?"

"I thought I heard someone outside."

"I could sleep," the man said, "but my wife's dog started yapping. It's my wife's dog. I don't even like small dogs. So how come I got to be the one to get up and walk it when it's got to take a pee in the middle of the night?" He looked down at the little animal as though he'd gladly wring its neck.

"Maybe he heard something, too," Whistler said, joining the man at the curb. The little dog sniffed at his leg.

The man's expression changed, softened, grew thoughtful and almost fond.

"They say little dogs make the best watchdogs," Whistler added.

The man stooped down and patted the dog on the head. It went bug-eyed with love. The man straightened up and looked carefully at Whistler again. "You're visiting Miss Jones?" A little smile quirked his lips like a twitch, a conservative comment, proving he was no fool and knew what was what.

"Using her house for a few days while she's out of town."

"Oh, yes. The other young woman gone as well?"

"My sister? No, she's still here."

The man shook his head slightly at the wonder of it all. "Well, good night. Maybe I can get back to sleep, but I doubt it."

He went slap-slapping on down the road in his slippers. Whistler watched him, but when the man turned around to look back over his shoulder, Whistler looked down at his feet. Something glittered there. He reached down, picked up a piece of crumpled cellophane and smoothed it out. It was a candy wrapper printed in black, pink, and gold. On one side it said, "French Secrets" and "Club Armentières." On the other side there was a risqué limerick.

> There was a young man from Wick
> Who had a marvelous prick.
> It was two inches long,
> But if you sang it a song,
> It grew to be ten in a lick.

He put it into his pocket, crossed the street, went back into the house, and down the hall to Nell's room.

She was cuddled over the phone, her head bent to one side as though resting while talking. "Good night. Ah, Jesus, Roger," she said very softly, "don't say things like that. It won't do any good."

She hung up the receiver and wiped her hand across her eyes. "I shouldn't have done that." She stared up at Whistler, her face white and nose red, tears streaking her cheeks. Her nose was running, too, and she wiped it off on her sleeve like a kid. "You said not to."

"What did he have to say?" Whistler asked.

"Oh, he said he didn't send anybody over here to do anything."

"But he knew where you were staying?"

"I had to leave a number in case anyone called."

"So he knows this house?"

"Yes, but he says he'd never do anything like that. He was very convincing."

"Oh?"

"Well, he can be very charming when he wants to be. I mean, after all, I didn't walk into marriage with a man who treated me badly. But then, men always treat women very well before they get them, don't they?"

Whistler didn't want to get into that.

"So, what else did he say? I mean you got very quiet and reasonable there all of a sudden."

"He reminded me about Jenny's twenty-first birthday party tomorrow night."

"Somebody, you think probably your husband, takes pictures of you naked at one-thirty in the morning. You call the sonofa-bitch up to accuse him of doing it. You tell me he's a cross between Dracula and Attila the Hun. And now you're telling me what a charming guy he is, and how he reminded you about his daughter's birthday party?"

"Well, I've got to make an appearance."

"What?"

"People like us are in the spotlight, Whistler, and when you're in the spotlight you've got to keep up a front."

FIVE

THE COMMISSARY OF the network's main building in West Hollywood had been known for the worst food in town for almost ten years. Even after they tried to steal a page from the film studios and tarted up the dining room, drawing in the geeks and gawkers with a five-dollar hamburger, a two-dollar Coke, and a chance to see their television favorites eating with a knife and fork off plates in the adjoining private dining room, where deals were cut and lies exchanged, the quality of the food, if anything, went down instead of up.

The anchormen and women, the talk and game show hosts, the visiting actors, directors, and cocaine dealers threatened to take their business away altogether, but there's something about the adulation of the rabble that's much more tasty than the bullshit of one's peers. The collection of one-lip smiles to be had at any one of the dozen watering holes that pass around the hat of popularity are never *ever* as satisfying as the slobbering grin of a fawning fan.

". . . as long as they don't touch," Twelvetrees said. "As long as they don't put their pasty little paws on me."

"He got past me, Rog. He blindsided me," Walter Pulaski said.

"Stop with the sports talk. I don't care that you worked seven and a half plays with the Rams in spring training before they found out you were queer. Who do you think you are, the Gipper? You think you're Ronnie Reagan? I'm just tellin' you, the next time you let some sticky-fingered gazoony get past your arm, I'll poke out your eyes and give you a white cane."

Billy Britain, the television critic, chuckled his filthy hyena's chuckle; Millie Bothwell, Twelvetrees's agent, screeched like a goosed peahen; Harry Klorn, the business manager, snickered like a monkey; and Manny Arbutus, the producer of "Midnight America," brayed like a jackass.

None of it was lost on Twelvetrees, who, fool though he might be in other ways, had an ear for comic nuance. "A zoo. I got me a goddamn travelin' menagerie," he said to the pretty girl who stood beside him.

Jenny Denver, Twelvetrees's firstborn by the first wife he'd unloaded when Jenny had been ten, was turning twenty-one that very night. She'd come back to him without invitation or warning six months before, as pretty as her mother once had been, calling herself Jenny Twelvetrees again. She smiled stiffly, apparently uncomfortable with the manners and language of show business, a much prissier girl than the one who'd asked Spinneran to show her the freaks along the Hollywood stroll the night before.

"Sonofabitch," Pulaski said, pulling in his shoulders with glee and sticking out his ass as though he were about to fart.

"Stick it in your dipsy-doo," Twelvetrees said.

Pulaski nearly had a fit of laughter.

Twelvetrees looked at his daughter. "How'd you like to have his brains?"

"I don' like frozen peas," she said as though reciting it from memory.

Pulaski roared.

"How'd you like to have his cock?" Twelvetrees asked.

When Jenny didn't respond right away, Millie Bothwell said, "I don't like Polish sausage."

It was a formula. It was a number Twelvetrees did with variations a dozen times a day. Pulaski almost always fell down anyway.

Nobody seemed to think it strange that Twelvetrees should talk filthy in front of his daughter, even if she was out of Atlanta only six months, even though she plainly didn't consider the conversations very elevating or the jokes very funny.

Millie knew that Twelvetrees would talk toilets to Queen

Elizabeth and anatomy with the pope if he thought it would get
a laugh. So what was a little joke about a cock?

The little twat might act like she thought a cock was for
making pee-pee, and the men might even buy her act, but Millie
knew goddamn well that Jenny wasn't a virgin, or her treasure
only rarely tasted. There was even something odd in her slanted,
twisty eyes, something kinky, something hungry, like the eyes of
the rubes Millie remembered standing in front of the pitch on the
midway, gawking at the attractions of the traveling freak show
into which she had been born.

Jenny touched her father's arm and let the rest of them walk on
ahead, preparing the way for the king to sit down to table.
"Daddy, I don' like you talkin' that way in front of me when
there's other people aroun'. They might just get the wrong idea
an' think me loose." She spoke in a voice like a stale, rock-hard
piece of corn bread smothered in a pour of honey. "Now you
know that. You just know that."

Twelvetrees took her hands and looked into her amber eyes
and thought, you look into somebody's face and you see a
person, and you also see another person. In fact, you see a lot of
people. You see a baby, naked on a blanket, kicking its little feet,
pumping its little hands as though it was racing to a moon made
of milk and honey, round little belly, little slit making like a pink
plum. And you see a little kid, maybe five years old, with a back
like a bow. Standing there naked after her bath, or half naked at
the seashore, shoulder blades sticking out like wings, little ass
humped out behind like you could use it to set a glass of
lemonade on a shelf. At least that's what he would say he was
thinking after consultation with his scriptwriters. But this time
he really was thinking something like that, though there were no
words, just images moving across the screen of memory like old
faded prints of out-of-distribution movies.

There was a person for every year, sometimes it seemed every
month, until this Jennifer, this person gets to be ten, and things
fall apart between her mother and you, like things do, and you
don't see your daughter anymore.

He hadn't been there to see the important changes, the hips
filling out, the chest developing like they do with girls, making
them look all tender and easily bruised.

Now here she was, looking like her mother, looking like

Marilyn when he'd been in the army and she'd been a dead farmer's daughter with snaky hips, and perky tits, and slanty eyes, and a tongue that flickered like a snake's.

He remembered how she'd played him like a fish until that New Year's Eve night, after the party at the grange hall with her deaf mother and her five brothers. After he got her home, and the mother and the youngest brother went up to bed, and the other four went to their own houses, Marilyn fixed up his bed on the living room couch. He was just drunk enough to get bold. Tired of waiting, he about knocked her down on the floor, dragged up her skirts, pulled down her underwear. She fought and thrashed her legs, but not too much, not enough to maybe damage his equipment so he couldn't do her any good on a night when she was as horny as he was; she had moaned softly, saying his name, biting his neck after he plunged into her like a ram taking a sheep. They called it tupping in the barnyard, like there was no fucking to be had down on the farm. Well, he'd tupped her for what seemed like hours, the drink giving him an everlasting boner that wouldn't break and wouldn't die, humping away, as deaf as her old lady, until she'd gotten through the haze of drink to say she had to go take a pee.

He'd let her up and sat there bare-assed on the worn carpet waiting for her to come back. But she hadn't come back. So he went up the stairs to the second floor, the bedroom floor, with the mother sleeping one door down from the bathroom where a sliver of light shone out from under the door, and the brother sleeping in the bedroom at the back of the long hall, and tried to get into the bathroom.

"Go away, go away," Marilyn had said.

"Come out of there, you bitch," he'd said.

"Go away, you'll wake my mother."

"Your mother's fuckin' deaf!"

"My brother isn't, and he'll beat the crap out of you."

"I got to come, goddamn it."

"You already done," she'd said. "I'm washing you out so I don't have a baby," which was the thing she'd told him a hundred times she feared the most. "I'm afraid of having a baby by a soldier who won't stay around to even greet the child," she'd said.

Well, she hadn't cleaned him out of her good enough, or

maybe didn't even try, or tried and it was already too late. Because she'd gotten pregnant, hadn't she? And what she hadn't had to say was that if he didn't do right by her, all *five* brothers would beat the shit out of him.

He couldn't remember, then or later, if he'd actually come that New Year's Eve night. But there'd been other nights right after, so it was no surprise to either of them when Jennifer came along.

He hadn't run off on her. He'd quit the army. Started cracking jokes in a saloon where he tended bar. Then he started working little clubs, doing better and better, until, pretty soon, he was a somebody, with women practically throwing their asses at him. So one night he walked out the door after one last big fight.

Eleven years later this girl comes back saying she's your daughter, but you know it's Marilyn come back to you, making you young again, ready to live and fuck forever.

Twelvetrees felt a tapping on his forehead. What the hell was Marilyn doing tapping him between the eyes with her finger?

"Come back," Jenny said, smiling so sweetly Twelvetrees thought his heart would break, remembering where he was, feeling the shock of growing a dozen years older in the tap of a finger.

"The words are nothing special," he said. "It's like hello or good morning. It's like nothing, you understand what I'm saying?"

"I don' know what these people are used to aroun' here, Daddy, but I do know I'm not gonna allow anyone to treat me like a whore, a fool, or another one of the boys. You play your little games an' talk dirty just to make them laugh, I understan', but you do that aroun' me an' you give fools like Pulaski the idea they can be loose with me, too. That nonsense starts, an' my poor little foot's gonna get tired stompin' on their fuckin' faces."

"Listen to the mouth on you," Twelvetrees said, mocking her, opening his eyes wide in shock not altogether pretended.

"That was just to show you I can say words like that an' not turn to stone. I'm no ten-year-old, but I don' have to talk dirty to prove it."

"Well, don't I know you're all grown up? Can't I just see that?" Twelvetrees said. He was about to put his arm around her, but she slipped away. He put his hands behind his back.

He was ready to toe the mark a little so far as Jenny was

concerned. There'd been two kids by Marilyn, Jenny and a boy. The boy wanted nothing to do with him. And that was all right, because the little bastard went out there on the road, stealing and doing drugs, getting himself a dose of this and that, getting himself murdered. Jenny was the one who showed him that she would or could love him. The one who had some backbone and some brains.

There'd been one wife, Maude, between Marilyn and Nell, a flashy blonde with big tits who'd been his idea of the kind of wife a successful entertainer should have. Then the fashion in wives changed, and all the producers and television stars were getting wives who were very demure, more like librarians or social workers. Maude hadn't given him any children. She'd practically cleaned the vault when he kicked her out. Now this one, Nell, meant to do the same. But if she did, it'd be over his dead body.

He held the chair for his daughter as everyone put down in their mental notebooks that he'd been scolded and had taken it without a squawk. They also wondered how long it would be before he got tired of playing the doting father and gave the stuck-up little cunt a public spanking.

At the next table four women beyond middle age, three of them looking like Norman Rockwell grandmothers, the fourth like an aging chorus pony, threw Twelvetrees glances and giggled around the straws in their Cokes.

"Look, Manny, I'm not going to say it again," Twelvetrees said, not having said whatever it was he was about to say a first time. "No more writers on the show. I can't stand writers. They suck adjectives." He looked at Jenny. "That's not dirty, honey."

Jenny let the jibe fly past her ear out into space, just shaking her head and smiling like a female Buddha. That is if Buddha had a face featuring amber eyes set a trifle too close together and slanted under dark, severely arched brows that made Jenny look like she doubted you. Her mouth was like a little bunch of red berries, full of juice and drunkenness. All of it was framed within a waterfall of hair, as straight and shining as black ice. She was beautiful in a way Hollywood thought was beautiful when Myrna Loy and Sylvia Sydney lived and loved up there on America's silver screens.

"We're talking Mailer," Arbutus said. "We're talking Vidal. They both got new books coming out the same month. We're talking maybe Mailer calls Vidal a fucking queer—"

"Watch your language in front of Jenny. My daughter isn't used to it."

"—and Vidal tells Mailer all his brains is in his . . ."

There was a long pause while everybody waited for the train to come in, but nobody was about to help Arbutus flag it down.

". . . penis," Arbutus said on a note of triumph. "Maybe Mailer punches Vidal in the chops, maybe Vidal kicks Mailer in the cozies."

"The audience wants phony mayhem they can switch to wrestling. No more writers, even if you promised to get me Hemingway and Steinbeck to punch it out on stage."

"Hemingway and Steinbeck are long gone."

"There you go. What am I tellin' you? Who gives a rat's ass about writers?"

The ex-pony girl had made it up to their table when nobody was looking. The waitress hadn't even come to take their orders yet, because nobody had given her the high sign they were ready, but here was this stranger, this lady with her dyed hair and her uplift bra zeroing in on Twelvetrees like he was a plum and she was Jack Horner's thumb. It was like someone stuck rods up everybody's ass, except Jenny's, the way their backs stiffened up. They knew how dangerous it was to bother Roger in the middle of the day before he got something in his stomach.

"Mr. Twelvetrees," the old doll trilled like a penny whistle.

Twelvetrees turned his whole body around as though just turning his head wouldn't be enough to pay her honor, and a smile like snow sparkling on Mount Wilson raised the temperature of the room two degrees.

"Roger. Call me Roger, love. What can I do for you?"

"I have a little niece . . ." she started to say, pen and paper napkin in hand.

"And I'll just bet she's a honey-baby. You sure this isn't for her aunt . . . what's your name, dear?"

"Rose."

"Auntie Rosarita. You've got Spanish blood, isn't that right?"

"How can you tell?" she simpered.

"*Corazón mío.*"

"Wha?" she said, having about as much Spanish as a towel girl in a Chinese whorehouse.

When he put his hand on his heart she got the meaning and blushed.

Twelvetrees took the napkin and started writing on it, while murmuring the words aloud, "To Rose. Was ever another quite so sweet? Roger Twelvetrees."

After she'd gone back to her table and her friends, who were close to passing out with the thrill of it all, Twelvetrees managed to look proud and humble, as if he didn't really believe he had the right to be treated like a king.

The waitress, known to one and all as Mamie, was unimpressed by celebrity, having had a hundred try to goose her up her skirt. She stood there sprung-hipped, elbow leaning on the shelf of her bones, waiting for Twelvetrees's pleasure.

"Reuben, swiss cheese on rye with mayo, fruit salad . . ."

"Dynasty Delectable Delight," Mamie murmured as she wrote it down.

"You're kiddin' me. Dynasty Delectable Delight? I'm gonna f'ow up," Twelvetrees said.

"You do and you'll clean it up," Mamie joked.

It wasn't the right thing to say. The king was being generous. The king was being affable. The king was being wise and good. But the king was still the king. His eyes got narrow and cold. Just who did this raggedy broad in her nurse's shoes and stained apron think she was swapping toppers with the king?

"I ever fuck you?" he asked.

"Wha?" Mamie's mouth fell open in the middle of a chew. She saw herself in the unemployment line right that minute.

"I mean, I have to tell you, I only allow women I've fucked crack wise with me."

He stared at her, backing her into the corner from which there is no escape. No matter what she said, he could make it the wrong thing to say. The silence was humiliating. She just stood there, pencil poised above her book of meal checks, rapidly changing color; fear, rage, and frustration washing across her face and skinny neck. What good would it do to remind him there'd been days and meals when they'd slugged it out comedically toe to toe, when he'd sometimes lost and taken it, almost rolling on the floor at the quickness of her wit. Even copping some of her remarks for his own and recycling them on his nightly show. She was red, then white, and finally a mottled wreck, the first torture of nervous eczema urging her to scratch her crotch and bosom.

Damn it, she thought, these assholes could blow hot and cold anytime they wanted to. There were always plenty of people around ready to kiss their asses and never remind them that they were probably wearing dirty underwear.

Twelvetrees let the silence stretch out and break.

He finally pointed to the next person in the circle and went on ordering for all. "Cheeseburger medium rare, with everything. Tuna fish on white toast, pickle on the side . . ." He stared at Arbutus slyly, waiting to see what the producer would do.

Everybody knew Manny Arbutus couldn't stand tuna fish and hated pickles. The combination gave him serious indigestion. He didn't say a word.

Twelvetrees turned to his daughter.

"Rye toast," she said.

"You got to eat."

"Rye toast with a pat of butter."

Sonofabitch, Twelvetrees thought, what a pistol my kid is. What a goddamn pistol. Ready to face me down and shoot it out right here. Has more balls than any guy at the table. Even has more balls than Millie Bothwell, the iron twat of La-La Land. He grinned and put his hand over her hand.

That should have been the end of that, but one of the old dolls at the nearby table, seeing the success of her red-headed friend and wanting to match it, came toddling over with her own pencil and napkin. Twelvetrees pretended she wasn't even standing there, her old biddy-bosom practically leaning on his neck. Finally he did turn around, looking her up and down as though she'd just walked off a UFO.

"What do you want?"

She stepped back like he'd slapped her in the face. "My friend got your autograph . . ." she started to stammer.

"What is it with you fuckin' people? You want to fuckin' eat me up? You want to gobble up my life? How am I supposed to get some food into me so I can entertain you, you don't let me eat in peace? I mean, goddamn it."

The woman was close to tears, wanting to run, but pinned there motionless, clutching her pencil and napkin to her chest. Jenny stood up and touched her elbow, turned her around, started her toward her table and her friends, walked along with her for several paces, then, avoiding the older woman's thanks, walked on to the exit.

Twelvetrees threw down his napkin and was up and after her, catching her at the door.

"Hey, ease off," he said, taking her arm and holding her in place. She started to pull away, then decided not to make a scene.

He took her arm and led her over to a table backed against a wall near the door. She sat down without protest and he sat down across from her, taking her hands in his.

"Look, I'll try to watch my temper. I'm uptight, you know? I mean, this business with Nell divorcing me, threatening to come after me for everything I got. Take my goddamn pants right off me. Leave me bare-assed out in the cold. Hard as I worked. All these years. I mean, for Christ's sake, Jen, gimme a break. Your old dad's gonna be a three-time loser."

"Maybe you only really lost once."

"Your mother. You mean when I lost your mother. You're right, you're so goddamn right." Tears came up and misted his eyes, watered his tonsils, gave him that compassionate doglike stare that had the television audience saying what a really nice and decent man he was. "That was my big mistake. Letting your mother get away from me was my big, big mistake. I was just a kid when we got married. We were only babies. I was fighting like a sonofabitch to give her and you and your brother the world."

"You didn' do very good, Daddy," Jenny said.

"So all right, don't abuse me. Don't be like everybody else. Don't be like that cunt . . . excuse me . . . that bitch, Nell, who calls me up in the middle of the night . . . I'm fast asleep, the first time in months I'm getting a good night's sleep . . . she wakes me up and starts shouting at me. Some goddamn babble about sending some cat burglar into her bedroom to scare the shit out of her, taking flash pictures that don't mean what they look like they mean. Whatever that means. So don't you be like everybody else, taking a piece out of me then telling me what an asshole I am, making my life miserable. Don't go getting on my back because once in a while I forget myself around you and say maybe a fuck or a shit. Don't do that." He wound down like a tin toy. "Don't fuckin' do that."

SIX

WHISTLER HAD ALREADY been in the kitchen reading the morning paper for half an hour when Nell came wandering in. She had a sheepish grin on her face, as if she thought she was the cause of all the turmoil of the night before.

She pulled her hair back with both hands and said, "I must look a wreck. You see me looking like this early in the morning that's the end of the romance."

She was doing the same thing so many other women did, trolling for compliments, feeding out innuendo like chum thrown upon the water. If he bit, there'd be the quick retreat, the patient smile as if she'd thought he was the kind of man who could enjoy a little kidding around without taking it too seriously. Then she'd act like she should have known better. He realized that he was hoping for things from her that would keep her special.

"Your divorce is in the gossips with a picture of you."

"Does it look like me?"

"Enough. You want breakfast here or out?"

"Out. But I'd like a cup of coffee now."

He got up and poured her a cup.

"The dogs look all right," she said. "They were glad to see me this morning."

"They weren't glad to see me. I was going to feed them. I called them by name, just like you said, but they wouldn't touch it."

"I'll see if they'll eat for me. I should have the vet look them over anyway."

The dogs ate for her, but they dropped them at the vets for a checkup about two hours later. It was noon by the time they got to Gentry's.

Bosco sat reading *Through the Looking Glass*. He had a handkerchief tied around his neck and was wearing a short-sleeved shirt. The stump of his missing arm was a net of shiny white scar tissue and looked as hard as a knob of marble.

He took their order at the register, and they went to sit in a booth by the window. Outside, half-dressed baby whores, gaudy pimps, flash acts on roller skates, and undercover cops in lavender net shirts were already on the stroll. When some of them looked into Gentry's and saw Nell, they discussed their impression that she was a celebrity of some sort.

If Nell's divorce was in the papers, it had probably already been on the morning television shows. Twelvetrees would be working it into his monologue and into the repartee with his announcer, MacDoone, by tonight, tomorrow the latest. Taking profit where it could be found.

For a while people would recognize her on the street and in the restaurants. There'd be anonymous telephone calls at all hours. There'd be letters dunning her for a piece of the money strangers knew would be settled on her. Strangers might even accost her on the street. It might be a while before it became stale bread. It was a price she'd have to pay.

Nell was wearing a white blouse, champagne linen slacks and a matching vest. She carried the jacket that completed the outfit and a linen envelope purse. She looked a million with her red hair tied back in a long ponytail with a lime green chiffon scarf.

Bosco brought the food himself instead of sending the waitress. He made a fuss over the preparation of the eggs—were they soft enough?—and the bacon—was it crisp enough? He was plainly glad to see Nell again. He poured their coffee and left them to it.

Nell glanced at Whistler from time to time, but he kept his eyes outside or on his plate.

"I've been giving you a hard time," she said. "Last night . . ."

"You didn't offer any provocation last night," he said, making a joke.

"Some men would have made a thing."

"Well, I would have made a thing—if I'd thought it would've worked."

"It looked like I started something and then called it off in the middle."

"More like at the beginning."

"Then, this morning, I wouldn't leave it alone. I had to go poking at you, looking for you to tell me I was a baby doll even in the morning without my makeup."

"You're no baby, but you're a doll," he said, then wished he hadn't because it had come out sounding foolish.

"You know how to sweet-talk a girl, I'll give you that."

"Well, that's a start."

"I want you to know something. Any other time, any other circumstance, I think we could have had a dance, you know? But when we say goodbye it's . . ."

"I know the words," Whistler said. "Forget about it, before I start to cry."

She smiled. A small dimple flashed under each corner of her mouth, and almost pulled Whistler's heart out through his mouth.

Bosco's timing was right on the button without him knowing it. He filled the awkward moment by returning with the coffee-pot. He waited for the nod, then topped them up.

Nell looked at the stump of his arm without staring or flinching. Bosco caught her looking. She caught him looking at her looking.

"That give you trouble, any pain?" she asked.

"Now and then I feel the ghost."

"We all have one or two of those."

"Oh, yes."

"You lose it in a war?" she asked.

"I lost it in an argument with a pimp over one of his ladies."

He smiled and went back to the counter where two kids with orange and purple hair had just stepped up to pay their tab.

"The whore was twelve and Bosco thought she should be home in Ohio or wherever it was she came from," Whistler said. "The pimp blew off Bosco's arm, but Bosco came at him all the same. Before he passed out Bosco broke the pimp's neck."

"Did the girl go back to Ohio?"

"She cried for the pimp but not for Bosco. Found another

daddy before Bosco's stump was even healed. Worked a double
shift on the streets every night for two years until she got her
throat cut." He looked out the window. "Right down the street
under the marquee of the movie house. Right where famous
people put their feet."

Nell put down her cup and wiped her mouth with a paper
napkin. She took a compact from her pocket and snapped it
open, looking at herself in little patches. "This needs more than
I can manage at the table." She slid out of the booth and
pussyfooted down the tiled aisle toward the rest rooms.

Bosco came back again and sat where she'd been sitting.

"You took the job?"

"I can use the money."

"Can you use the grief?"

"Are you going to live my life again?"

"Trust a pretty woman and you'll sleep on straw."

"I thought you liked her, the way you act."

"What's not to like? But we're not talking about me, we're
talking about you."

"What about me?"

"You're a sucker for a pretty face."

"Never mind," Whistler said.

"Her husband's got a reputation."

"For what?"

"For having guys punched out."

"I heard. Doormen at discos. Parking lot attendants. Photographers. Half the celebrities in town got a reputation."

"The word is he also punches out whores."

"Half that word is bullshit and the other half blue smoke most
of the time."

"Not this time. I know for a fact."

Whistler was about to ask what it was Bosco knew for a fact
when Isaac Canaan came into the shop, spotted Whistler and
Bosco, and came over to sit.

He had a face like a hound's and a heart that was a stone one
minute and a bag of tears the next. His little niece had been
abducted, raped, and murdered by a pervert, and the fire it lit
had never gone out. Whistler had stayed up day and night
helping Canaan look for her. He might even have helped Canaan
from going crazy when they found her.

There were a lot of people on the street who swore the vice cop never slept. There were some who had dreams of Canaan coming to get them for their sins.

"There's no justice," Canaan said. "That twist I seen you with the other day. A twist like that, a gonif like you. Like Bambi and Godzilla."

"I'm still with her; but don't worry, I'll always love you in my fashion."

"You're a comic is what stuns her mind. Where the hell you find her?"

"She found me."

"Curiouser and curiouser."

Whistler looked at Bosco, who shrugged and raised an eyebrow. "I gave him my *Annotated Alice in Wonderland* to read."

"What's Mrs. Midnight America doing with you anyhow?" Canaan asked.

"So you know who she is."

Canaan tapped his ear, then pulled down the lower lid of one eye. "I hear the news. I see the news. She's cutting the knot."

"That's right."

"So tell me again, what's your connection?" Canaan asked.

"I didn't tell you once, but she came to me for a little body care."

"You gonna make a life's work out of it?"

"I'm escorting her around town for a few days, she shouldn't have an accident."

"Is she expecting one?"

"It could happen."

Canaan nodded, knowing that the worst could always happen.

"You know this Roger Twelvetrees?" Whistler asked.

"I know him when he's nothing but Mr. Three o'Clock in the Morning America."

"I don't remember that show."

"I mean out there. Cruising the talent."

"Lately?"

"No, not lately."

"You think he's cleaned up his act?"

"It's possible he lost his appetite, but I doubt it. I think you get that rich, that famous, you do better with home delivery. Who needs the crowds? All them autographs to sign. But he might

have changed his diet. I hear he has a taste for young whores
lately. He used to like them old enough to take it."

"Take what?"

"A little kicking around, a little punishment."

"Bosco told me he was a hitter."

"What Bosco don't know, ain't worth knowing."

"You think he's capable?"

"You mean would he do somebody who got him mad enough
or excited enough? I think so."

"What gives you that idea?"

"Because I think he might have done it once. You could call
battering a hooker until she died of the injuries an accident, but
to me it's murder. And some people do it once, it's all they can
do to keep from doing it again."

"Who was the victim?"

"A whore he picked up from the stroll right out there. A
punching bag. She'd do it all."

"She have a name?"

"I don't know about her real name, but I think her street name
was Boots," Bosco said. "It's the kind of name sticks with you.
She was also called Felitia's Mother," he added, as though
reluctantly giving away a confidence.

"Felitia?" Whistler inclined his head toward the window.

"Yeah, that one. The kid what wears pleated skirts and middy
blouses. She was maybe seven when her mother got busted up so
bad she died."

"How long ago was this?" Whistler asked.

"Six years?" Bosco turned to Canaan for confirmation.

"Maybe seven," Canaan said.

Whistler stared through the door as though he could spot the
hooker called Felitia out there in the crowd. "Felitia's only
thirteen, fourteen?"

"That's about right."

"For Christ's sake, she looks to be a hundred around the eyes."

"Give or take," Canaan said dryly.

"What came of the investigation?"

"What investigation?"

"You said Felitia's Mother died."

"A streetwalker died. She was busted up, but how you gonna
say what really killed her? I never saw her when she wasn't

drugged up to the eyes. That's why she could take so much punishment. She didn't even feel it," Bosco said.

"You sure the beating is what killed her?"

Canaan shrugged. Bosco looked off into space.

"How can I find out?"

"It should be in the records down at the morgue," Canaan said.

"I'd need a name. There's so many."

"You got Boots. You got Felitia's Mother. Sometimes that's how they got them identified, by the street name."

"What happened about Twelvetrees?" Whistler asked.

"What I remember is they brought Twelvetrees in for questioning. He wasn't the big man then that he is now, but he was big enough," Canaan said. "Big enough to get some help from here and there. Important people who wouldn't believe a funny man like Twelvetrees could do such a thing. There were other customers brought in for questioning, too, you understand? It wasn't as though his name was the only one in her book."

"So Twelvetrees got away."

"Fachrissakes, I just said he was brought in for questions, just like some others. What makes you so sure he was the one who did it?"

"Because you just said you thought he did it."

"Well, that was my impression at the time. But it wasn't my case."

"So how come you know so much about it?"

"I was worried about the kid. I was told Felitia had an older sister—I don't know how much older—living with some relative. I couldn't find her. I thought if I found her she could take care of Felitia and the way she turned out wouldn't have happened. So there she is, out on the stroll wearing the soles of her feet off just like her mother."

They all looked out the window as though expecting Felitia to light up or otherwise identify herself. "What can you expect? Before she died, Felitia's Mother was already turning the sister out doing triples. I talk to Felitia sometimes, but she tells me to mind my own business. I try to keep an eye on her. Oh, me; oh, my," he said looking over Whistler's shoulder.

They all turned around to watch Nell's approach, breasts softly moving inside her blouse, long legs taking strides. She sent out signals as if she was sugar and every man was a fly.

She reached them and tucked herself against Whistler as if she belonged there, baiting every other man in sight.

She looked at Canaan. "I don't think we've met."

Whistler introduced them, and Canaan removed the hat he never took off, so far as anyone knew. People said he even wore it to bed.

"Did I interrupt something? Were you talking shop?" Nell asked.

"We're through," Whistler said. "You want another cup of coffee?"

"I don't think so."

"Well, could you let me out? I've got to go somewhere. Only take me half an hour, an hour tops."

"Can't I come along?"

"This is something I had left over when you hired me yesterday," he lied. "You understand?"

"Confidential?"

"Well, it calls for some discretion. You'll wait here?" He looked at Bosco and then at Canaan. "You'll be all right?" he said, asking a question of Nell and assurances from his friends.

"She'll be all right," Canaan said, smiling like everybody's favorite uncle. "I'll tell her stories."

Nell got up and stood there while Whistler got out of the booth.

"Well, just don't scare her to death," Whistler said.

Nell caught his arm and kissed him on the cheek.

For Christ's sake!

SEVEN

SPINNERAN WALKED INTO the dining room half a stride, saw Jenny and Twelvetrees, and stopped on a dime. He watched them, waiting to be recognized, standing with his weight on one leg, the knee of the other slightly bent, posing for a Cerutti ad.

A swimmer's body, slim and long-boned, pared down for speed.

He was wearing a casual suit with natural shoulders and push-up sleeves over a short-sleeved white silk shirt unbuttoned at the throat with a tie pulled down beneath it. His boots were Spanish. The outfit was as much a costume as the World War I airman's uniform had been.

He made a picture. A pale picture of a young aristocrat out of some high-key photo of the decadent twenties.

But it was the face, the jaw sharp and tapered, the mouth shapely, the brows light brown and even, the hair, pale as wine, parted in the middle and combed back so severely it looked like a metal cap, that added most to the impression that he was lost but unafraid in an alien world he found hardly bearable.

Jenny glanced his way. He stepped forward, taking a leather envelope, nearly the color of his hair, from under his arm. Jenny nodded and he came over, stopping a stride away, striking the waiting pose again, a tall water bird completely at his ease.

"Daddy, this is Connor Spinneran. My father, Roger Twelvetrees."

Spinneran reached out a hand. Twelvetrees didn't take it.

"This is a friend, Jenny? This is a friend I don't know about?"

"Your daughter and I are cordial, Mr. Twelvetrees, but I wouldn't presume to say that we were friends," Spinneran said in the flat Boston accent that emphasized the lightness of a voice that had the clarity of a boy tenor's.

"So what are you?"

There was a moment of silence while Spinneran glanced at Jenny and raised an eyebrow slightly.

"Well, I'm waiting, Jen," Twelvetrees said. "What's this all about?"

Spinneran was watching Jenny as though he appreciated how pretty she was, his good manners sticking out all over him, in the calm of his attitude, the position of his hands on the slim leather envelope, the attentive thrust of his head. Jenny glanced at the portfolio and nodded. "Are they in there?"

"Yes, Miss Twelvetrees."

"Please sit down."

Spinneran glanced around and, after asking permission, took an empty chair from a nearby table. He sat down and opened the leather envelope on his lap, removed a manila folder, and drew out two eight-by-ten glossies. He held them against his chest until Twelvetrees asked to see them with a nod, then laid them face down on the table in front of Twelvetrees.

Twelvetrees turned them over one after the other. He saw his wife and Whistler, naked, locked in each other's arms, staring into the camera with that terrible, bone-bare look of fear that etches the faces of anyone startled in that awful way, their bodies as white as the bellies of night-roaming fish at the bottom of the sea.

"Where'd you get these?"

"I took them last night at the home of Miss Mary Beth Jones, a prostitute on a working holiday in Palm Springs."

"I know about her. Nell's using her house until she gets settled in a place of her own or until we work things out."

"I understand. I'll give shorter answers."

"Why'd you take these pictures?"

"I asked him to, Daddy," Jenny said.

"Why the hell would you do that?" Twelvetrees asked.

"I hear you cursin' around the house that you don' intend to let Nell pick your pocket on her way out of your life." She seemed close to tears.

"So what am I supposed to do with these, blackmail her?"

"I just asked Mr. Spinneran to see what he could find out. I didn' expect . . ."

"Okay. You were trying to help your old man. How can I get mad at that?"

Jenny got up and touched Twelvetrees on the neck.

Spinneran moved smoothly to his feet.

"I thought I was bein' of some help, Daddy," Jenny said.

"I know, kitten. I know you meant the best."

"I got to go on home an' get ready for the party tonight." She glanced at Spinneran. "Thank you, Mr. Spinneran. If there are any other charges . . ."

Spinneran gestured as though dismissing the rest of any payment due.

"Then, I'll see you tonight, Connor."

"I'll be there."

"Here, give your old man a kiss," Twelvetrees said, and reached up to pull her head down. His mouth met her's and lingered a moment. "You're all right, kid," he murmured.

"If you need me just whistle," Jenny kidded back in the voice of Lauren Bacall.

They watched her walk out of the commissary, drawing appreciative glances from men and speculative glances from women.

Spinneran sat down.

"What are you?" Twelvetrees asked.

"I'm an investigative consultant."

"Gimme a break. Are you an eye?"

"This isn't nineteen-forty, Mr. Twelvetrees."

"And you're not Humphrey Bogart. I can see that."

"Different times need different titles, different definitions."

"So who do you work for?"

"I'm about to sever my association with Tregaron and Wales."

"What did my daugther pay you for slipping around photographing my bare-assed wife and her stud?"

"We never settled on a fee."

"You do charity work for pretty young women?"

"We happened to meet at the Museum of Art while looking at

a minimalist painting by Ellsworth Kelly," Spinneran began, as though determined not to be intimidated.

"And you just happened to say you were a private dick, and she just happened to say she wanted you to spy on her stepmother, and take her picture bare-assed if the occasion should arise?"

Spinneran resisted Twelvetrees's belligerent sarcasm with imperturbable calm, though two spots of heightened color appeared high on his cheeks. "That is essentially what took place," he said.

"How long ago did this happen?"

"We met ten days or so ago. She didn't ask me for the favor until last night."

"So now it's a favor. You do favors like this on such short notice?"

"It wasn't difficult."

"And on such short acquaintance?"

"It wasn't expensive."

"And you figured it might lead to something with me?"

"I'm not playing games, Mr. Twelvetrees," Spinneran said smoothly. "A man in your position sometimes needs service. If I were a top automobile mechanic, would I be out of line bringing myself to your attention?"

"You know to the inch how to slice the bullshit, don't you? So let me ask, what kind of service do you think I might require?"

Spinneran took out one of his business cards, which had only his name on it. He wrote a number on it.

"You're going to have to make up your own mind about that. You might decide that you want to avoid the emotional stress and possible financial loss of a divorce settlement. I'm expensive, but not as greedy as some people we might mention. If you need me, Mr. Twelvetrees, I can be reached at that number, anytime, day or night."

Twelvetrees went into his pocket. "Wait a minute, sonny." He peeled off two one-hundred-dollar bills and put them on the table. "For the photography."

Spinneran smiled and shook his head. "No charge for the photographs. I don't think they'd be very useful in persuading your wife not to steal your shoes."

Twelvetrees pushed the money at him. "You took the trouble."

"I'll take it as an advertising deduction."

"How's that?"

"They're proof that bodyguards wouldn't do her any good if I wanted to get her."

"Bodyguard?"

"That man in the picture isn't a boyfriend."

"So the two hundred's for finding out who he is."

"He's a gypsy private ticket by the name of Whistler who works out of his hat," Spinneran said.

Mamie came up to them at just that moment, summoned by the restaurant manager who'd been watching with dismay as Mr. Midnight America and his guest had gone unserved. She stood there, pencil and pad poised.

"Can I get you anything?"

Spinneran shook his head, smiled, and got up to leave.

"Hey, don't forget your money," Twelvetrees said, jerking his head to the two bills still lying on the table.

Spinneran met his mocking eyes, picked up the money, folded it, and tucked it into the pocket of Mamie's apron.

Mamie looked at Twelvetrees, wondering what she should do with the two hundred. Twelvetrees got up and patted her hand.

"Can you believe that sucker? He gives away two hundred bucks just for the pleasure of sticking it up my ass for five seconds. I tell you, babe, that makes me the highest priced hooker in town."

"I been saying that for years," Mamie cracked warily.

Twelvetrees started laughing fit to bust. He threw his arm around her shoulders as if they were old, old friends.

"You figure how to clean that up, babe, and I'll use it on my show tomorrow night," Twelvetrees said.

EIGHT

WHISTLER HAD KNOWN the Club Armentières in one of its previous incarnations. He used to come listen to poets read their works, thinking they were wise and himself wonderful. Since then he'd been there once or twice when on the prowl. Enough to know the proprietor called himself Maurice and his "wife" Esme, but not much more.

The alley didn't seem much changed. The dog turds petrified among the weeds might have been the same ones, stored away in some warehouse full of urban props and trotted out to dress the sets of a hundred cheap flicks recorded on reels of stock ends by nonunion camera crews and young directors trying to kick down the door to honor, power, fame, riches, and the love of women. Or men.

The door was open to air out the place. When he walked through the door he could tell the strategy had done no good, the place smelled terrible and was heavy with the heat of the Santa Ana winds as well.

Whistler nearly didn't recognize Esme, dressed in jeans and sweatshirt, a knotted half-stocking covering his balding head, swamping down the floor with a sour-smelling mop. Maurice was nowhere to be seen.

Esme looked up. "Not open. Not open," he trilled.

"I wasn't looking for a drink or anything to eat," Whistler said.

Esme squinted his eyes. "Do I know you? Get out of the doorway so I can see you."

Whistler came farther into the room so that he was no longer a silhouette against the harsh light.

Esme leaned the mop handle against the zinc-topped bar. "Sure, I know you. Let me think." He threw his head back, flattening out the wattles of his neck, dramatically placing a thumb and finger on the bridge of his nose between his eyes, pulling out the memory.

Whistler could see that Esme was a person who prided himself on his memory.

"You've got something to do with the law. You're something to do with detectives." He brought his chin down and stared challengingly at Whistler with nearsighted intensity. "Am I right? Am I right?"

Whistler smiled the brief, secret smile common to officers of the law, as though he were reluctant to answer questions or affirm a speculation, because that's what only officers of the law were authorized to do and citizens should not presume to usurp the power.

"I knew it. You want a brandy? You want a glass of wine?"

Whistler shook his head and poked a finger into the little bowl of cellophane-wrapped candies beside the cash register drawer.

"How about a beer? I can serve you a beer." Esme said, wiping his forehead with his forearm. "No? So all right, you came to talk about what happened the other night. I'm so warm. My God, I'm sweating like a pig. I shouldn't be mopping the fucking floor, you know. I keep telling Maurice to get a boy to do it. He's too cheap. He says he'll do it himself and then he never does it. He wouldn't care if this place turned into a pigpen. So then I have to do it." He'd made his way around the end of the counter and was behind the bar pouring himself a glass of white wine. "I shouldn't be mopping the fucking floor, you know. You want one of those?"

"Candies?"

"Well, go ahead, take one."

Whistler picked one off the top.

Esme was staring at him, smiling. "Well, go ahead, unwrap it and pop it into your mouth."

"I'll save it for later."

"No, go ahead. Unwrap it and see what it says inside."

Whistler unwrapped the piece of hard candy and put it into

his mouth. It was licorice-flavored, but was stale and had an undertaste of soap.

"So read it. Go ahead, read it out loud," Esme said, staring at Whistler's mouth now, still smiling a smile that looked as though it had been cut out of a magazine ad for toothpaste and pasted on his face.

Whistler read it:

> There was a young boy from Des Moines,
> His sister's pants he purloined.
> Stole a bra from his ma,
> And told them ta-ta
> To set up shop on the old Tenderloin.

"Priceless," Esme said.

Whistler returned Esme's stare with a blank one of his own. "I don't get it."

"Well, you know, it means he became a TV—you know, a transvestite—and went into business on the street."

"Oh," Whistler said.

"You are the dense one, aren't you," Esme said, dropping his gaze to his glass of wine.

"You remember last night as well as you remembered me?" Whistler asked.

"Of course, I remember. The biker was a periodic regular. He didn't really have a bike, he just dressed like he had a bike."

"What is a periodic regular?"

"A customer who comes in every night, every other night, for seven or eight nights at a stretch, then we don't see him for maybe three months."

"Why is that?"

"Well, either the urge to come out of the closet and go fagging only comes on him every so often—you know, like a nasty fever?—or his wife goes to visit her folks for three months at a time and he can go out and be a pig. He was a middle-aged closet pervert from over in the Valley. He thought we didn't know."

"How did you know?"

"Well, the damn fool would get drunk and pay with a credit card sometimes—wouldn't he?—the stupid peckerhead."

"This other customer, the one who was dressed in a flyer's outfit . . ."

"Oh, yes, him. Very pretty, very Valentino—black hair parted in the middle—and very chilly. Little pussy tickler on his lip. Unfriendly. He was also about as cheap as Maurice."

"What makes you say that?"

"We charge fifteen percent *service compleat*, just like they do in the bistros and restaurants in France—you understand?—but we really do expect our patrons to be a little more generous than that. Another five percent. Ten percent would be better."

"And he didn't leave an additional tip?"

"Not a sou."

"Did he pay with a credit card?"

"Cash. A five-dollar bill, a one-dollar bill, and a thin dime. His tab had come to six dollars and five cents for two Napoleon brandies. And he stood there, right where you're standing, waiting for his nickel."

"His nickel change?"

"I mean, after all, a nickel. What can you buy for a nickel nowadays?"

"That's right. What can you buy?"

"Well, you can buy a French Secret."

"A what?"

"A candy like the one you're eating."

"So he took his change in candy?"

"And acted a little surly about it. But I was ready to wait him out. I mean, it wasn't the nickel—my God, what can you buy with a nickel nowadays?—it was the principle of the thing."

"Were these two ever together at any time during the evening?" Whistler asked.

"It was very early and pretty slow. Maybe thirteen, fourteen people in the club. I knew the Valley businessman, so I said hello to him and forgot about him. The flyer was very good-looking and new, so I paid a little more attention to him, perhaps. Quietly. I mean I didn't try to strike up a conversation or anything. I wanted him to get the feel of the place."

"But he was in costume?"

"When he was leaving, he mentioned that the club had been recommended to him by somebody back in New York. I thought at the time that it was very nice of him to take the trouble to dress

up the first time he visited us . . . even if he didn't leave a tip and
wanted his measly nickel in change."

"Because what can you buy with a nickel nowadays?"

Esme's eyebrows went up. "Yes," he said, instantly offended,
thinking he was being made fun of.

"He might have dressed that way so he'd look like he knew his
way around, wasn't just some turkey off the farm," Whistler said
quickly, anxious to retrieve his gaffe.

"What difference would it make?" Esme said, flat-eyed and
remote.

"No difference. We're just kicking this around, maybe we can
figure something out together," Whistler said, leaning on the bar
top and smiling into Esme's eyes.

Esme lost his chill. "Phillip and Charles started swapping
tongues, which is something we don't encourage. I mean, a show
of affection is all right, but we frown upon any excess. I might
have said something, but no one seemed to object too much, so
I let it pass. Harry took the opportunity—"

"Harry?"

"The Valley businessman biker."

"Gotcha."

"Harry used it as an excuse to try to strike up a conversation
with the flyer. But the dark knight of the air wasn't having any.
I could have told Harry the flyer wasn't the type that went for
leather and chains."

"Then you didn't get the impression they knew each other?"

"Sometimes my customers play little games. You know, old
friends will make believe they're meeting for the first time.
Recapturing the romance of those first moments—you understand? I mean, my God, they've probably just shared a bathroom
and here they are pretending their eyes are clashing, simply
clashing, across a crowded room."

"Like in the song?"

"I think it's sweet. Well, this wasn't that. The flyer put Harry
down and took a walk a couple of minutes later. A minute after
that Harry followed him out. So I started to follow them."

"Why would you do that?"

"Harry had been drinking before he got here. I'd seen him
mean before. As long as he was inside we could handle it. I was
afraid he was drunk enough and mad enough—I mean, he'd been

rejected very strongly right in front of everybody—to go after the flyer outside in the alley. We don't need the kind of trouble that would bring." He stopped, as though just that moment realizing the facts. "The kind of trouble it *did* bring, for heaven's sake."

"Did you get to the door in time to see anything?"

"I had my hand on the latch when I saw two flashes through the stained glass. I thought it could be lightning. I thought a thunderstorm was going to break up the heat. That's what was going through my head."

"So you opened the door to see?"

"Maurice called me from the bar and told me not to go out. He always tells me, if anybody is supposed to go out there and see there isn't any trouble, it should be the man of the establishment. He's the man of the establishment, but he doesn't do it. I always do it. Like I always mop the floor."

"So by the time you got out there . . ."

". . . Harry was laying in the middle of the alley pumping blood."

"And the flyer?"

Esme shrugged.

"So you didn't even see him get into a car?"

"I didn't see him at all."

"Was Danny Cortez around today?" Whistler asked, moving away from the bar.

"He was here this morning, and he said he might be back again."

"Did he get Harry's real name?"

"I gave it to him."

"Have you still got it handy?"

"You police should really get your act together, you know," Esme said, but he opened the cash drawer, took out some credit slips, and copied a name off the top one. Then he wrote down the telephone number that Harry the businessman biker had jotted down as required by the management.

Whistler came back two steps and took it from Esme who held on to it for a second. "You're not a cop," Esme said. "I just remembered. You're private."

"Well, for God's sake, Esme, isn't that practically the same thing?"

"I don't know if Cortez would like you nosing around."

"Now that the cat's out of the bag, can we keep it our little secret?"

"If you promise to be nice to me."

"Well, I don't know how nice you want me to be, but I'll tell you what, if you keep this quiet I promise not to burn your wig and hide your padded bra," Whistler said, making sure to smile.

Esme squinched up his face and made a little mew. "Oh, you're such a beast. Get out of here before I call a cop."

NINE

THERE WERE PLACES along a stretch of Sunset Boulevard between Crescent Heights and Doheny Drive that looked like a city struggling out from under siege. Small hotels and ancient office buildings were pocked with broken windows and other windows were boarded up. The handles of double doors were wrapped with padlocked chains. Pieces of stucco had fallen away leaving gaping wounds, and walls were striped with graffiti the color of old saber slashes.

There was no foot traffic along the street. Anyone who had a need to walk there wore the anxious look of a soldier plodding through no-man's-land. The empty sidewalks spoke of muggers and rapists everywhere, even in broad daylight.

One or two buildings were still occupied, struggling to stay alive amid the general forlorn decay. A pink one, with green trim and a plastic palm in the lobby, sheltered a marginal talent agency, a dating service, three writers who ground out pornography, a radio ministry in the age of television, and the offices of Tregaron and Wales, a security agency that provided rent-a-cops for parties, retail sales, and the openings of gasoline stations and head shops.

The offices were composed of a waiting room about as big as the customer's john in a whorehouse, and a room large enough to accommodate a fake antique partner's desk, four chairs—two swivel and two straight—a water cooler, a metal typing stand with an electric typewriter resting on it, a worn leather couch, a four-drawer filing cabinet, four telephones, and one answering machine.

Tregaron had been Philly the Fink Torino back in New Jersey, a running mouth who'd somehow escaped the wrath of the mob by telling as many tales on the cops as on the families, thereby buying important favors from executives on both sides of the street.

There came a day when both sides advised him to travel west and keep in touch.

Wales had been known as Mocky Hush in her hooking days. She'd earned her name because she'd once been known as the quietest whore in the tri-state area around Cincinnati. Saying nothing, she heard much, finally eavesdropping on a conversation about a killing that convinced her to travel west in the interests of her health and welfare.

One of her favorite poems went, "Fuck a bartender, you're a two-dollar whore. Fuck a banker, you're an entrepreneur." She was long past it, though still a pretty fair-looking piece. But there was no living to be made on her back anymore.

When they weren't playing cards with one another, Torino and Hush spent their time on the eary here and there, this watering hole and that country club, trolling for gossip that could be turned into gold.

Occasionally they got a call for a uniformed cop. In the Rolodex they had names of unemployed actors, broken-down winos, failed confidence men, one-legged tap dancers, and a few junkies—all of them armed, most of them unbondable.

Occasionally they arranged contract murder for respectable citizens tired of wife, husband, boss, or lover.

In Spinneran they had found a treasure.

Connor Spinneran had come to them with written references from Pug-Nose Codigora of Chicago, Judge Mortimer Cromarty of Boston, and Professor Stanley Pardubica of New Haven, home of Yale University.

When queried further by telephone, each of them acted in a sudden hurry and, without going into much more detail, urged the partners to give the kid a chance.

This immediately told the partners that Spinneran had talents that would certainly prove valuable to the firm, a nose for blackmail on the one hand and a mouth tutored by discretion on the other being not the least of them.

Since Cromarty had a taste for boys, Codigora for young and kinky whores, and Pardubica of Yale favoring cross-dressing, S and M, and the occasional flirtation with self-hanging, it meant that Spinneran was either a twangie boy, an accomplished pimp, or a willing playmate in games that could only be surmised. His hobbies and pastimes were, of course, his own affair. The only thing Torino and Hush cared about was that he was, at the very least, a nasty piece of business, which suited them very well.

He did, however, have his faults. For one thing, it had proved difficult, almost impossible, to track his history beyond the three recommendations without an effort so expensive it was hardly worth the cost. For another, his discretion, while valuable from one point of view, was a definite pain in the ass from another. The only secrets people like kept are the ones that are kept from others.

Also he didn't gamble, which was a disease Torino and Hush had in common. His refusal to take a hand of cards or put down a hundred on a pony's nose was a quirk they considered unnatural. Whenever he walked in on their permanent, ongoing marathon gin rummy game, they always offered him a chair and he always refused to sit in.

During these games, in the long afternoons inside the nearly airless room, they had occasion to discuss their most valuable employee up one end and down the other.

"I told Connor just the other day," Mocky said. "A young person's got to take chances. If you can't take chances when you're young, when can you take chances?"

"So what did he say?"

"He just smiled."

"Why does he do that? Why does he always smile like that and don't say nothing? It makes me nervous. There's something not quite right about that gink."

"He's not all man, I can tell you that."

"Well, no kiddin'. For chrissakes, Mocky, a blind man could see his feet ain't touched the ground in fifteen years."

"He ain't a faggot neither."

"So what is he?"

"A neuter," Mocky said.

"If he's a neuter, maybe that's what makes him so good at what he does. Nothing to distract him. I knew a wise guy back in Jersey, name of Harry the Wire, liked to practically take a person's head off with a loop. You know how they do? We'd have these parties, six or seven guys, eleven, twelve girls. Enough for seconds, you know what I mean? The main course and dessert, you don't got to wait. Harry the Wire never partook. I thought that strange, so I asked him was he religious. He says not especially, though he goes to confession and makes his Easter duties every year. I ask him was he saving himself for marriage. He says he don't believe in it. It's costly, he says. It's cheaper to have a dog. I ask him did he have a dog. He said he didn't."

"What the hell's the dog got to do with it, Philly?" Mocky interrupted as she frowned over her cards.

"I thought you'd like to know. So I asked him did he have a chronic disease. I thought maybe like high blood pressure. A man could have a stroke in the middle of a kazotski, you know what I mean?"

"I had it happen," Mocky said.

"So I asked him, how come he don't partake. He looks at me this funny way and tells me he goes off like a rocket every time he ices somebody, and how much of that kind of excitement could a reasonable man take? The way he looked at me was like he was thinking about doing me and getting his rocks off right on the spot. I never asked Harry the Wire about his personal life again. Our employee has got the look. I think Spinneran would kill a person just as soon as kiss 'em on the cheek. Maybe he goes around at night killing people for free instead of fucking."

"Are you crazy? Fachrissakes, the way you talk, makes a person crazy."

"I'm not crazy. I'm just saying you can't be normal to do good in certain professions," Torino said philosophically, "otherwise you're pissin' in the wind."

Spinneran walked in on them just then. Mocky waved him to a chair, which he pulled back from the table several inches before sitting down and crossing his legs.

Mocky glanced down at his ankles. "How do you keep your socks so neat?"

"I tack them to my shinbones," Spinneran replied.

Mocky laughed. "Now that's what I call tough."

Spinneran went into his briefcase and came up with a manila envelope like the one he'd given to Twelvetrees, and threw it on the desk on top of the cards. Mocky pushed it toward Torino so she could get to the ten of hearts. She discarded a queen of spades. Torino picked up, discarded, said gin, and laid down his hand.

He opened the flap as Mocky totted up the score.

There were two prints of the body of the man in the alley. Torino tilted his head this way and that.

"Okay," he said.

"Have you heard from the wife?" Spinneran asked.

"Not yet. Maybe the cops ain't yet informed her of her husband's death."

"It's in the papers."

"Unidentified. I don't hear from her by tomorrow, I take a little ride over to Van Nuys, make sure she isn't under surveillance, phone isn't tapped, and I present our bill for the rest she owes us."

"I'd like my wages now, if you don't mind."

Mocky's hands faltered as she shuffled the cards. "What's the hurry. You work by the piece, you get paid by the piece."

"So? There's the pictures. There's the proof I did the job."

"Who's saying you didn't? What I'm saying is you get paid when we get paid."

"And all I'm saying is I don't want to wait."

Mocky Hush had an ear for what people were really saying when they were saying something else. She laid down the cards. "All right. What's the rest of it?"

"Rest of what?"

"I just mean don't you want to tell us why you need your money before we got our money?"

"I need it for personal reasons."

"I can understand that," Torino said. "We all got personal reasons, but personal reasons ain't good enough for when we got twenty-five hundred dollars involved here."

Mocky picked up the cards and started dealing them out, acting very casual. "You got to be more specific than that," she said. "Your mother sick? You got a girlfriend in some kind of trouble?" She kept tossing little glances at Spinneran, wondering if she could finally trap him into giving something about himself away.

"As a matter of fact, I have a friend who needs an operation."

"Watch yourself," Torino advised. "I myself have been taken by the old 'I need an operation' dodge."

"This is no dodge. This is a necessity."

"So it can't wait? Your friend's having it done right this minute? Even as we speak? The hospital won't sew her up unless you bring the cash?"

Spinneran got up.

"I can wait. I can't stand the conversation."

"Don't go away mad," Torino said, picking up his cards and setting up his melds.

The outer door closed. Not hard and not soft. Spinneran didn't even let you know what he was feeling by how he closed a door.

After a minute Mocky said, "You know what? I think that boy has got himself a hidden agenda."

"A what?"

"I think he might be going into business for himself."

"So what do you think we ought to do?"

"I think we should put somebody on his tender ass."

"You got anybody in mind?"

"You remember Mike Rialto?"

"The one-eyed pimp, Mike Rialto?"

"Well, he's not really a pimp, more like a talent scout," Mocky said. "He's also got a private ticket, and I understand he could follow a fly up a cow's asshole and neither one would ever know it."

"Why don't you give him a call then? We'll look him over."

"If it's all the same to you, Philly, is it okay I look him over by myself?"

Torino leered. "Jesus Christ, Mocky."

"Nothing like that. I ought to wash out your brains with soap. It's just we was friends once upon a time and I'd like to talk about old times a little."

TEN

"TO WHAT DO I owe the honor, Roger?" Bernie Mandell asked as he got up from behind his acre of desk to greet his most valued and valuable client. "The meeting's not till four o'clock. It's only two."

"So I miss my afternoon nap. I can make the sacrifice," Twelvetrees said. "I mean, if you don't make a sacrifice one way you'll make a sacrifice another."

"Sit down. You'll have a little something? Coffee? Tea? Hot chocolate?"

"Nothing."

Bernie Mandell's suit fit like a sausage skin. It was dove gray with paler stripes running through it, producing a moiré effect. When he sat down he rippled. He seemed to ripple even when he was still.

His skin fit like a sausage skin, too. His complexion was tinged with gray, the pale sheen of a bratwurst, with little circles of color on his cheeks and the point of his nose. On first meeting most people thought it was rouge, until they noticed how the flush moved around his cheeks and jowls according to his temper.

He had pale eyes, pale hair, and yellow teeth.

He was on permanent retainer to Roger Twelvetrees. His fees were very high. His specialty was speed. He hated long delay. He enjoyed slicing up pies. He was greedy and thorough, not a single berry or crumb of crust got away if he could help it. But he knew when it was smart to give the enemy a cut.

He called himself a full-service office, and made jokes about how he'd pick up a client's cleaning or get his car lubed if the price was right.

Now he sat there contemplating his asshole of a client and wondering what Twelvetrees was being so goddamn smug about. It no doubt had to do with whatever was in the manila envelope he held on his lap.

"I thought you could give me an idea of how this thing today is supposed to work," Twelvetrees said.

"The way it works is when two people decide to call it quits there's a certain amount of property has got to be shared out."

"Half of all I made after taxes and expenses during the time we were married, right?"

"Not exactly. There are factors."

"Like what?"

"Like children."

"We haven't got any."

"I know that. You asked me about factors that could alter the equation, I'm telling you."

"Nell's not sick, and she's not old, and she could go out and get a job if she had to," Twelvetrees said.

"Nell's not twenty-one. She hasn't got any marketable skills."

"She's always telling me what a great club singer she was."

"She had the makings of a career. She interrupted it for marriage. Five years puts a hole in something like a singing career."

"Whose lawyer are you?"

"I'm your lawyer. That's why I'm going to do everything I can to do what's best for you. But there's no reason why we should let this turn into a bitter fight."

"What do you think she's going to ask for?"

Mandell held his arms out from his sides, palms up. "Who can say? Married to you five years? A million? Say five million?"

"Jesus Christ!"

"I'm giving you a low figure. What's five million to a man with your income?"

"What the hell do you mean?"

"I'm quoting from an imagined conversation between Nell and

her attorney, Hindy Reno. Look, what's to worry? Whatever they
ask is just a point of departure. They ask, we offer, they counter.
That's how it works."

He leaned forward, starting to enjoy this opportunity of
making it clear to his client.

"Like you go to a bazaar in Afghanistan. There's a rug
merchant got plenty of rugs. You see a rug you like. You know a
little something about rugs. This one rug is worth maybe eight
hundred dollars. That's a good price, a fair price. Eight hundred
dollars. So you ask how much is this rug."

Twelvetrees was looking at his lawyer as though he couldn't
believe his ears, but Mandell was on the wing and didn't notice.

"The rug merchant says four thousand dollars," Mandell
continued.

"For a lousy eight-hundred-dollar rug?"

"That's what I'm illustrating. That was his ploy, you see? So
what do you say?"

"I tell him to take the rug and stuff it up his ass."

"No, no, no. You offer five bucks."

"So now I'm as big an asshole as he is?"

"So now you start the negotiation. After a while you get the rug
for maybe seven fifty, maybe eight fifty, but you get it for a price
that's right in the neighborhood of what it's worth."

"How long does this take?"

"That isn't the point."

"How long does this take?"

"Depends."

"And during all this bargaining back and forth, maybe I have
to call in an expert to represent me?"

"That's possible."

"And the rug merchant calls in somebody to make his case?"

"Also possible, but that isn't the object of the story. The
object—"

"Maybe I don't know the object of the story," Twelvetrees
interrupted, "but the object of the experts is to make a buck. To
keep the negotiations going on as long as possible so they can
charge by the hour."

"I'm not charging you for this, Roger," Mandell said quickly.
"This is friends. This is off the clock. Even though you arrive
unannounced, without an appointment, two hours early."

"So never mind rugs," Twelvetrees said. "Let's talk about tits and ass."

"You're going to sing me a song from *Chorus Line?*"

Twelvetrees unclasped the flap on the manila envelope he'd been holding in his lap, took out the photos, and threw them face up onto Mandell's desk.

Mandell was saying, "I wish you wouldn't worry about this afternoon. I'm here to—" when he picked them up, took a look, said, "Not a bad pair of boobs for a girl Nell's age" without missing a beat, then went right on to finish "—look after your interests, and that's all you've got to know."

"What you're holding in your hands is what I'd call a factor," Twelvetrees said. "Wouldn't you say your wife fucking around before the divorce is even in the works is a factor?"

"What I hold in my hands is nothing but some photographs of two naked people."

"One of which happens to be the cunt who is out to steal my socks."

"Where'd you get these?"

"A private detective."

"A detective hired by yourself?" Mandell asked with some reproach in his voice, his expression saying as loud as words, how come, if Twelvetrees needed a soft-shoe act, he didn't let his old friend and loyal attorney, Bernie Mandell, do the hiring.

"Hired by somebody else."

"And paid for by somebody else?"

"I gave the detective a bonus for the pictures."

"How was entry effected?" Mandell asked, returning the photos to the envelope.

"Come again?"

"Did the detective have authorization to be in the house? Was he there in response to a need to be there? Was he, for instance, investigating a criminal affair? Or was he hired to watch over the premises for fear of burglary while the owner was away?"

"I don't know anything about any of that."

"The point is, if these photographs were obtained inadvertently while in the execution of lawful guardianship of property, there might, just might, be some way to enter them into evidence at the hearing. If they were obtained as the result of an action taken for that single, specific purpose—"

"Will you speak plain English?"

"—then I doubt we could even get the photographer to take the stand explaining the circumstances under which they were acquired, since he would immediately be placing himself in what is known as the shit. A charge of illegal breaking and entering—"

"Never mind," Twelvetrees said, reaching over and retrieving the envelope. "Can we use the pictures?"

"We can let the judge have a look at them. He rules them irrelevant and immaterial, but he's had a look at them all the same. But first we see how it goes this afternoon. First we hear what they want, then we offer them five dollars. Why don't you leave the pictures with me?"

"Well, I don't want pictures of my wife in this condition floating around."

"They wouldn't float."

Twelvetrees stood up, tucked the envelope under his arm, and went to the door. Mandell hurried to open it for him.

"As soon as possible, after this is settled, we should sit down and rewrite your will. Unless I'm very much mistaken, you'll be wanting to make special provisions for Jenny. It's like a miracle how she came back to you."

"That's right. A miracle," Twelvetrees said.

Walter Pulaski was waiting in the outer office. He got up when Twelvetrees came out, ready to guard his body.

Mandell didn't even say hello. Pulaski was like a fixture. He'd have received more attention if he'd been a dog.

"You got a little time to kill," Mandell said. "By the time you go home, you'd have to come back. Go around the corner to the delicatessen. Have a nice corned beef on rye. Ask for Gertie to wait on you and tell her to put it on my tab."

ELEVEN

MIKE RIALTO HAD a private ticket, made his living as a procurer, and had only one eye. He'd lost the other to iritis, an infection some wags claimed he'd acquired blinking off a whore down in Tijuana. Sometimes he wore a patch, most of the time the socket was fitted with a glass eye that didn't match the color of the good eye.

He was afraid of the dark and wouldn't go to bed until dawn. He sat all night at well-lighted bus stops all over the city. If you asked him what he was doing, he'd say he was on a stakeout. He was thought to be as good at stakeout and running a tail as anyone in the business.

Rialto and Mocky Hush had been lovers once upon a time. But she'd been ruthless and looking for class, and he was not very classy. They parted because Mocky didn't want losers for friends.

Sitting in her office in a sports coat that looked like a corduroy horse blanket, his shirt collar unbuttoned, and a rag of a tie pulled down, he still looked like a loser.

"Long time no see," he said.

"I see you still got good taste in clothes, but ain't the horse cold?"

Rialto frowned. "I hope that's a joke, Mocky, because I didn't come here to be insulted."

She lifted a hand heavy with rings, and said, "Take a minute, Mike, before you get mad. Didn't we always used to joke?"

Rialto's face looked sad for a second, as though he couldn't remember if they'd ever joked around or not. Then he grinned, "Don't your arm get tired carrying around all that glass?"

She looked at her jewelry. "These are glass, but the ones in the deposit box ain't."

"Oh, sure," Rialto said, looking around the room with exaggerated care.

"I don't spend it on overhead, Mike. That ain't the way to do it if you want to be left alone. So how's it goin', Mike?" she asked brightly.

"Can't complain."

"Making plenty?"

"Making a living."

"Streets are crowded with merchandise."

"Well, I'm not a pimp, Mocky. I just do the occasional favor for a friend."

"So you're making it with your good private eye?" She pulled down the lower lid of her own eye.

Rialto laughed. "A little joke, there."

"How are your rates?"

"Depends on the girl and the services required."

"I'm talking about a tail."

"Oh, I thought you meant you had some firemen visiting town."

"No, I'm talking about the other kind of tail. I want whores I know how to get whores."

"Three hundred a day and expenses."

"I think we've had enough jokes," she said.

"Two hundred, I'll pay for the gas in town."

"Professional courtesy, Mike?"

"A hundred and a half?"

"And a quarter? That sounds fair. Don't you think that sounds fair?"

"Can I look at it like it was an investment?"

"Will you run that horse by me one more time?"

"I mean, like, can I look forward to more business from you in the future?"

"Well, you can always do that. But this is a one-time-only situation at the moment."

"I understand. Who you want covered?"

From the desk drawer Mocky took a four-by-five blowup of the photograph taken of Spinneran for his license and handed it over. He was wearing an open-collared sports shirt and his hair was half falling across his pale forehead.

Rialto looked at it and said, "I can't tell, is it a man or a woman."

"A mule."

"What color hair?"

"Brassy."

He put the photo in his pocket. "Okay. He got a name?"

"Connor Spinneran."

"Funny name. Got an address?"

"He'll check in here sometime today. If he don't he'll be at the address on the back of the photo tonight."

"He work here?"

"That's right, and he lives at the other address."

"You want me to check up on one of your own people? What am I looking for?"

"Well, we don't know, do we? That's why we're putting you on the case, Mike."

"Okay, then."

Mocky straightened up, but didn't stand. She handed over an envelope. "There's three days' advance, cash, in there."

Rialto struggled to his feet. "What kind of wheels?"

"He drives a maroon BMW 633CSi."

"Jesus, maybe I should work for you, Mocky."

"The car's the only thing the kid owns, and that's in hock. You know how kids are."

"Oh, I remember, Mocky."

Mocky watched him lumber across the room. Why the hell did she feel her heart squeeze for a second? He turned around.

"You're really looking very good, Mocky. You ain't changed a bit."

"Neither have you, Mike."

He made a face as if he were going to say she shouldn't lie to him.

TWELVE

IF HE WENT over into the Valley now, Whistler thought, the passes would be fairly free of traffic. Then, say it took an hour to talk to the widow of Harold Vyborg—that was the name Esme had taken from the charge slip—he'd be going into Hollywood to pick up Nell while the commuter crush was going the other way.

He crossed the street, walked down two blocks to the gas station on the corner, and stepped into the phone booth. He called Gentry's, and Bosco answered.

"This is me," Whistler said. "You doing all right?"

"Nell's enjoying the show out the window, and Canaan's still telling her stories about some of the entertainers. He can be very
. . ."

Whistler had to shut the door against the roar of the traffic. "What did you say?"

"I said Canaan can be very funny when he wants to be."

"When does your shift end?"

"Half an hour."

"Can you keep Nell company if I don't get there until maybe an hour and a half after that?"

"I don't mind. What are you doing?"

"Nothing much. Just nosing around a little. This is between you and me."

"I understand."

"Last night somebody busted into the house where Nell's

staying. I wasn't fast enough to keep him from getting away. I wasn't even fast enough to see what he was driving, but I think I've got a pretty fair idea."

"Got all tangled in the sheets, did you?"

Whistler ignored the insinuation. "I looked around outside, over by a construction site across the street, which is the place I think this gazoony watched from and waited until he figured the house was asleep. I found a candy wrapper with the name of the Club Armentières on it."

"I like matchbooks better. There was this picture with William Powell and Myrna Loy—"

"*The Thin Man.*"

"—where the clue was a paper napkin from a nightclub."

"It's getting so whatever happens in real life feels stale because it's all happened before in the movies," Whistler said.

"Yeah," Bosco agreed. "Pretty soon you won't have to bother living your life. All you'll have to do is buy the movie."

"In this movie with Myrna Loy, was a murder committed at the nightclub earlier that same night?"

"Not as I recall."

"Well, there you go. I got a candy wrapper from the Armentières and I got a murder there, too."

"You think the gazoony what killed the person at the Armentières is the same one busted into the house?"

"I'm saying it's a possibility."

"Because of the candy wrapper?"

"It's all I've got. It could be the end of a piece of string."

"I think you got a boarding house reach."

"Well, my old man always said you had to have a boarding house reach if you were ever going to get your share off the table. I'm going out to speak to the wife of the dead man, if she's available."

"Well, good luck."

"Don't let Nell get impatient," Whistler said.

"Are you kidding? She'll be with me."

Whistler hung up and then called Benny the Booster, a hustler who sent shoddy merchandise that had never been ordered to names and addresses harvested out of the reverse directory. Seven days later he sent a bill. Twenty-one days after that he made a telephone call asking for his money. Out of every hundred people, seven paid up when they got the invoice with the merchandise, another five when they got the bill, and three more when he made the call. The other eighty-five told him they hadn't ordered the crap and didn't want it, that they'd call the police if he called again, or that they'd already called the police and why was he still at large.

Benny said he had a very good thing going. How many mail-order businesses had a fifteen percent return? On the few occasions when a district attorney's office finally acted to restrain him and bring him to court, he folded his corporation; changed his business address, phone number, and letterhead; let things cool; and got back in business sixty days later. He knew the world was so full of violent crime, and the courts so clogged with cases, that they were glad to let him disappear without punishment, thereby letting themselves off the hook until he resurfaced another time, another place.

It was a matter of a promise to get the address of Harold Vyborg of 37797 Sunnyglen Lane, Van Nuys.

The heat was starting to build up in the booth. Whistler dialed Vyborg's number. The voice of an old woman answered.

"Can Mrs. Vyborg come to the phone?"

"Mrs. Vyborg is . . . who is this?"

"A friend of Harry's."

"Who?"

"Harold. Is this the Harold Vyborg residence?"

"Yes, yes."

"Will you tell me who I'm speaking with?"

"Mrs. Jensen, Carla's . . . Mrs. Vyborg's mother."

"I was very sorry to hear about Harold, Mrs. Jensen. I'm not sure if we ever met."

"I don't think so. What is your name?"

"I knew Harold through business, but I was at his home three or four times. I remember a party he gave—"

"Your name?"

"I wanted to know if there was going to be a service."

"Oh, yes?"

"I'd like to pay my respects."

"Not a church service," she said, anxious to be helpful to someone who wanted to do a decent thing for her son-in-law. "He'll be buried from the chapel at Forest Lawn."

"The one in Glendale?"

"No, the one over by Warner Brothers."

"Has he been laid out?"

"You can view the body any time during the day until ten o'clock at night."

"I wanted to deliver my condolences to Carla personally."

"Yes?"

"Do you have any idea when I could do that?"

"Well, I was going to say when you called that Carla's been over at Forest Lawn since this morning. She should still be there. She said she didn't want any lunch." Mrs. Jensen sounded worried about her daughter not wanting any lunch.

"I'll tell her she should have something to eat if I see her before you do," Whistler said.

"Thank you, Mr. . . . ?"

Whistler hung up and left the phone booth.

He drove through the pass along the Hollywood Freeway to Barham Boulevard, then along Forest Lawn Road, through the cemetery gates, and up to the parking lot in front of the colonial building that accommodated all the services Forest Lawn had to offer. There weren't many cars in the lot.

The change in temperature from the outside to the inside made the backs of his hands and his cheeks feel damp. A very attractive woman was sitting at a desk that was placed at the natural focal point of the heavily carpeted reception hall. It was so quiet in the place Whistler could hear the hiss of his footsteps and the rale of his breathing.

There was a discreet nameplate on the desk identifying the woman as Ms. Wilda Pigeon. The way she looked him over as he approached, Whistler didn't know if she was measuring him for a coffin or a bed.

"Mr. Vyborg?" he said.

"That would be room seven. You may sign the registry just inside the door."

"Is anyone in there? I mean besides Mr. Vyborg."

Ms. Pigeon's mouth twitched. "I believe the widow of the deceased is with him."

"How is she taking it?"

"With considerable calm and fortitude. Are you a relative? A friend? Are you a cop?"

"What makes you ask that?"

"We've had one or two stop in from time to time."

"Has one stopped in to see Mr. Vyborg?"

"Earlier this morning. The deceased hadn't been laid out yet."

"He died last night, he's laid out today. Quick service."

"The widow paid extra."

"About the cop . . ."

"Daniel Cortez."

"Did he speak to the widow?"

"She hadn't yet arrived and the deceased hadn't yet been laid out for viewing."

"So what did Daniel Cortez do?"

"He waited for her, sat over there in the corner and watched the door when he wasn't looking at my legs. You haven't told me if you're a cop."

"Outside of a chance of spending a nice morning looking at your legs, why do you suppose Detective Cortez sat over there?"

"Do you suppose it was on the theory that the killer would want to have a look at his victim?"

"Killer?"

"Well, Mr. Vyborg didn't cut himself shaving and die from loss of blood, did he?"

"You had a look at him, did you?"

"I'm an apprentice cosmetologist. So?"

"I'm a private cop."

"How come you don't look like Humphrey Bogart?"

Whistler walked across the sea of carpet to room seven. The door was open. The coffin was on a bier at the back of the room with flowers at the head and foot. A woman who just missed being matronly, who seemed lush and sexually provocative instead, sat off to one side, her white-gloved hands resting on a folded newspaper in her lap, her eyes staring straight ahead at the face of the corpse with a look of disdain, disgust, anger, and satisfaction such as Whistler had never seen before.

Whistler looked at the open guest book on a stand beside the door. The pages were untouched. He picked up the pen beside it and wrote "A Friend" at the top of the clean page. The hiss of the ballpoint was loud enough in the silent room to break the spell that gripped Mrs. Vyborg. When Whistler turned to her, she was looking at him, a studied look of quiet mourning on her face.

He went to her and took her hand. "My name's Whistler."

"Yes?"

"I didn't know your husband."

A look of consternation moved across her face like a shadow. "Then why are you here?"

"The papers didn't give the details, but I know what happened to your husband."

She looked terrified. It was all she could do to sit there with her hands folded in her lap. "How do you know that? Do you work for . . ." She stopped.

"Do I work for the same company you hired to get the goods on your husband?"

She stared at Whistler as though he were the head of Medusa and she'd been turned to stone. Finally she managed to say, "The goods?"

"Did you think he was running around on you with other women?"

Her eyes cleared. She relaxed.

Whistler had the feeling that he'd almost had something, that she'd almost let the cat out of the bag, but he'd let it get away.

"If I hired anyone to find out if my husband was running around, I certainly wouldn't have expected to find out that he was running around with queers." The word turned her mouth sour. "I was going to ask if you worked for the police. If you're not from the police, there's no reason for me to answer your questions, is there?"

He took out the leather case with his private license behind the plastic window and held it open in his hand. She took his wrist, and bent her head to look at it. Her fingers dragged across his wrist as she withdrew her hand.

"I still don't understand what you hope to get from me."

"I have a client," Whistler said. "I've got reason to believe the same man who killed your husband could be checking up on her."

"Do you mean he wants to kill her, too?" she asked, burlesquing her disbelief.

"He took some pictures of her, checking out any indiscretions. He may have been checking out your husband's indiscretions, too. Your husband may have challenged him. They had a fight and things ended up the way they did. That is, if you hired anyone to check up on your husband."

"But I didn't. I just said so, didn't I? My husband was an

insurance executive. Very conservative. Very circumspect. He put in long hours. His work was everything. I had no reason to suspect anything. Certainly not . . ." Her mouth went wry again.

"Perhaps his company ordered the surveillance."

"I doubt it very much. But then that shouldn't carry much authority, should it? After all, it seems like I knew practically nothing about Harold."

She looked at the face of her husband rising from the billows of cream-colored satin, and the same hating and hateful expression she'd been wearing when Whistler walked through the door twisted her face like a spasm of pain.

"Has the man they believe might have killed your husband been described to you?"

"Yes, a detective named Cortez asked me if I knew a slender man, with black hair and a mustache, wearing a military uniform from World War One."

"You never saw anyone like that with your husband?"

She raised her eyebrows, making fun of Whistler. "A man in a World War One uniform?"

Whistler didn't reply. He sat down, bent toward her, one elbow on his knee, head raised, staring up into her face. She recoiled a little, rocking back in the chair until she was sitting up very straight.

"I can't answer anything about my husband's secret life. I knew nothing about it. Absolutely nothing." Her voice was rising and thinning out.

"You had no suspicions?"

"Suspicions of what? That my husband was a homosexual?"

"He may not have thought of himself that way."

"He was in a gay bar and—"

"What I mean is, some men—plain everyday businessmen—like to dress up in leather and pretend they're outlaws. They like to hang around gay joints. Some of them maybe even like to rough them up a little."

"Perverts!" The word snapped and popped like a little firecracker.

Whistler stood up. She looked up at him now, and that seemed to make her feel more comfortable, a woman of her generation looking up to the man, a position from which she knew how to manipulate, how to endure, how to prevail. She even tried to smile, acting out the part of the grateful widow receiving condolences.

Whistler said goodbye. He walked across the thick carpet that muffled his footsteps, turned at the door, and glanced back at the widow. She sat there hating the dead man.

THIRTEEN

THE BUILDING WAS faced with red brick, with a glass and bronze canopy over the entrance in case of rain in a climate where it was never supposed to rain. The lobby had a white marble floor and pink marble walls. The two elevators had doors of brushed copper. There was a little directory in a gold frame behind some glass. There were four floors and only three tenants.

Whistler and Nell stood in front of the elevators, Whistler having finally collected her from the care of Bosco and Canaan, driven her back to Brentwood for a change of clothes, and then driven back into the boil and turmoil of Beverly Hills.

One of the elevator doors opened and a young woman stepped out, looking very poised in a blue dress with white collar and cuffs.

Whistler stepped back to let her pass, but she stood there, folding her hands in front of her just below her waist.

"Mrs. Twelvetrees?"

"Yes?"

"Mr. Mandell sent me down to show you to the conference room. He didn't want you to have to present yourself at the reception desk."

She looked at Whistler, smiling slightly, inquiringly.

"I'm with Mrs. Twelvetrees," Whistler said.

She nodded and stepped aside so that Nell could precede her into the elevator, letting Whistler bring up the rear. It was done without hesitation or misstep, as though she expected everyone read Miss Manners and knew what to do in every situation.

The elevator was air-conditioned, the air lightly scented, the ride to the fourth floor too short. Whistler hated to leave the car.

The young woman saw them safely off the elevator, inclined her head toward the facing doors across the narrow hall, smiled, her hands still folded beneath her little belly, then the doors closed and she was gone.

They went into a reception area. There was no desk, just four uncomfortable-looking chairs, one on either side of a pair of doors to the inner office, and one on either side of the entrance doors.

One of those was occupied by Walter Pulaski, who was wearing an electric blue sports coat and staring at his shoes.

"Hello, Walter," Nell said.

He started as though he'd been given a jolt, his mouth working itself into a smile as he raised his head. Then he half stumbled to his feet, looking for a place to put his hands.

"Miz Twelvetrees," he said. His glance flashed to Whistler, then away, looking down at the floor.

The floor was an expanse of polished hardwood with a yellow, white, and cream oriental carpet, much longer in one dimension than the other, inviting you to follow it to the pair of very tall polished oak doors.

Whistler grinned. "Want to come with me down the yellow-brick road?"

"We should have brought along a dog named Toto," Nell replied.

Before they reached the doors they were swung open by Bernie Mandell.

Whistler could see two men inside the room sitting in black Eames chairs on one side of a slate coffee table as big as a double surf board. He recognized Roger Twelvetrees. He didn't recognize the other.

"On the button. Right on the button," Mandell said in a voice that sold jovial by the pound.

Nell had to dip a little to take his kiss on her cheek.

"How many times have I said you should run away, leave Roger, come to Spain, Tahiti, someplace, anyplace, with me?" Mandell asked.

"With Sophie and the four kids?" Nell teased back.

"Just the two of us, such a beautiful shiksa you are, such a dream. Did I mean it? Of course, I meant it. In my dreams. In my fantasies. But did I want it to actually happen if it meant my two favorite people truly had to go and do it? Split up, I mean? Come to the parting of the ways?"

Twelvetrees was up and grinning in the easy way known to millions, ambling over in a cloud of goodwill. The other man unfolded himself, he was that tall, and stood there giving carefully controlled looks of welcome, pleasure, doubt, sarcasm, and expectation to everyone.

Twelvetrees craned his head forward and pursed his lips. Nell moved her torso so he could get to her cheek without making chest contact. He gave her a noisy smack under the ear. "Long time no see," he said.

"Hello, Roger."

Mandell hadn't missed a beat. "Of course I didn't mean it. I meant it, the running away, but at the cost of a divorce, of course I didn't mean it. What am I, a barbarian?" He stuck his hand out at Whistler. "I don't know you. Were you invited?"

"I invited him," Nell said.

Mandell held on to Whistler's hand and twisted around like a Thanksgiving Day parade float to look at the tall man. "Another lawyer is it? Are you ganging up on me?"

"A friend," Nell said.

Twelvetrees wanted to shake Whistler's hand. Mandell gave it up right away. Twelvetrees applied the pressure. Whistler raised his eyebrows a little, as if he were asking Twelvetrees did he want to arm wrestle in such a place at such a time.

"What do you mean 'friend,' Nell, for Christ's sake?" Twelvetrees said.

The tall man laughed and came over to join them. They were all gathered in the doorway, not in and not out.

"I know you don't I?" he asked. "My name's Hindy Reno. I represent Mrs. Twelvetrees."

Whistler's hand was passed again. Reno shook it while leaning over to give Nell the obligatory peck on the cheek and cop a peek down her front.

Whistler recognized him then. Hindy Reno's real name was Hindemuth Renkowski, the son of a Polish father and Irish mother, born and bred in the slums of Chicago, educated at a small law school with no name or reputation. He'd changed his name by legal petition about six months after he'd passed the bar in Illinois and bought his first pair of high-heeled boots made of lizard skin. He was six feet three and skinny as a fence post. He looked a lot like the late Gary Cooper. He'd come out to Hollywood because he figured he could work the resemblance. It was a way to meet people in the business. La-La Land loves a gimmick.

Whistler knew him because he'd looked him up once when Reno and his client, Cholly Ludovicki, the wrestler, had come to him asking him to bend the truth in a case Ludovicki was bringing against some television show about a doctor and a gypsy with a cauliflower ear. He'd never actually met Reno, only talked to him on the phone, but he knew as much about the lawyer as anybody in town probably knew.

"Sure I know you. Your name's Whistler." Reno grinned. "Whistler's—"

"Not a lawyer," Whistler said, cutting him short. A look passed between them. Reno nodded slightly. He wouldn't give anything away until Nell told him why she'd brought a detective along.

"A safety engineer," Reno said.

"You don't mind waiting out here with Mr. Pulaski? Private matters are going to be discussed this afternoon," Mandell said.

Twelvetrees was looking at Whistler as though he'd like a copy of his pedigree and a sample of his blood.

"Bernie, I'd like Mr. Whistler to—" Nell started to say.

"I'm sure Mr. Whistler doesn't mind," Reno interrupted her, taking Nell's elbow and leading her over the threshold. "People talk about their sex lives, politics, and religion anywhere, anytime, nowadays. But when they talk about money, it's a big secret."

"That's right," Mandell said, starting to close the door. "You want something to do while you're waiting, check the elevators. I could use a little reassurance those little cars can keep on carrying me up and down. That was a joke, Mr. Whistler. A little safety engineering humor."

Whistler took two steps backward, and Mandell closed the door on him politely but steadily. The latch failed to engage.

When Whistler turned around, he caught Walter Pulaski staring at him.

"Mr. Reno knows you," Pulaski said. "I know you?"

"I don't think so."

"I work for Mr. Twelvetrees. I'm his bodyguard. You work for Mrs. Twelvetrees?"

"I work for myself," Whistler said.

It was frigid in the waiting room. The air conditioner was pumping away. Whistler went over to the window and cranked it open a few inches, letting in the hot breeze of the Santa Anas. The draught pushed the door to the conference room open an inch or two.

Whistler wandered over and sat down. Pulaski was looking at his shoes again. Whistler looked at his shoes.

"So we'll all sit down around the table," Mandell said. "Who wants what to drink? Coffee, tea, hot chocolate . . ."

"Please, Bernie. It's a hundred and four outside," Reno said.

"But it's nice and cool in here. So we'll stay here forever drinking hot chocolate."

The table was bare except for four blue-lined yellow legal pads in leatherette folders, four ballpoint pens that retailed out at five ninety-eight apiece, and a Sony recording and transcription machine with an omnidirectional mike on a chromium stand.

They arranged themselves around the table, Twelvetrees and Reno in the chairs they'd had before, Mandell in one with a high back at a short end, and Nell on a small leather couch. Reno had his briefcase on the carpet beside him. Mandell kept eyeing a manila envelope on the floor under Twelvetrees's chair.

Mandell moved the pad and pen in front of him an inch this way, then an inch that way, getting ready to open business. His hands were small and fat, the nails beautifully manicured and buffed. They drew everyone's eyes. They never stopped moving, clasping and unclasping, pointing out this detail and that of any conversation with a busy index finger. Sometimes they detoured long enough to pull at the underwear binding his crotch or straighten out his pecker when it got caught crosswise.

"Is anyone intimidated by a recording device?" he asked. "No? You don't mind if I turn it on instead of calling in a steno?" He punched the necessary buttons. "Technology, it's wonderful."

"But can it sit on your lap, Bernie?" Twelvetrees asked. "Has it got good legs? Can it cop your joint on the lunch hour?"

"Roger," Mandell said, laughing but shaking his head as though Twelvetrees were a naughty child. "Mind your manners. This is being taped. You want another Watergate here? You want a tape running around full of blue jokes?"

"Maybe we could issue a bootleg record and cassette, this business shouldn't be a total loss," Twelvetrees said. "Would you want half the royalties, Reno?"

Mandell reached over and stopped the recorder, rewound the tape, then looked at Twelvetrees with his fingers hovering over the record buttons. "Are you going to be good, Roger? Can I depend on a little serious attitude?"

"Ready when you are."

Mandell hit the buttons again.

"Who the fuck's the character in the twenty-dollar suit?" Twelvetrees said, fixing Nell with a belligerent stare.

"Where can you get a suit for twenty dollars these days?" Reno countered, trying to stave off Nell's angry response.

"In the fuckin' ragbag at the Salvation Army is where," Twelvetrees said.

Nell looked at Reno. "Hindy, would you ask my husband to watch his language a little?"

"For chrissakes, will you listen to that?" Twelvetrees said with a great show of disgust.

Mandell patted his client's sleeve. "I think Nell's just trying to—"

"I know what she's trying to do. She's trying to act la-de-fucking-da, as though she's a queen and I'm some scumbag crawling around the gutter. I gross twenty million a year—"

"Rog!" Mandell said sharply, reaching for the stop button. "We don't know that. I mean, we have to look over the books. You understand what I'm telling you?"

"He's telling you not to show me your bankbook, Roger," Nell said, smiling sweetly.

"This is a preliminary discussion," Reno said. "I think we're all in agreement that our purpose is twofold. First, to see to an equitable division of the property acquired by Roger and Nell during their marriage. Second, to see it's done in such a way that the I.R.S. doesn't loot the proceeds of the division."

"That's a given," Mandell said. "We can agree on that. Can't we agree on that, Roger?"

"I think we should also have it understood going in that my client was an entertainer with a substantial career," Reno said.

"She was a bar entertainer, for chrissakes," Twelvetrees said. "She was singing for beer and pretzels anywhere she could find a bar stool to sit her ass down. She was probably selling it on the side."

He stared daggers at Nell, who seemed to be taking his abuse very calmly, though a shine of color under her skin and the fixed little smile on her mouth gave her distress away.

"That's not exactly true," Reno said smoothly, reaching down for his briefcase beside his chair. "I have here advertisements from lounges and supper clubs—"

"We'll agree that Nell had a career," Mandell interrupted. "We've got to be fair about this, Roger. Nell has a lovely voice. You know, Nell, that tape you made?"

"The one I paid for," Twelvetrees said.

"Sophie plays it for the grandchildren every time they visit. Puts them right to sleep."

"Thanks," Nell said, and laughed.

"Well, what's wrong with that? The title's 'Lullabies for Lovers,' isn't it? Lullabies is for putting to sleep, isn't it?"

"I was making a little joke," Nell said.

"Everybody's a comedian," Twelvetrees interjected, as though he was seriously annoyed by the observation.

Reno took out of his briefcase five copies of a document three pages long. He gave one to Twelvetrees, one to Nell, and two to Mandell.

"This is a list of acquisitions over the last five years that might be considered common property. I gave you an extra copy for your files, Bernie."

Mandell waved the thin sheaf of papers. "Wait a second here, Hindy, this was supposed to be a preliminary discussion of policy."

"I don't see any reason why we can't add a little something specific, do you? Someplace along the line we're going to have to call in a couple of accountants, a couple of appraisers . . ."

"We've got an inventory ready for you."

"Well, you've got your inventory—we understand that—but we have our inventory. That's what I'm saying. Why can't we compare the lists? At least do that . . ."

"Let's start dickering about the fuckin' rug," Twelvetrees said.

"What?" Reno said, a questioning look on his face.

"Let's look at the inventory you prepared for us," Mandell quickly said. "Any place to start is a place to start. You want to read it off, Hindy, while we follow along?"

Reno cleared his throat as though he were about to perform.

"Seven million in cash and securities, two New York City apartments furnished, the Hollywood Hills estate with furnishings, the Malibu house furnished, one Rolls-Royce, one Mercedes-Benz, one Alfa-Romeo, one Masarati, one seventy-seven Toyota hatchback . . ."

"Three rusty nails and a bag of horseshit," Twelvetrees said. "How come my dirty socks aren't on that list?"

"Take it easy, Roger," Mandell said. "We're just trying to establish a basis for negotiation here."

"Well, now, Bernie," Reno said, "as long as you're bringing up the subject of negotiation, we're trying to come to an agreement on this inventory here. Negotiation doesn't come into it. We're ready to simplify that part of it."

"Simplify? How simplify?" Mandell asked, as though he expected Reno to pull a gun.

"Half. That's what we expect to settle on here. Negotiations don't figure into it."

Twelvetrees leaped to his feet. His face twisted up in rage, the muscles of his neck standing out, his eyes pushing at his eyelids with the pressure of his blood. Instant boiling rage produced from a standing start. Fifteen-second fury on demand. "Half? What the fuck half!"

"Now sit down, Roger," Mandell said, getting to his feet.

"You'll get half a rap in the mouth," Twelvetrees screamed. "You'll get half a punch in the belly."

Mandell hit the wrong button on the Sony. It played back at speed, the ducklike garble counterpointing Twelvetrees's fury, creating an ear-shattering din.

"Whistler!" Nell shouted, adding her voice to the general uproar as Twelvetrees went on and on, accusing her of every vile act he could get his tongue around, Mandell trying to calm him down, Reno threatening legal action, and the Sony hooting away like a penny whistle.

Whistler glanced at Pulaski, who was on his feet, not sure what he was supposed to do. Whistler charged into the conference room.

Twelvetrees was bending down and picking up an envelope.

"Don't do this, Roger," Mandell said. "Please don't do this."

Twelvetrees tore off the flap and ripped the envelope down the side in his haste.

"This doesn't maintain the proper judicious atmosphere," Mandell said.

Nell was on her feet, moving toward Whistler.

Reno was reaching out to her. "It's all right, Nell. Let's just calm down everybody."

Twelvetrees threw the pictures of a naked Whistler and Nell down on the gray slate.

"Is she kidding? Is she fuckin' brain-stunned? You think I'm going to stand still and get robbed by a fuckin' whore with an ass so goddamned hot she picks up the first male tramp she can get her hands on?"

"I knew you hired that goddamned photographer," Nell screamed.

"I didn't! I didn't goddamn hire him. He came to me with that filth for sale *after* you called me. You're as crazy as a loon, you are. You're cock happy. You're one of them won't do it at home. You're one of them has got to have it down and dirty in the gutter."

Nell turned around, pushed past Whistler, and started running out of the room.

"Wait a minute. Just wait a goddamn minute," Twelvetrees said.

He started after her. Whistler stepped in his way.

"Jesus Christ, I'm sorry," Twelvetrees said. "I didn't mean what I said. Please, get out of my way. I got to catch her."

"Let him by, please," Mandell said.

"It's okay, Whistler," Reno said.

Whistler couldn't believe it. The color was out of Twelvetrees's face, his expression was calm and clear. The fury was gone as quickly as it had come. It startled and confused him for a minute. Twelvetrees made his way between the couch and table, and past Whistler very carefully.

"Do you understand a gazoony like that?" Whistler asked.

"What's to understand," Mandell said. "The man's a talent. The man's a celebrity."

Whistler left the office, hurried through the waiting room and out into the corridor. Nell was huddled in the corner by the elevators, her face to the wall, her head down. Twelvetrees was behind her, speaking very softly, as close as he could get to her without touching her. Pulaski was halfway down the hall.

Nell lifted her head and shook it. Twelvetrees backed off and Nell turned around. She cast a baleful look at him and waited until he stepped out of her way altogether. Then she walked down the corridor past Pulaski and said to Whistler, "Let's take the stairs."

Twelvetrees and Pulaski were already out the building entrance by the time Nell and Whistler reached the ground floor. The glass doors were just hushing shut.

"So did you get an earful of that?" Nell asked.

Whistler said that he had.

"You should have been in there getting a gander at the way that sonofabitch was staring at me."

"I saw a piece of it."

He pushed the outside door open and held it for her, then followed her out into a wall of heat. It almost rocked them back.

"So do you think I could use a safety man?"

"I'll hang around," he said.

"I'm glad. I wouldn't like going to that party tonight by myself." She stopped walking and half-turned to him before he could say anything. "Don't say it, Whistler. I know it's crazy. I'm not going to explain it."

She looked rumpled and distressed, not so neat and cool, ready to cry if he started an argument, or even a discussion.

"Something to drink," she said. "I'd like something to drink. There's a place on the corner."

She took Whistler's arm and leaned into him lightly as they walked.

Whistler shivered when they stepped inside the cocktail lounge. He'd be coming down with something, in and out of the cold and hot the way he was doing. Hanging out at Gentry's was safer, the air-conditioning didn't work too good.

The bar was tiny but half full. A few of the upwardly mobile young men and women were working one another for what they could get—a job, a promotion, a dinner, a weekend in Hawaii, an hour on the mattress.

Whistler and Nell settled themselves on two bar stools. The bartender wore a neutral mask.

"A ginger ale with a dash of grenadine, no cherry," Nell said. "Scratch that. Make it a daiquiri. No slush, but run it over the rocks."

Whistler took a ginger ale.

"What happens next?" Whistler asked, after the drinks had come.

"God knows. If this was the opening round, I'm not sure I can make the distance." She went into her skinny envelope purse and pulled out the inventory. "Want to see?"

"I heard some of it."

"Isn't it something what a funny man accumulates?"

"Do you expect him to stand still for you taking half of all that, and whatever else I didn't get to hear?"

"I've got him by the balls and they know it," she said. There was something not so likable about the way she said it.

She sucked up the last drops of sweetness.

"You finished?" she asked. "Maybe we should get going, then. I've got a lot to do before tonight. I plan to knock them right on their asses."

FOURTEEN

WHISTLER WAS OFFICIALLY hired, and on call to guard her body, but it didn't mean he couldn't wonder why he was all dressed up in his best black suit and silk rep tie escorting Nell Twelvetrees to a party given in honor of a stepdaughter she scarcely knew, in the house of the man she hated, who'd been screaming in her face and calling her every kind of whore not more than four hours ago.

The ways of La-La Land were bizarre and devious, Whistler thought, having much to do with face, panache, and grace under pressure. Not only Papa Hemingway but the inscrutable Chinese would have found them to their liking.

Whatever impact she'd dressed for when striding into Gentry's to hire herself a male companion was nothing to the care Nell had taken before presenting herself for this long goodbye.

The dress she was almost wearing was of a shade of emerald that caught the color of her eyes and complemented her red hair. It had the obligatory slit that rose higher on her thigh than ever, promising glimpses of hidden mysteries. The stockings she wore were the color of moonlight and shone with an odd fluorescence. Her shoes were little cages of thin green leather thongs.

Whistler felt like a chauffeur in his black wool suit.

They were riding in his old beat-up Chevy, Nell having opted for his car over her Mercedes for reasons he could only guess at.

He and his car were a stick in Twelvetrees's eye, proving that Nell didn't think money was the measure of a man. Twelvetrees could take all that he had and shove it—after she got hers.

The Chevy labored along the curving roads that climbed toward Twelvetrees's walled estate at the top of Skyline, far above the Strip and the sprawling city, which glittered down below like a bejeweled and sequined scarf tossed aside by a careless woman.

"I'd just as soon take you to Gentry's for a cup and a burger," Whistler said, "or I could find a beer joint where every man would kill every other man in the joint for the chance to sip lager from your shoe."

"You'll sweet-talk me into early diabetes, Whistler. But I do make a smashing picture, don't I?"

"Are you looking for a reconciliation with Twelvetrees?"

"I'm reminding the sonofabitch of what he's losing."

"Okay, if that's your pleasure. But can I just ask one more question?"

"As long as it doesn't have to do with love or marriage."

"Are you sure you're not going to fall out of the front of that dress?"

"Wouldn't it be interesting if I did," she said, grinning at him.

"That may be, but warn me before it happens. I don't want to get trampled to death."

She leaned across the short width of the car seat and laid a light kiss on his cheek, marking him a little but not smearing her lipstick. Then she settled back against the worn vinyl slipcovers, holding her little gift for Jenny Twelvetrees, all wrapped in pink paper and silver ribbon, in her hands.

Skyline was lined with cars on both sides all the way down to Green Valley Road. They passed a youngster in a red monkey jacket, blue jeans, and electric-green-and-yellow running shoes pumping up the hill like a marathoner. Another red-jacketed kid passed them in a white Rolls going the other way. Whistler drove through the open wrought-iron gates, huge panels of iron bars twisted into the shape of twelve fir trees, six to a side.

"Is this where you kicked off your shoes?" Whistler asked.

"This is where I was imprisoned in the tower," Nell said, laughing as though making fun of such extravagance.

Whistler pulled up and got out before another kid in a red

jacket could open the door for him. The kid acted as if it was just as well, pulling his hand back from the door handle very fast, as though afraid he'd be soiled forever if he touched it.

"Don't let it bother you, kid," Whistler said. "I rent cars to the studios. This is a classic."

"A classic what?"

The kid on the other side wouldn't have cared if they'd driven up in a wagon full of horseshit. He was handing Nell out of the car as if she were made of glass, and looking down the front of her dress at the same time. He was in love.

Twelvetrees and Jenny had a regular reception line going just inside the door.

He was in a dinner jacket of electric satin plaid. She was wearing a black dress that fit her like a glove missing three fingers.

Nell let some space grow between the last guest in line and herself. When there was enough ground to make an entrance, she composed a symphony in the seven steps it took to reach Twelvetrees and present her cheek for a kiss.

He made a try for her mouth, and his hand hovered around back as though he meant to grab her ass, but she ducked his lips and said, "Don't do it. You gave up your fondling privileges."

She and Jenny kissed the air somewhere in the vicinity of their mouths, and Nell handed over her offering.

Twelvetrees reached out and laid a hand on her arm, holding her there as Whistler took up the slack and stopped right by Nell's right hip. "Jenny?" he said.

Instead of handing Nell's gift to the maid who stood nearby, Jenny walked it over to the pile of packages herself.

"You're a private eye, are you Whistler?" Twelvetrees asked, with the smirkiest smirk Whistler had ever seen slipping around his mouth like a smear of jelly. "I hear you've got a full-service agency."

"I do what I can."

"You do pretty good for a guy who works out of his hat."

"Well, that's because I've got my head in it and my head's on straight."

Jenny came back with a flat package, about nine by twelve, wrapped in pale blue metallic paper, white ribbon, and a yellow bow.

"A little something for you," Twelvetrees said.

"Bernie convince you there was no way to use them?"

"I don't want us to be mad at one another, Nell."

"You're as changeable as the weather off the ocean," she said.

"It's always calm and blue, calm and blue, don't you remember?"

"I've got a little present for you, too," Nell said. She dipped into her little beaded bag and came up with a package about three by four by half an inch thick, just the size of a tape cassette. It was wrapped in brown paper and held together with a rubber band.

"This a copy of your lullabies?" Twelvetrees asked.

"Play it and see."

"Your gift to me isn't wrapped as nice as my gift to you," Twelvetrees said.

"My gift to you needed a plain brown wrapper."

A flash of fear and then one of anger passed across Twelvetrees's face as he watched Nell walk away with all her motors softly running.

Whistler looked around and wondered which of the guests were having a good time. The wheelers and dealers were having a good time because contacts were everything to them. Appointments were gold. Meetings were money in the bank. It wasn't the product they cared about, it was the deal. The deal was mother, father, wife, and sweetheart. It was the fucking godhead!

The deal that was going to happen tomorrow. The deal that was just around the corner.

Just the other day Whistler had been in a building in Century City, a beehive of deals, caught in an elevator with two types talking over their day.

"So you had a good one, Harry?"

"I took three meetings."

"Three? That's marvelous. Three! Do yourself any good?"

"I took a great meeting with Ivan Kipplinger."

"This the Ivan Kipplinger that packaged *Disgusting Tortures*?"

"No. He packaged *Disgusting Tortures Two* and *Three*."

"A fucking genius."

"And a very nice guy. He gives very good meeting."

"I wouldn't know. I haven't had the pleasure."

"Take my word."

"I do, I do. So what happened at the meeting?"

"We agreed to take another meeting next week. We set the date."

"That's good. That's very good."

"It gives me confidence. I really feel this package I brought to him is going to grow some legs and fly."

"Wings."

"Wha?"

"Wings and fly."

"Whatever."

"What's the project?"

"It's too soon to talk about. Know what I mean? I'm superstitious. I could jinx the deal."

"I understand. You know, maybe I'll put together a little proposal for Kipplinger myself. How do you think he'd go for it, I worked up something like *Disgusting Tortures Four?*"

"Save yourself the time and trouble. He's already up to *Five.*"

"A fucking genius."

"Also a very nice guy."

"I could use a laugh," a very husky voice murmured at Whistler's shoulder.

"Christ, was I laughing?" Whistler said, turning and smiling at Ann Malloy, a red-haired aging beauty who'd played second fiddle to twenty stars in a hundred trivialities and kept a photograph of herself in the title role of a road company production of *Medea* framed on her apartment wall. Times, Whistler had been told here and there, had grown very hard for Ann. She hadn't saved her pennies and her fiddle was out of tune. "People will think I've gone off my rocker," he said.

"Nobody's taking any notice. The only time they'll notice is when a person acts halfway sane, or when they fall on the floor foaming at the mouth, threatening to knock over the coke dish."

"How's it going, Ann?"

"Would I kid you? It's going great. I've got so many offers my agent is going to need an agent."

"Who's your agent?"

"Huggy Baer."

"I had him for an agent once. A long time ago. I thought . . ." He caught himself.

"That Huggy was dead? Well, I'll tell you Whistler, I go over to see him at his office, sometimes I wonder if he's dead. He should retire."

"You want to sit down?"

"You mean before I fall down?"

"I didn't mean that. I meant my feet hurt already. You're looking great, just great."

"Sure I am, but it was like pulling teeth to get you to say so."

"I didn't know you needed it."

"Any woman over thirty—scratch that, over fifteen, nowadays—needs compliments. It's what we use for wool to knit the afghans we wrap around our legs on lonely nights to keep us warm. There's the sonofabitch."

"Who?"

"Twelvetrees. Huggy tried to get me on his show. You know, one of those nostalgia bits? Whatever happened to? It could draw a little attention."

She was staring at Twelvetrees. Whistler thought of that old phrase, "if looks could kill."

"What happened?"

"He said no."

"Did he at least see you?"

"Oh, sure."

"What did he say?"

She looked squarely into Whistler's eyes. "He said for me to get down on my knees, if I could manage, and do him."

"Sonofabitch."

She held her gaze. "I did it, goddamn it. I fucking went and did it. He still didn't give me a spot. I'd like to bite out his throat."

Whistler turned his head away as though he was looking for a place for them to sit, not wanting to read any more of what was in her eyes.

"Never mind, Whistler. I think I'll circulate. Do myself some good. Maybe some of my old fans are here tonight." She took a step and paused. "Maybe I'll put an ad in the trades. Throw myself on their fucking mercy. Bette Davis did that once. Remember? It got her started again."

Ann wandered off. She was still a lot of woman. She'd be a treasure nearly anywhere else but La-La Land.

*   *   *

L.A. is the kind of town where people leave changes of clothes at the office, the health club, or a favorite bar. Some even carry a spare wardrobe in the trunks of their cars. The distances are so great from home to work to playpen, the traffic such a killer, that hustlers of every persuasion on a tight schedule make provisions.

It figured that if Spinneran lived way out in Sherman Oaks and had business or pleasure planned for a Friday night, he'd make his change at the office.

Rialto had parked across the street from the offices of Tregaron and Wales after talking to Mocky, and was pleased to see he'd worked it out right when the red BMW pulled up and parked in a twenty-minute zone around eight o'clock. At eight-twenty, right on the button, Spinneran was changed and back in his car.

Rialto followed him, buried in the heavy traffic along Sunset, until the BMW peeled off at Sunset Plaza and started climbing into the hills. Rialto didn't go all the way. When he saw the attendants in red jackets doing the up-and-down quarter-mile shuffle, he parked the Cadillac, got a camera out of the glove compartment, and walked over to a kid who was just that minute parking a Mercedes.

He handed the boy a five-dollar bill and said, "I already parked my car. I'm not a guest. Loop me up there, will ya?"

"The kid looked at the camera and then at the five, and said, "Get in." Spinneran's BMW passed them going down as they were going up. The kid dropped Rialto off at the bottom of the drive, hung a U, and went back down the hill with the five in his pocket.

There were half a dozen people with cameras hanging around the gate, hustling for a shot they could sell to the magazines.

Rialto started walking through the gate. A uniformed rent-a-cop asked him was he a guest. Rialto put out a folded ten.

"You're joking," the cop said.

"I'm free-lance. I can't afford more."

"It's not worth the bother to me if one of these clowns makes a beef about getting their picture took. You could be a nut with a gun hidden in that camera."

"If I was an asshole who wanted to off somebody coming to this party, I'd slip you a hundred. What the fuck would I care?"

"Ten bucks is an insult."

"Well, it's not worth a nickel more to me," Rialto said.

"Then why don't you just go and join the herd over there?"

Rialto gave him the finger and went across the street. He leaned against the gatepost of another estate. All he wanted was an excuse for being there. He watched the photographers taking pictures of arriving guests through the windows of the cars. The flashes would blind the drivers for a second and they'd turn their heads away. Some smiled and took it. A couple asked the photographers why they didn't go fuck off.

The driveway curved up and around to the foot of the steps leading to the front door. Rialto could see the people going in under the lights from where he sat. There was security all over the place. He thought about living like that and decided he'd like the money, houses, cars, and broads, but he wouldn't want somebody in his ear all the time just to keep some asshole from kidnapping him, or somebody he cared about, and holding him or them for ransom.

That's what he told himself, but in his heart of hearts he knew he was a liar. He'd kill to get his hands on just a piece of that kind of money.

Whistler had found a chair in a corner. He wasn't having a very good time. Parties reminded him of parties in the past when he got drunk and made a fool of himself.

Across the room he could see Jenny, the birthday girl, smiling and accepting congratulations from people she didn't know. She was tracking the room over their shoulders while she smiled and exchanged a word or two. She found who she was looking for. Whistler looked where she was looking.

There was someone else not having a very good time, Whistler thought. The pale young man standing on the dining room level, four steps higher, looked down on the chattering crowd as though willing them all to drop dead. It wasn't an angry or hateful look, just one of the coldest disdain and disregard. He smiled slightly as he watched Jenny making her way toward him. He accepted her kiss on his cheek as though she were paying him a tribute.

The drink in Whistler's hand had long since grown warm. He put it, untasted, on a marble table and wended his way out toward the garden, passing within six crowded feet of a tightly smiling Nell and a tightly angry Twelvetrees whispering together in a corner.

He overheard a scrap of conversation as he passed.

"Who the fuck told you that?" Twelvetrees asked.

"I've got my sources, just like you've got your sources," Nell replied.

"I was questioned. That's all it was, I was questioned."

"Well, we know about how that works, don't we Roger? An important man like you."

"Listen, you rotten cunt ..." Twelvetrees started to say, moving in on her, his face red, his jaws working.

Whistler hesitated just a second, but Nell smiled into Twelvetrees's face and said, "Go ahead, Roger, make an asshole of yourself in front of everybody. Make my case for me."

Twelvetrees backed off.

"I'm ready to be reasonable," he said, but didn't look it.

Whistler went on through the tall french windows out into the garden toward a stone wall that was glowing with a blanket of flowers like red and orange straw. The Santa Anas couldn't reach this high. A wind from the coast topped them and brought the distant smell of the sea.

Whistler closed his eyes. Right away the magic of La-La Land when it was young and he was young came rushing back and smacked him in the mouth so hard it brought tears to his eyes.

He stood there, rocking slightly, feeling glad and sorry, memories of old mistakes and lost chances rushing up to take him by the hand, trying to drag him back. All the way back to the time when he was in love the first time with a truly beautiful girl. A girl of innocent beauty, soon spoiled.

A girl who'd colored her hair, fixed her nose, lifted her breasts, and, when that wasn't enough, took a whole bottle of pills and died, leaving him to wonder why he'd never been able to teach her that they didn't always give you the real reason for withholding the prize.

You're too fat, too thin, too tall, too short. You've got blue eyes, you've got brown eyes. Fix your nose, your bows, your little toes. Be this, be that, be something other. Lay on your back and let me tell you how to work the street.

"I'm not sure I want to know," a soft, throaty voice said.

Whistler opened his eyes. Jenny Twelvetrees was standing there, half in the cool light of the moon, half in the warm wash of the lights spilling through the doors. For a minute she looked just like that girl from long ago. Innocent. Mouth like a child.

Eyes almost frightened. For a minute Whistler thought she'd read his mind.

"What's that?"

"Who're you thinkin' about? The way you're lookin' makes me jealous."

"Jealous? Don't tell me you fell in love with me at first sight?"

"On second thought, if you were thinkin' about a lost love, don' tell me about it."

"Not even if the lost love looked like you?"

"Like me?"

"Yes, like you."

"That, I think, is what used to be called a line."

"But true."

"Well, that's nice, then. I don' mind lookin' like a memory. What happened to her?"

"The town raped her, ruined her, changed her face, and gave her appetites she couldn't satisfy."

"Not such good memories. I've been warned this town does that a lot."

"So what do you think?"

"I think it might be true."

"But you think you'd never let it happen to you."

"I know I'll never let it happen to me."

"How come?"

"I've got a head start. My father's Mr. Midnight America." She grinned, making fun of herself and Twelvetrees.

"So, okay, you have it easy getting inside the house. Now somebody asks you to sit down and play. Are they going to laugh?"

"If they do, I'll do somethin' else."

"We're very good at laughing up our sleeves around here. You might not know when to walk away."

"I'll know. Believe me, I'll know. There's no law you have to be born dumb in Atlanta."

"That's your home?"

"That's where my mother took me after she divorced my father. I was ten."

"Don't you like it in Atlanta?"

"It's not heaven. It's all right."

"Your mother ever marry again?"

"She married Martin Denver, M.D. A nice man with a nice practice. OB/GYN. He looks at girls and women all day long. Maybe that's why he doesn' really like us very much."

A little crystal cage of silence dropped down from the night sky and surrounded them. They both looked out toward the city.

"My stepfather's a very good, kind man," she said after a while.

"Do you call him pop or daddy?"

"I call him Martin."

"You call Twelvetrees daddy?"

"Yes."

"You like Twelvetrees?"

Her eyes looked cloudy. "I think he's sad. Maybe lonely." She didn't try to hide her disdain, but she didn't lean on it.

"He's always got people around. At least bodyguards," Whistler said.

"You know that's not the same thing. He's been doin' without family."

"But now you're back with him?"

"I didn' say I was family," Jenny said softly. "I grew up without a daddy."

"So you're just here working the relationship."

"Why not? Nothin' wrong with that. Everyone's tryin' to get out of the blocks in a hurry."

"You a runner?"

"The hundred-yard dash. But life's more like the marathon, ain' it? Thousands of people pile up at the beginning of the Boston. If you're in the pack, you jog in place for twenty minutes an' don' break out for an hour. Sometimes you're so boxed in you never break out. That ain' gonna happen to me."

"Okay."

"Mr. Whistler?"

"Never mind the Mister."

"I'm not sayin' I'm altogether as tough and sure of myself as I might pretend to be."

"I know what you mean."

She took a step closer to him so she had to tilt her head back a trifle and look up at him from beneath her brows. He could feel her body warmth. He knew if he touched her the flesh would be resilient, resisting his fingers before giving way. Her mouth glistened in the moonlight. He'd missed the moment when she'd wet her lips. It had been neatly done.

He was swaying toward her as though powerless in her gravitational field.

"Can I call you if it gets too much for me?" she asked. "I've got a feelin' you could be a friend."

"Speaking of friends. What happened to the young guy with the blond hair? Isn't he a friend?"

"He's very shy. Confident, but shy. Is that possible? Anyway, he just made an appearance because I invited him and he's got perfect manners. But he didn' stay. So what do you say? If I need a friend real bad?"

Whistler was about to say take my house, my car, my sword, my heart when Nell cleared her throat.

He looked over to see her standing in the doorway, a funny knowing smile on her mouth.

Twelvetrees was at her shoulder. His expression was knowing, too, but he wasn't smiling.

"Time to open up your presents, kitten," he said.

They all trooped inside and stood around oo-ing and ah-ing with everybody else while Jenny opened up one expensive present after another from grinning people she didn't know.

Nell's gift was a silver case for birth control pills. A kind of joke that was no joke. Jenny and Nell smiled at one another across the room as though they were as close as sisters, as though they were having so much fun.

If looks could kill, Whistler thought. If looks could kill.

FIFTEEN

IN NO MORE than an hour, Spinneran was out again. He handed over his parking stub and the attendant got into a Rolls that had not yet been parked and took it down the hill.

Rialto waved the Rolls down and knocked on the window on the passenger side. The kid he'd given the five hit the electric button and lowered the window.

"I'm gonna give it up," Rialto told him. "Can you drop me down to the foot of the hill?"

The kid hesitated, maybe hoping for another five, but when Rialto didn't offer, he said okay and unlocked the door by punching another button.

Rialto looked back through the window and caught a last glimpse of Spinneran standing like a white knight at the top of the porch.

"I didn't see you take any pictures," the kid said.

"What kind of pictures you gonna get? A bunch of people behind the wheel of a car? Who the hell am I gonna sell that kind of crap to?"

"So why do you bother hanging around at all?" the kid asked, with the eagerness of a true believer who thought you could pick up valuable bits and pieces nearly everywhere.

"You hope for lucky. You hope some gazoony slaps his date in the mouth. You hope one of them celebrities gets drunk and hits a photographer."

"Not you?"

Rialto laughed. "Hell, no, some other schmuck trying to make the rent taking pictures of people who already got their pictures took two million times. Sometimes you wonder why you keep going. It's all the same. One day and another day."

The kid went into the pocket of his shirt with two fingers as if he were going to give Rialto back his five, and then thought better of it. When Rialto got out of the car, huffing and puffing, the kid bent over and looked up and out at him. "I'm going into production," the kid said.

"God bless you," Rialto replied. "You ever need a still cameraman on your first epic gimme a call."

He got into the Cadillac and backed up into a driveway. When the BMW went by, Rialto fell in behind.

It wasn't as easy following the BMW at nearly ten o'clock. There was plenty of traffic but Spinneran knew how to work it, taking chances Rialto didn't like to take, car repairs being what they were nowadays, cutting in and out, threatening to get lost so far ahead that Rialto would lose him. Spinneran wasn't heading home to the Valley. He was going downtown, toward the center of Hollywood. Rialto followed him all the way down Hollywood Boulevard to the parking lot behind the bookstore on the four corners. He parked seven spots away and followed Spinneran inside after a minute or two.

Rialto knew the bookstore very well. It was a place where the hookers and other street people went to get out of the rain. The management didn't want to bring grief down on their heads, so they let them come in as long as they didn't soil the books or sit on the counters.

A bookstore had its good points and its bad points when it came to tailing somebody. One good point was that so many people went in just to browse around that you didn't look suspicious if you were just browsing around. In a jewelry store you'd stick out like a sore thumb, and in a shoe store some clerk would draw attention to you by coming up and asking what he could show you. The bad point was this particular bookstore had three levels and four exits. If somebody had an idea they were being tailed, they had choices for ducking out on you.

But Spinneran probably had no reason to think there was somebody on his tail. At least there he was, right out in the open, talking to a salesclerk. It was somebody Rialto knew. Its name was Jan Savoda.

Rialto knew Jan Savoda from way back, back before Savoda stopped wearing men's clothes altogether and bought himself a black wig and a set of thirty-eight C-cup falsies. Back when Savoda was dragging around with Steve Chicago, the ugliest queen who'd ever smeared his lipstick.

So what was this? It looked like Savoda had given up being a he-she and was a more or less respectable she-she, living the part in life and not just for parties. For all Rialto knew, Savoda might have already had his balls and pecker chopped.

Once, some time before Twelvetrees had his great success, Rialto and Twelvetrees were walking the stroll. Twelvetrees, more than half in the bag, spotted Savoda and told Rialto that that was the playmate he fancied for the night. Rialto had clued him in, playing tricks on a valued customer being very bad for business, but Twelvetrees hadn't changed his mind. He'd just said, "What the hell, don't knock it until you've tried it, right?"

That was how Rialto knew Jan Savoda.

Savoda gathered up his purse from under the counter and went out the back way with Spinneran at his elbow. Rialto had his head down in a book as they passed.

"Well, damn it, how soon *did* they say they'd have it ready?" Spinneran was saying.

"They said a week, but you know these mechanics," Savoda answered in a high, fluting voice.

Practically every man in the bookstore was watching the couple leave, practically every one of them lusting after one or the other.

Time was, when he was young and hopeful, on the hustle and looking for a score, Whistler would still have been in there at two or three A.M., propping up his eyelids with matchsticks, afraid to miss a thing, a glimmer of interest in a small-time gonif's eye, a flash of some beauty's inner thigh that was as good as an engraved invitation.

Time was that Nell would have been hanging in there, too, scared that the chance would present itself just two minutes after she walked out the door, on the way home to her single bed and a bite of chocolate to soothe the disappointed child in her breast.

When you got older, you got wiser, and you went home early to get your sleep.

Leaving was quicker and more honest than it was going in. There was no glad hand at the exit. There was just a kid with a pimply neck and a red jacket copping a smoke at the bottom of the front steps, stashing it on the stone balustrade as he hurried over to take the ticket, folding the five before loping off like an easy-running miler, off to search out the battered Chevy.

"You gave the kid a five?" Nell asked.

"What the hell. I shagged cars more than once. Besides, if I tipped him a buck I might never see my car again. When you're that age you can't stand poverty on anybody but yourself."

On the drive back to Mary Beth's, they kept a comfortable silence at first. Whistler was even feeling domestic, as though he and Nell were man and wife, he an insurance salesman maybe and she a housewife with a part-time job at the local department store. On their way home after a dinner with friends or in-laws, his or hers.

"She's a little bun, isn't she?" Nell said, looking straight ahead.

"Who's a what?"

"A little bun. A honey bun. Little raisin eyes. Sweet icing lips."

"You mean Jenny?"

Nell turned her head sharply. "Well, I don't mean that aging red-headed ex-feature player who had you cornered by the aspidistra."

"What the hell's an aspidistra? I always meant to look it up."

"It's a tall houseplant."

"I've got a tall houseplant. A ficus benjamina."

"Is there no end of wonders to you, Whistler?"

"Tell me about Jenny."

"You mean she didn't tell you everything? Didn't she do the number about calling on you if she needed a friend? I see she did. She worked that one on me, too."

"She's just a kid."

"She's twenty-one going on sixty."

"Maybe it comes out a little phony because we get most of our act out of the movies."

"Dream on, babe. Let's just say that child brings out the bitchiness in me."

"Like the red-headed ex-feature player?"

"Her, too, you bastard. She gets it out of a bottle, mine's the genuine article."

"I know."

"I could take that as a smart remark," Nell said, smiling.

"What about Jenny?"

"She's Roger's oldest, born back when Roger was just a small-time comic with straw in his ears, working the little gin mills across the country and trying to figure out which of the big-timers he should imitate.

"One thing about Roger, whenever he tells stories about those days he doesn't get all wet-eyed like some of them do. He says it was the pits and he wouldn't go back to play one of those toilets if the proprietor gave him his wife and seven virgin daughters. Coming from Twelvetrees, who collects pussy like old maids collect cats, that proves just how low his opinion of the good old days is."

"A lot of people talk about hard times like they were good times because they were young."

"That's right. But Twelvetrees doesn't think he ever grew old. He thinks he was born when he started his midnight show. There was no life before that, and now he's just a teenager."

"You know Jenny's mother?"

"Of her. I know every sickening detail of practically every lady and every lady's orifice he's ever had. He told me Jenny's mother, Marilyn, had a nest like a mousetrap. I'm not sure I ever knew what that was supposed to mean, but apparently, according to Roger, it was enough to make him think he was in love. Enough to marry the girl and stay with her long enough for her to have two kids."

"You ever meet the other one?"

"Jenny's brother? Roger Junior passed through one time and one time only. That was before Jenny arrived on the scene. He came to Roger looking for money. The kid hated him and let it show. Roger let him sleep in the pool house for a week, slipped him a hundred bucks, and sent him on his way. Told me the kid would end up dead in some alley. He was right. The boy was found with his throat cut in Seattle about three months ago."

"How did Twelvetrees take it?"

"I couldn't read him. He hardly knew the kid, and the kid

wouldn't pretend to love him that one time. So there was nothing in the relationship for Roger. He can always tell if he's lost the audience or never had it. That's what he always told me. Well, he never had young Roger. He was four years younger than Jenny. Only six when Twelvetrees left them."

"Over another woman?"

"Women. Nothing serious. Among others, he was making it with the floor girl at the station and the singer on his daytime show."

"I remember."

"Why do you remember?"

"I knew the singer. We were almost friends."

"For Christ's sake, this is a town full of alley cats," Nell said, but she said it sadly as though fidelity and true love could not hope to flourish in such a place. Then she fell silent.

Whistler thought back to that girl.

Her name had been Gina Bacolla. She'd had short black curly hair that danced around her head when she talked. She was forever touching it back into place and doing no good at all. It was in her eyes more often than not. And there was always a smudge on her face somewhere. Eye shadow or chocolate or a smear of dressing from the salad she'd had for lunch. Or a streak of paint. Or a track through the matte finish of her cheek made by a tear that had escaped her almost constant laughter.

They'd met somehow, Whistler couldn't remember where or exactly when. What he remembered most was how she desired fame so badly. Every little thing that happened was triumph or disaster. Night or day. Black or white. Storm or doldrums. There was nothing in between.

Making love to her began in wild abandon and ended with a laundry list of damage done to her, advantage taken, until Whistler had learned to grunt or sigh from time to time while he thought of other things. She never knew the difference. She was on about herself and the complicated tactics and strategies that would determine her future.

Once, when she had him on the phone, he'd run out of smokes. He'd put down the phone and gone across the street to the liquor store for some cigarettes and a six-pack of beer, He was gone ten minutes. She never knew it. She was still talking when he picked the receiver up again and said, uh-huh.

She used him for a wailing wall. She paid off with sex. She was the child conning the grown-up by any means possible so he'd listen to her stories.

"The trumpets. I told that bastard, Roger, about the trumpets. They were riding right in on top of my high note, drowning it. Right there where it goes 'over the raaaaainbow,' you know, there's this horn stepping on it. I told him Judy Garland would never have sold that song if they'd let the trumpets shit on her high note like that. You understand what I'm saying?"

"I do, I do."

"And the spot was right in my eyes. You see that?"

"It didn't look to me like—"

"Right in my eyes. How does it look, me hitting the high note with the brass dumping on me and the spotlight burning my fucking eyes out?"

"Speaking of that . . ."

"Of what?"

"Fucking. Are you fucking Twelvetrees?" he asked, staring at her, his head propped up by his hands folded under his neck.

"You're not putting your mark on me, are you?"

"I'm just asking. I'm interested."

She lay down on him, every swell and curve ready to weep oil, her dark eyes like olives, glistening, staring into his face.

"I've got to be famous," she said, as though refusing his proposal of marriage.

All of a sudden it was truly important to him. "So tell me, are you fucking him?"

She got out of bed and into her robe. She went into the bathroom and didn't come out. After a little while he'd gotten up, too, dressed, went home, and never saw her again. Except once, three years later, in a bar along the strip.

She'd been off the air and out of sight for two years. When Twelvetrees had moved on to the late late show, he took the trumpets with him, but he didn't take her.

So she was sitting at the end of the long bar with another woman Whistler knew. A woman named Frannie, still beautiful and leggy, though going to lard around the middle. A hooker of some reputation who no longer had the wind, and made her living by doing triples and showing younger, fresher talent the ropes. Both women were wearing little shoulder furs and Gina's mouth looked like it was bruised, stretched out by too much singing about the goddamn raaaainbow, Whistler thought.

He'd turned around and walked out before she saw him. Because, if he'd gone up to her and said hello, he knew somehow that she would have thrown herself on his mercy and that would have been more than he could have handled.

"So?" he said.

"So you're back, are you?" Nell said in a voice that told him she'd been somewhere else, too, while he'd been remembering.

They passed the new house not yet built, pulled into the driveway, and cut the motor, drifting to a stop before the door.

She turned to him, looking at his forehead, then his eyes, and then his mouth. Her breasts were as white as bone, scattered with little marks like drops of drying rain.

He reached out and pulled her in close.

"It's just a good-night kiss at the door, Whistler. This isn't picking up where it left off last night."

He kissed her. She wasn't stingy with her mouth or tongue.

"When we get inside that door, we go to our separate beds. You're just a man I hired for some temporary work."

He kissed her again. It was just as generous, but she held that little bit back that told him he wasn't to try for more.

When they got out of the car, Bip and Bongo were racketing a greeting.

"Honey, honey, honey, honey," Nell crooned in a high, sweet, melancholy voice.

Once inside she said, "You want to watch 'Midnight America'?"

"Who's subbing?"

"It's a repeat. One of those best of Mr. Midnight America nights." And she laughed.

They took a pass on "Midnight America" and had a hot chocolate instead. Then they went to their separate rooms. This time Whistler could hear Nell turn the lock on her door.

SIXTEEN

THE APARTMENT IN the new building in Sherman Oaks cost plenty.

It had a feature advertised as a harvest kitchen. There was a long counter made of fake chopping block extending out from a wall shared in common by the living room and kitchen. It was all open, and the big, scrubbed pine kitchen table was also half in the kitchen, half in the living room.

Spinneran and Savoda sat there some evenings drinking coffee. Savoda told stories of Hollywood and Spinneran listened.

Savoda had been the "other woman" in one of the first divorce cases Spinneran had been handed when he'd gone to work for Tregaron and Wales, where enough straight business was transacted to cover their occasional, but far more lucrative, murder-for-hire services. During his surveillance, he'd found out that Savoda was a man. It had been enough to make the husband, an industrialist of considerable wealth, pay off the wife in a very large way so that the news about his kinky sex habits wouldn't be broadcast from the top of Mount Wilson. The wife had also demanded, for the sake of her sanity and the children she'd said, but probably out of pure spite, that he kick the gay transvestite's ass out of their little love nest.

Just before that happened Spinneran had given Savoda fair warning so that he could save what he could from the wreckage.

Since Savoda was without accommodations, and Spinneran had this very big apartment with plenty of extra space, they struck a deal. Savoda got room and board in exchange for keeping the house and cooking dinner every now and then. Besides, Spinneran reasoned, Savoda was better company than a cat, and, from the listening post provided by his job in the bookstore, knew just about everything that was going down on the street.

It had worked out all right. Neither made emotional or physical demands on the other, though Savoda was given to passionate rages about his fate and long wearisome crying spells during which he threatened suicide. Spinneran put up with it because he felt that both of them were outcasts in the land of outcasts.

Savoda was sitting at the table in robe and slippers, his wig cast aside, a half-stocking holding down his hair. He looked like an actor or dancer ready to put on his makeup.

Spinneran was wearing a light silk Japanese lounging coat.

"Maybe you should spring for a new car," Spinneran said.

"For heaven's sake, dear, where would I get the money?"

"You could get a job someplace that pays better than the bookstore."

"Doing what? Just doing what? I could go back to tramping the streets and doing extras?"

"I'm not telling you to do extras."

"I'm *already* doing extras and saving every penny I can put aside for my operation. But I can't work forty-eight hours a day."

"You're only getting three forty-five an hour at the bookstore," Spinneran said conversationally, "and you go out and buy hundred-and-fifty-dollar shoes."

"Oh, my God, you want me to dress like a tramp?"

"I'm talking about three forty-five an hour."

"I make contacts at the bookstore. I don't like selling it out on the sidewalk like a fishmonger. My God. Besides, the competition is getting vicious. And the pimps are going around putting the squeeze on. I get threatened three times a week just walking from the shop to the bus, for God's sake."

"Well, there you go. You've got to get wheels. The car you've got is in the garage more than it's under you. What do you need a Jaguar for anyhow?"

"What do you need a BMW 633CSi for?" Savoda retorted, indignantly.

"A ten-year-old Jaguar that breaks down all the time is what we're talking about."

"No, we're talking about me selling blow jobs on the street like a candy butcher."

"Don't say that."

"Yes, we are. We're talking about my dignity. My life-style."

"Well, about your life-style . . ."

"I want to change it."

"I know that, goddamn it!"

"You don't have to yell."

"Did I yell?"

"Yes, you did."

"I didn't mean to," Spinneran said mildly. "I know you want things to be different."

"And I'm working very hard to effect a change. I'm saving every penny I can beg, borrow, or suck up off the pavement for the operation."

They fell into a little pool of silence while they sipped on their coffee.

"You sure about the operation?" Spinneran finally said.

"It's the only way I can see to change my life. I mean, I don't want to go around being a faggot. I'm—" He hesitated, tears flooding into his eyes, threatening to spill over. "—I'm a woman. That's what I am. God made a mistake in the recipe when he made me."

Spinneran winced and turned his head away from so much weak emotion.

"He put in a little too much of this and a little too much of that," Savoda said. "So here I am a woman with a cock and balls, and hardly any tits."

"At least you haven't got a beard."

"That's the hormones. And look." He opened up his robe. He was naked except for his shorts. His chest was like that of a very young girl or a fat man, though Savoda was thin otherwise. "I think I'm getting some results, don't you?"

"Oh, yes. So when are you going to schedule the operation?"

"I'm afraid," Savoda said, his face screwing up as if he were going to scream and weep. Some tears did well out and trail down his cheeks.

"You don't have to be afraid," Spinneran said soothingly. "It's a very commonplace operation nowadays."

"I'm afraid that after it's done, I still won't be one thing or the other. I've been warned it's very hard for a man to accept a loving relationship with a transsexual who's had the operation."

"So when you meet *the* man, don't tell him."

"How could I do that? How could I lie to the man I loved?"

"Maybe he'll be able to handle it," Spinneran said, after a long, thoughtful pause.

"They say it's very hard for a man to accept it. It's the masculine ego thing."

"You want to watch a little television?" Spinneran asked.

"Oh, why the hell not," Savoda said, drying his eyes with the corner of his sleeve. "I mean, at least those fucking people on the tube live halfway normal lives. Nothing but a little garden-variety incest, sodomy, cross-dressing, infanticide, larceny, murder, a little pushing acne cures to Indians. My God, you got to laugh or you'd go crazy."

They went into the living room and turned on the television. Spinneran watched the screen like a man who wasn't watching, who was a million miles away and wanted to stay there. Savoda looked at him every once in a while, always afraid that one of these nights he'd go too far with his worries and woes, and Spinneran would tell him to pack his bra and high heels and get the hell out.

"Aren't you the unlucky one," Savoda said, "getting saddled with a thing like me?"

"Watch the television," Spinneran said.

Whistler felt brain-stunned as he watched the station logo fade out and the "Midnight America" logo fade in. He thought about the millions of silent people, sitting in the same room together, who were about to waste their time watching a bunch of people gabbing with one another.

Maybe Roger Twelvetrees would execute a bad buck and wing with some guest dancer to the insane applause of the studio audience. Maybe he'd do a number with the lady from the zoo and hold a baby this or that in his lap, making believe it pissed on him. That one got them rolling in the aisles every time.

The program logo faded. Then a disclaimer appeared saying, "This program was previously recorded."

A big moon face appeared.

"Are you ready for it, night birds?" Jocko MacDoone brayed into his hand-held mike.

"Reaaaady!" the studio audience shouted back.

"Are you ready for the man, night owls?"

"Reaaaady!"

"Are you ready for the man of the wee small hours?"

"Reaaaady!" they shouted back, whistling, stomping, applauding, carrying on like fools right on cue, overjoyed by the chance to be part of an American ritual, hoping and praying the cameras roving the audience would stop on them and make them immortal for five seconds.

"Are you ready for Mr. Midnight Americaaaaaaa?"

The place exploded, and out ran Roger Twelvetrees through the part in the curtains, crooked teeth flashing, arms pumping, putting on the brakes right under the spot as though he'd just run a mile to get there, throwing up his arms, shaking his head modestly, shy and humble before so much adulation. Country boy who'd made good, never mind everybody knew, if they took the time to remember, that Roger Twelvetrees had been born and raised in a slum back in South Philadelphia.

There he was, wearing his cords, sleeveless pullover, and tweed jacket showing a little wear at the elbows and collar. The same man you'd see if you were driving through the country's heartland in the middle of the night and stopped at an all-night diner west of nowhere, sitting on a stool at the counter having a cup of coffee. Worried farmer, weary traveling salesman, small-town doctor cooling out after being dragged out of bed at three in the morning to birth a child or close the eyes of an old man just dead. All alone, the great American archetype, sleepless dreamer, salt of the earth, somebody to talk to when you were lonely and couldn't sleep. Because you were on the road, too. On the long, long lonely road, going somewhere, going nowhere.

"Gimme a break, will ya?" Twelvetrees said. "Gimme a break."

There was a television set of one size or another in every room in Twelvetrees's house. That was over and above the bank of eight twenty-five-inch television sets that filled one wall of the "media room," which was nearly as large as one of the theaters in a multiple-screen house.

Most of the party, certainly anybody who was out to gain favor

with their host, were in that room, ready to fall down every time
the two-dimensional icon on the screen cocked an eyebrow.

Some were scattered in little groups elsewhere. There were a
half dozen, who fancied themselves distinctively common, hanging around the thirteen-incher in the kitchen, sucking on their
glasses and getting in the Nicaraguan cook's way.

There was even a couple screwing in one of the bathrooms, the
man looking over his shoulder at the television screen, the girl
straddling his lap looking into the image reversed in the mirror.
It was insanity, but one never knew when questions might be
asked.

Jenny was in her room, lying on the bed, looking at her bare
feet and a pile of gifts she'd had Pulaski tote in to keep her
company as she wondered was it really worth it turning twenty-
one in La-La Land without a boyfriend to squeeze her tit. Her
nineteen inch was on low volume, but loud enough to hear the
jokes that just missed turning blue.

"There's this farm boy sitting on the barnyard fence with this
healthy farm girl—I mean she's really biiiig." Twelvetrees stuck
out his chest and held out his hands, fashioning watermelons in
the air. The audience guffawed, a burst of sound that had
probably been juiced up in the taping studio. "They're watching
the rooster having a good time with a chicken. Farm boy starts
squirming around. Girl says, 'What's the matter with you?' Boy
says, 'That rooster's giving me ideas.' 'Well go ahead, do what
you want,' she said. 'It's your chicken.' "

The audience fell out, they laughed, they shrieked, they
groaned. Because they were smart, they were with it. Some of
them had sat through four hundred and fifty programs in a row.
Twelvetrees called some of them by their first names. They knew
the jokes. They knew there was always going to be an old yawn
for an opener, and they were *supposed* to groan, letting Twelvetrees know that they knew he was just a good old boy who'd
rather be sitting around the cracker barrel—where the hell would
you find a cracker barrel nowadays?—chewing the fat with them
instead of being up there under the spotlights making ten million
a year.

"Gimme a break will ya?" Mr. Midnight America brayed into
fifty million homes. "Just gimme a break."

Twelvetrees was alone in his bedroom. He took Nell's little

package from his pocket. He took the cassette out of the plastic case. There was a handwritten label on it with nothing but a date. "September 13, 1980." He opened up a cabinet and revealed top-of-the-line stereo components. He inserted the cassette in the deck, punched the play button, and turned the volume down.

His own voice said, "I hired you for games."

A woman's thin, weary voice said, "Well, I know. But for Christ's sake, you got to promise not to go too far."

There was the sound of a slap. It sounded almost like a snapping rubber band up close to your ear.

"Oh, shit," the woman said.

After a while the slaps gave way to blows that sounded like a hammer striking a melon.

His rage against the blackmail Nell was laying on him started to build. At the same time he was getting an erection listening to the tape of that old experience.

The voice of the woman coming from the stereo speakers said, "Oh, no, that's enough." It didn't sound like a protest or even a plea. It sounded like somebody saying there was no reason to go on killing her, because she was already dead.

SEVENTEEN

THE NEXT MORNING Whistler and Nell got up within five minutes of each other, but Nell was first.

When he shuffled out into the kitchen in his shorts and the seersucker beach robe he hardly ever wore when he was home, she was at the counter putting the coffee on. She was wearing her ratty robe. Her hair hung around her face like rusty straw. She gave him a quick smile. There were little puffy pouches under her eyes that made her look cheerful.

Bip and Bongo were lying around on the tile floor. They grinned at him when he walked in.

The sliding glass doors were open to the patio and pool. When he walked over to look out, the shimmering glare from the water cut his eyes like dull knife blades. Even the blue of the cloudless sky was brighter than he could stand. He took a step and it was as though he'd broken an invisible shield between the air-conditioned inside and the Santa Ana scorcher outside. He stepped right back in and let the cold air surround him again.

"We died and went to hell," Nell said.

"You think they got air-conditioning in heaven?"

"I thought we'd do breakfast here, if you don't mind?"

"Gentry's will go on without me. Eggs over easy?"

"Bacon or sausage?"

"Either. Both."

"Can you make toast?"

"I'm always willing to try something new."

He looked into a huge bread safe. "We got a selection," he said. "English muffin?"

"Got one of those."

"That's what I'll have."

He took two from the package, split them with a fork, and put the first pair into the slick white toaster.

"Twelvetrees has a very bad temper," he said.

"You finally got the idea," she said.

"He ever hit you?"

"Was I a battered wife?"

"Did he ever hit you? I don't know how to work out the definition of the other."

"He hit me, but he didn't do it often and he didn't do it hard."

"How come?"

"Because I always told him I'd kill him while he was sleeping if he did."

"So it was like rough games? Sexual games?"

She lifted the eggs out of the pan with a spatula and placed them neatly on two plates. She laid bacon and sausage from another pan on a platter lined with paper towels. She brought it all to the table. The toaster popped and Whistler took the muffins out with a pair of bamboo tongs and put in the second pair.

"Look," she said, "we could have an intellectual discussion about hitting, punching, wife beating."

"I wasn't arguing a case or splitting any hairs."

"I know what you're saying. I don't know where one thing ends and the other begins myself. There have been times when I wanted to be pushed around a little bit. You know, pretend I was in danger. It's like fantasizing about rape. Women do that, and men think that means they want to be raped. But it doesn't. It just means they want to fantasize about it. You know what I mean?"

Whistler nodded, staring at the toaster, waiting for it to pop again.

"I really wasn't asking about rough contact sports," he said.

"Okay. Roger did both. Sometimes I joined in, until he started losing his head. Then I stopped him. Once in a while he got mad enough to really want to hurt me. That's when I threatened his life. That's when I meant it. And he knew I meant it. There was no confusion about which was which and what was what."

The toaster delivered up the second pair of English muffins. Whistler put them on the plate with the others and brought them to the table.

"He ever get into any difficulty over something like that?"

"Any difficulty?"

"Did he ever hurt some woman bad enough to bring the cops down on him?"

She looked at him carefully. His head was down, his interest apparently on his breakfast.

"Do you know something I don't know?" she asked.

"There's stories. Old stories."

"There's old stories about a lot of famous people."

"You don't know if the stories about Twelvetrees are true?"

"What stories?"

"About having a thing about beating up on women."

"Hookers?"

"Yes, professional women."

"He never talked to me about anything like that."

You'd think she'd want to put the Indian sign on Twelvetrees, Whistler thought. Nod her head to every nasty story anybody could tell about him. Build a case against him in everybody and anybody's mind so if they had to go to court there'd be things she could tell having heard about. Was she bending over being fair? Or was she being cute? Why did he feel he was being worked?

"You're working for me, aren't you, Whistler?"

"Huh," he said, startled at the word, as though she'd read his mind.

"Are you still guarding my body?"

"I'm still working for you."

"You'll have to wait for your pay."

He nodded. "I can wait."

"I want to go down to Venice today," she said. "This afternoon."

"Venice? What's down in Venice?"

"My mother."

"Is that where you come from? Venice?"

"Oh, no. I come from a lot of places," Nell said. "But I was in Venice with my mother before I hitched a ride to Hollywood to make my fortune."

*   *   *

They were sitting in the back booth, Bosco, Canaan, and Cortez, three unlikely witches in a modern version of Macbeth. Canaan had returned Bosco's copy of the *Annotated Alice in Wonderland*. It was lying on the Formica table amid the plates and coffee cups.

"Where's Whistler?" Cortez asked.

"How the hell should I know?" Canaan said.

"Don't he always come in for breakfast?"

"Sometimes he comes in for breakfast," Bosco said.

"He's always in for breakfast."

"*Most* of the time he's in for breakfast."

"Fuck it with this shit about breakfast, please. I got a sour stomach," Canaan said.

"So what do you think?" Cortez asked him. "You think Whistler's pussy-whipped?"

"I don't think he's even had a taste yet," Canaan said.

"That don't mean he can't be pussy-whipped."

"The way I understand it," Bosco said, "a man who's chained to the bed at the cost of all other activities can be said to be pussy-whipped."

"Well, he's not here for breakfast," Cortez said, tossing a look at Canaan, who pretended not to hear. "So all right," Cortez went on, "let's say this . . . can we say this? . . . Whistler's in *danger* of being pussy-whipped."

"That we can say without a doubt," Canaan said.

Bosco shook his head. "I don't think so. I don't think Whistler's going to wear some broad's leash. I don't care—"

"Hold it right there," Cortez interrupted. "That Nell's no broad. That Nell's a goddamn Masarati with gold headers."

"What do you know about her?" Bosco asked.

"I got eyes, ain't I?"

"Yeah, but what do you *know* about her? Whistler's just got over a skirt that did a number on him. You think he's gonna go ga-ga over this one before he checks her out?"

"Since when does a man with a hard-on check out the object of his affections?" Canaan asked, playing the old philosopher.

"Well, so is one of you gonna check her out?" Bosco asked.

The detectives looked at one another.

"I'll check her out," Cortez said, just as Canaan started opening his mouth.

"Yeah, we shouldn't have the sentence first and the trial later," Bosco said.

"Wha?" Cortez said.

"You wouldn't understand unless you read the book," Canaan said, placing his palm over the face of Alice on the dust jacket.

Cortez got to his feet. "I got people to catch."

"We don't tell Whistler we're minding his business," Bosco said, just as Whistler and Nell walked in the door. "We was just talking about you," he said, as they approached.

"Something good, I hope," Nell said.

"We was just wishing for your well-being," Bosco said. "Are you going to eat?"

"We've had. Maybe some coffee," Whistler said.

"How are you, Mrs. Twelvetrees?" Cortez asked.

"Nell."

"Forgot." He smiled one of his very white smiles and tugged a curly forelock as though he was just any old gardener or the man that washed her car. "I was just going, but it's nice seeing you again."

"Me, too."

"You two got anything on for today?" he asked as though they were a couple of tourists or friends on vacation.

"I thought we'd go down to Venice," Nell said.

"Oh, Venice? It's a very interesting place."

"My mother lives there."

"Well, then, you know," Cortez said, and then turned to Whistler. "Can I talk to you a minute over here, Whistler?"

They walked down half the length of the coffee shop to a spot where the counter and booths were empty.

"What were you doing over to the Armentières?" Cortez asked.

"Don't tell me that Esme told you I was there?"

"Yeah, and she told me you were asking questions. What I want to know is, why were you asking questions?"

It would be easy enough, maybe even helpful somehow, to tell Cortez about the sneak-photographer and the candy wrapper in the gutter. But he didn't like the way Cortez was hovering over him, pressing into his space, playing the intimidation game.

Whistler shrugged. "Curiosity," he said.

"I don't understand. Explain that."

"Well, you know."

"No, I don't know."

"Like this street is my neighborhood . . ."

"This is twenty, twenty-five blocks away and a boulevard south."

"So what? It's Hollywood, isn't it?"

"So Forest Lawn over to Burbank ain't Hollywood."

"The apprentice cosmetologist told you about that, did she? You're turning half the town into finks."

"I told her to call me and tell me whoever came to see Vyborg."

"Killer returns to the scene of the crime?"

"It happens."

"So all right, I had a couple of—"

"You're interfering in a homicide."

"—conversations."

"You figure there's some way you can work a client out of this business, a guy gets himself stabbed in the belly?"

Whistler smiled a crooked smile as though Cortez had found him out.

"You got a client," Cortez said. "Why don't you do a good job watching over Nell. You don't want the job, I'll take the job."

"You'd have to quit the force."

Cortez grinned, showing every friendly tooth. "Well, maybe even that could be arranged."

"Okay," Whistler said, and waited. He'd been told to mind his own business. That was the bitter. Now came the sweet.

"You understand what I'm telling you here, Whistler? Anything you want to know about any case I'm on—anything I can talk about—all you got to do is ask. But don't go poking around the garbage without permission."

"Okay," Whistler said again, and watched Cortez walk away and leave the shop. He turned when he was outside on the sidewalk and waved to Whistler, then to Nell.

Whistler went back to the others and sat down.

"I've got a favor to ask," he said to Bosco and Canaan.

"What's that?" Canaan asked.

"Same favor as yesterday."

"You keep dumping me on these people, I'm going to think I've got body odor or bad breath," Nell said.

"It's just that—"

"Whatever you were doing yesterday, you haven't finished doing?" she finished for him.

"That's right."

"Okay, boys," she said, folding her hands on the Formica and leaning over them to grin into Canaan's face and then into Bosco's, "what are we going to do today?"

"I could read to you from *Alice*," Bosco said.

Whistler knew a person down at the morgue by the name of Charlie Chickering. They weren't friends, but Charlie was willing to make accommodations for a finnif here, a sawbuck there.

He had eyeglasses like the bottoms of Coke bottles and his teeth were trapped in silver cages. He was sucking on a Dr. Brown's cream soda when Whistler approached his desk.

"You been promoted?" Whistler asked.

"How's that?"

"You're working days."

"That's no promotion, it's just more work."

"There must be more chances to make a buck on the side."

"How's that?" Charlie said again.

"More requests for information."

"You got a request for information?"

"I want to find out about an autopsy run on a hooker died from a beating about six, seven years ago."

"You're putting me on? That file would have been cleared out."

"Even if it was an unsolved homicide?"

"That might still be in the furniture."

"Could you get up and see?"

"The old stuff is kept downstairs."

"So I'll come down with you if you're afraid of the dark."

"Well, I mean, it could take some time, and I'm not supposed to leave the desk."

"This time of day I don't think you'll get a bunch of bodies rolling in, do you?"

"Regulations, you know what I mean?"

"You got to take a piss now and then, all the soda you drink."

"Jesus Christ, the expense."

Whistler tossed a five-dollar bill on the desk.

"Next thing a person knows, I'll have to switch to water," Charlie said.

Whistler added another fiver. "I'm not asking much."

"Well, for old time's sake," Charlie said, and finally got up off his ass. He picked up the two bills, folded them up into a little square, and tucked it into his change pocket.

They went down into the basement. There were mountains of papers all filed away in cardboard boxes.

"When does this stuff go on computer?" Whistler asked.

"Only new stuff goes on computer. This is the city of the dead."

"You got to have an index."

"Oh, yeah, we got one of those for every year."

"For Christ's sake, Charlie, show a little initiative for the ten," Whistler said. "Do I have to drag it out of you?"

Charlie went down the rows, tapping on the dusty boxes and turning on a line of naked bulbs with pull chains as they went deeper and deeper into the tunnel of paper.

"All right. Here's eighty-one. So what we do is look here in the index for what? For what, Whistler?"

"Boots. Her street name was Boots."

"Oh, that's helpful," Charlie said sarcastically.

"You must have them cross-filed with their street names."

"Sometimes. If that's all we could get."

"Not all the time?"

"Well, most of the time."

"Don't make it harder than it is."

Charlie flipped through the file. "No Boots."

"Try Felitia's Mother."

Charlie riffled through the cards again, raising a little atmosphere of dust. Whistler pulled out his handkerchief and caught the sneeze.

"Nothing," Charlie said.

"Let's go one year down the pike."

They found the reference in the index for eighty.

"Connors," Charlie said. "Her real name was Connors. Oh, fachrissakes."

"What's the matter?"

"It's that fucking box right there. We got to move the six fucking boxes on top to get to it."

"You collapse from exhaustion I'll give you mouth to mouth," Whistler said.

Charlie wandered off and came back with a ladder. He climbed up and started handing the boxes down. Finally they got to the one that held the file on Felitia's Mother or Boots.

Whistler took the top off the file carton and went through the tabs. He pulled the folder marked Connors.

He learned that Alice Connors aka Boots aka Felitia's Mother had died at Central Receiving having no known address. Her age was estimated to be under forty, though the M.E. had made a wry note that she had the organs and body of a woman of sixty. Primary cause of death was a ruptured spleen. There was a circulation log at the bottom of the last page.

"What does this mean, Charlie?" Whistler asked.

"Copies went to Chancery Court, Missing Persons, the District Attorney, and Homicide Division. Also a copy to Central Property, along with her package of goods."

"She had a couple of daughters. Wouldn't her effects be turned over to them?"

"Whatever cash she had on her would be. On an unsolved homicide like this anything else would go in a basket."

"You don't think anybody's still trying to find the killer after seven years?"

"No, I don't, but that's how it's done when there's an open file."

"Thanks," Whistler said and started walking back along the musty corridor of forgotten lives.

"Hey," Charlie called, "ain't you gonna help me put these boxes back?"

Whistler kept on walking.

"Thanks a lot, Whistler. Glad to be of service. And don't come back."

Of all the things Twelvetrees dreamed about and feared, ending up old without a cent, getting AIDS from a whore who'd been playing around with some fairy, kicking off in the middle of a threesome with two naked broads watching as your heart burst, falling off a boat into a guppie pool and drowning while little kids in two-piece bathing suits applauded the funny man, jumping off a tall building and breaking your neck on a bag of used condoms, or choking on a piece of steak at some restaurant decorated with plastic palms, the worst was waking up in the middle of the day after a sleep like death and finding out you were the only person in town left alive.

Twelvetrees swam up out of the grave and started at the horror of the silence and the empty bed. Even Millie Bothwell would be a comfort, he thought.

There was a time when her fat body had been familiar.

A couple of months there when he'd crawled up out of the roadhouses and pissy clubs, paid his dues on the talk shows with Douglas (Whatever happened to *that* gazoony, see how it could happen to you?), Griffin, and Carson, did the variety one-a-week on local television, the five-a-week in daytime syndication. Until he was ready for the big one. The network weekly variety. Better yet, a network slot at midnight.

He'd wondered who could get it for him? Who had the clout, the push, the key to the closets filled with dead bodies? He'd asked around and everybody told him that Bothwell, the iron-crotched twat, was the one. So he did what he had to do: spent some time in bed with her. What was so bad about that? He'd done worse when he was in the army or on the road, sucking toes in Needles and Fort Worth. Hell, he'd done worse for years, every night he got the itch. Down there on the parade ground, in one city or another, where the nolas, twangie boys, and creatures nobody knew what to call marched around. Creatures like that Boots.

He sat up as though somebody had stuck a hot wire up his ass. The memory of listening to the tape Nell had laid on him last night came thundering back. Jesus Christ! How did she ever get her hands on that? The police had taken the tape he'd made that time away with them and kept it along with the payoff. He'd had a spare. She could have found that, nosing around among his things, and made a copy for herself.

He'd been stupid making those tapes. It was just for chuckles. Something to scare the hookers with. Like making them watch bondage films, or even one of them goddamn massacre pictures, on the VCR. You could buy them anywhere. They were just for kicks.

But he should never have recorded his own scene. That was dumb and dangerous. On the other hand, how the hell was he supposed to know she'd go and die?

The cops had talked it out of him. Scared it out of him. He'd shoved it into their hands to prove he hadn't actually killed that hooker. It was evidence that he'd pushed the punching bag around a little bit, maybe, but it also proved that she'd been alive when she left his house.

Now Nell was warning him with it. Telling him she'd drag it all out again. Maybe spread copies of the tape around all over town. That kind of thing could chop him off at the knees, ruin him.

He put the fingertips of one hand on the wrist of the other. At first he couldn't find the beat. Another shot of adrenaline juiced his nerves. His pulse thumped. Then he could hear it in his ears. It was so quiet in the house.

Nobody in the goddamn house? What the hell kind of protection was that? What was he paying those two Polack bastards for?

He got up off the leather couch and lurched across the room to the door. He stood in the hallway on the second floor listening. Nothing. Just the sounds of traffic from way down at the bottom of the hill, like distant surf. His head felt fuzzy, as if he was straddling time.

"Hey! Is anybody here? Is anybody in the goddamn house?"

He heard Jenny's voice coming faintly from her bedroom suite. He couldn't make out for sure what she was saying. He thought it was, "Daddy, Daddy! Walter went to buy me somethin' at the store!"

He went into her bedroom saying, "Where are you?"

Jenny wasn't in the bedroom. The satin spread was mussed where she'd been lying on the bed reading a movie magazine. She shouldn't be laying on the bed on top of the spread, Twelvetrees thought, probably with her shoes on, too. Kids.

The door to the adjoining bath was open an inch or so. He could hear little splashes like a kid playing in the water. He walked across to the bathroom door. He was going to tell her not to lay on the bedspread. He pushed the door with his fingertips. It swung open like a trick set on Broadway, like a moving picture's lap dissolve.

Jenny was sitting in the bath. She looked scared for a second. She didn't say anything. She just smiled the way Marilyn used to smile when she wasn't sure what mood he was in.

"I don' think you should be lookin' at me, Daddy," she said.

"No, oh, no," Twelvetrees replied, but he didn't turn his back.

"I think you ought to leave the room."

"The last time I saw you in the bath, you were five, maybe six."

"No, I was older than that. I remember."

"I woke up and I didn't know where I was for a minute. In fact, I thought I was back home with your mother and you were ten." He gestured behind him and laughed. "I saw the magazine and your bed mussed and I was going to scold you for laying on it with your shoes on. Remember you used to do that?"

She was holding the washcloth over her breasts, staring at him.

"Jesus Christ, but you look just like your mother looked at your age."

"Please go," Jenny said.

EIGHTEEN

THE PROPERTY ROOM seemed more like a morgue than the morgue. Racks and racks of wire baskets held the last possessions of God knew how many people, the dead, the lost, and the strayed.

Barney Tesich, with his beer barrel gut and unloaded .357 magnum cradled in a braided holster on his hip, was the keeper of this human dead letter office. Very few ever came to call and claim their goods.

The things stayed stored here until the court finally issued instructions to dispose of them. Then the possessions were returned to relatives—if they, too, were not dead and gone—or relegated to auction or the furnace. Such things as guns, knives, umbrellas, overshoes, false teeth, eyeglasses, and snapshots of persons once loved and treasured.

"I'm standing here wondering, Barney," Whistler said.

"What are you wondering about, Whistler?" Tesich responded.

"I'm wondering if I should make an offer or ask the favor."

"What's your particular problem concerning this decision?"

"Well, if I offer you more than a sawbuck, you might get the idea that what I want is of so much importance to you that you'll try to raise the price."

"Is this favor of much importance to you?"

"On the other hand, if I offer you twenty in order to expedite—"

"Expedite?"

"Yes, speed up."

"I know what is expedite."

"—In order to expedite the process, will I be giving away a tenner I didn't have to spend?"

"There's another factor to be taken into consideration here," Tesich said.

"What's that?"

"If my keeping quiet about this favor is part of the deal."

"I thought that went with the package."

"Oh, no. It's separate."

"I have to buy this favor in sections?"

"Silence is a service I offer my best customers, they shouldn't pay for more than they need."

"Okay, here's your twenty," Whistler said, peeling a bill from the bottom of a flash roll.

"The favor without the silence," Tesich said, lifting it off the counter with naturally sticky fingers.

"Uh-oh," Whistler said, and put down another ten.

"We can speak in sign language from now on, if you want," Tesich said.

"Find me a basket on an Alice Connors, deceased August twenty-eight, nineteen eighty."

"That's a long time. Whatever's in it could've turned to dust."

Or been looted a dozen times as it was pushed to the back of storage in the passage of years, Whistler thought.

Tesich got out of his chair with some difficulty and a grunt of general discontent. He shuffled off into the gloom almost as thick as the gloom over in Morgue Records.

It took him so long to come back that Whistler half expected him to be changed by age and the passing of the seasons.

The wire basket was almost empty. A pair of electric pink satin hot pants, a bare midriff cutoff jersey top, a half-cup bra to show the merchandise on the upper shelf, a pair of spaghetti strap high-heeled sandals, and, in a brown circulation envelope, a zippered bag made of flowered plastic, the kind women carry toilet things in when off on a trip.

In the bag were a pair of prescription sunglasses, a lipstick, eyeliner, mascara, cake blush, a small bottle of hand cream, a packet of flavored douche, a roll of dental floss, one of those circles of elastic with a wooden bead for holding back a fall of hair, and thirty-eight cents in change.

No paper money, no credit card, no keys.

The circulation envelope had been signed in by Barney Tesich. The signature of the detective on the case, signing off the property, was a scrawled mess, scarcely legible between the coffee stains and the fading of time.

Whistler put his finger under it. "Can you read that?"

"It's not my handwriting," Tesich said, giving it no more than a passing glance.

"I know it's not. *This* is your signature. I'm asking do you know who signed this stuff in?"

"I wouldn't know."

"Somebody buy the complete package?"

"I can't hear you, Whistler. Can you hear me?"

"I can hear you."

"That's funny, because I ain't talking."

Whistler put his nose right down to the brown paper, so close that he could smell it. It smelled of newsprint about to crumple. After a full two minutes he could barely make out what looked like the first initial cee.

Twelvetrees sat in his own bedroom thinking that Jenny hadn't really chased him out. He sat there trying to sort out feelings that were frightening and painful. He hated it, hated how he'd always been led around by his cock. There was no let up.

Jenny had sat in the tub, so naked and so beautiful, probably spoiled already by somebody just like him. He'd been trying to think, ever since she'd appeared on his doorstep, how maybe she hadn't been touched yet. But how could he imagine a foolish thing like that nowadays? Even down in Atlanta, a girl of twenty-one would be a freak if she was still a virgin. What was the country coming to? Where had all the traditional values gone?

I mean, you work your ass off to make it good for your wife and kids—what else did a man work his ass off for?—so, all right, maybe you get a little tired of shtupping the same old cold cuts and poking the same old eclairs, but that's no reason a father should lose his chance to make sure his daughter doesn't lose her cherry to some boy who doesn't even value it. Who was it wanted the divorce, Marilyn or him? He couldn't remember.

All he knew was he'd give a bundle to screw Marilyn again.

Not the Marilyn who'd been married the last eleven years to some goddamn doctor down there in the benighted South, but the Marilyn he'd knocked down on the floor and screwed into the worn carpet. That Marilyn! That young Marilyn getting laid by that young Twelvetrees! The Marilyn who'd looked just like Jenny. Jenny who was twenty-one, but who'd been ten just a couple of days ago.

He had a boner like a steel rod.

Bosco was sitting across from Nell, drawing pictures on a menu with a marking pen, when Whistler got back to Gentry's.

He slid into the booth before they saw him.

"What's that you got there?" he asked.

"I was explaining to Nell about the Santa Anas. The experts call them 'drainage' winds, and plain folks used to call them 'witch's winds.' They say the Indians would go mad and throw themselves into the sea when the Santa Anas blew."

"Now the hookers, pimps, and gonifs throw themselves under cars," Whistler said, grinning at Nell.

"You can laugh," Bosco said, "but these winds can stir up a crazy kind of hell in some people. Ask Canaan or Cortez about what it does to the statistics on murder, rape, and suicide."

That bore too closely on the reason why Whistler was guarding Nell. He put away his grin. "So what does this squiggle mean?" He pointed to the graph Bosco had drawn.

"I got a theory. The Santa Anas have been blowing two full nights and one and a half days. According to my research, which I have conducted over the years, this spell of wind's going to last the rest of today and tonight, all of tomorrow and tomorrow night, and will probably blow cool around five o'clock the day after that."

"Where's your data?"

Bosco looked out the window and spotted what he wanted. "You see Bitchie-Boo over there?"

"Bitchie-Boo is the black hooker with the silver wig," Whistler said, as Nell leaned toward him and craned her neck to look.

"Notice the footwear," Bosco said.

"Ankle boots," Nell said.

"When the Santa Anas are blowing Bitchie wears sandals. When she senses the approach of a weather break, she switches to ankle boots. Sixty, seventy-two hours after that, almost every time, she switches to calf boots and the winds shift."

"Amazing," both Whistler and Nell said, as though they'd rehearsed it.

"I think so," Bosco said.

"I'd like to start down to Venice now," Nell told Whistler.

"Okay," he said. "You want to take care of anything before we go?"

"Not a bad idea. I'm floating with all the coffee."

She pushed against Whistler's leg with her leg. He slid out of the booth and let her out. He watched her action as she walked through the arch to the rest rooms. He couldn't help himself. No man could help himself from watching that action, he thought. He sat down again.

"Where have you been?" Bosco asked.

"Oh, doing this and that. Canaan leave?"

"You see him hiding under the table?"

"I just meant I don't see him."

"Well, he left an hour ago."

"You remember the other day we were talking about this Boots?" Whistler asked.

"Boots?"

"Felitia's Mother?"

"Oh, yes."

"Did Canaan catch that case?"

"Why would he catch the case? He never worked homicide."

"Well, it wasn't homicide until after. I mean, she wasn't found murdered on the street. She died in the hospital from a beating."

"So?"

"Well, so Canaan hasn't been working kiddie vice all his life. Only the last few years. Only since his niece."

"So?"

"So I was just wondering, did he work regular vice back then, seven years ago."

"You check that? You find it was seven and not six?"

"Yes, I checked it."

"What for? What's going on?"

"Nothing's going on. I'm just looking into a little something about this Twelvetrees, that's all."

"That he might have killed that hooker and some cop helped him cover it up?"

"Well, it's a thought."

"That Canaan helped cover it up?"

"I didn't say that. Hey, for Christ's sake, don't growl at me. I'm not out hunting for Canaan. You read goddamn books like *Alice in Wonderland*, you start thinking crazy."

"Hey, what're you getting your balls in an uproar, babe?"

They stared at each other for a minute.

"You think maybe Cortez was catching cases for homicide back then?" Whistler asked.

"It's more than possible. Why don't you ask him?"

Whistler took his key ring out of his pocket and removed the key to the Chevy. "Trade me for a couple of days?" he asked.

"Sure." Bosco went into his pockets and pulled out the keys to his van. "It could use some gas."

"Use the door through the kitchen?"

"Anything you want, Whistler. Anything you want. You know that."

NINETEEN

"WHY BOSCO'S VAN?" Nell asked.

"I'd just as soon we don't make it easy for that gazoony who snapped our picture the other night."

"You think he's watching us?"

"I don't know, but why take the chance?"

"My God, I'll be glad when this is over."

"If you're afraid, I think it could be over with pretty quick. All you've got to do is go into that lawyer's office and say you don't want to play games. You don't want to negotiate. You don't want to play one for you, one for me. You don't—"

"That's not the way it's done."

"It's the way it's done when some working stiff and his old lady break up. They say, what have we got here, and how do we divide it. What's fair?"

"What would you say is fair?"

"I'd say a hundred thousand—could you live okay on a hundred thousand—a year would be fair."

"For how long?"

"For maybe five years. You gave him five years, you get five years."

"He's been making twenty million a year."

"He's got expenses. So let him worry about it. Take a hundred a year tax-free. Who wants twenty million?"

"You wouldn't want twenty million a year?"

"No, I wouldn't. You ask a person a question like that, first thing they think is, I want it, I want it. I've thought about it. No, I wouldn't want it."

"How much would you want?" she asked, a smile starting up at the corners of her mouth, watching him as he considered her question.

"A million," he said. "I think I could use a million."

They started to laugh.

At La Brea he turned south.

"Aren't you going to take the freeways?"

"They'll be like ovens."

"You're right."

She put her head back on Bosco's mauve plush seat covers.

Whistler glanced at her. He liked the way she looked, almost plain, more like the girl she'd once been, the lipstick off her mouth, the strong bridge of her nose, the high cheekbones stretched and shining, the freckles showing up more than usual, her hair grabbed back and caught with a piece of ribbon.

"You say you lived down to Venice when you came to Californa?"

She knew he was looking at her. She lowered and raised her chin a couple of times.

"Just you and your mother?"

"What makes you say that?"

"When you said you wanted to come down to Venice, you said to see your mother. You didn't mention your father."

"I came out alone at first."

"How old were you?"

"Fourteen."

"Then your mother came out?"

"That's right. When I was seventeen, eighteen."

"After your father died?"

"No. After she left him."

"So after your mother came out, she stayed with you? How did that work out?"

"We managed. But it didn't last long, mother and daughter pretending to be sisters. Then my old man came chasing out after her. He'd said the hell with her when she took off, but after a while he couldn't stand the deprivation."

"The what?"

She looked at him as though he were being deliberately dense. "You know what."

"Oh."

"That was always a problem for Pa, getting enough of my mother. They've been living in Venice the past twelve, thirteen years. I think he's still not getting enough."

"You visit them often?"

"Not too often."

"Where'd you come from originally?"

"Bunt."

"Oh, yes?" Whistler said, as if he probably knew where Bunt was but it had just slipped his mind.

"On the Skunk."

"Utah?"

She laughed. "Iowa."

"What does your father do?"

"Now? He and my mother manage a roach hotel filled with winos, druggies, and artists that live in the storefronts that used to be shops in the great long ago."

"How about when you were a kid?"

"Daddy was a farmer for a while. His father left him the farm when he died. It'd been in the family three generations before that. My father figured out a way to lose it."

She turned her head again and stared up at the odd marks in the lining of the cab above her head. Bosco had once told Whistler that they had been made by the thrashing feet of various ladies transported by passion.

"Up the Mississippi from where it meets the Skunk is a town called Muscatine with factories that produced pearl buttons from freshwater oyster shells," Nell said. "Big business back in the fifties. Plastics closed down all but a few in the seventies, but Daddy was bust before that, so it wasn't much to worry about."

Her voice had picked up an accent, slightly flat and drawn-out, the voice farmers and ranchers used to tell their stories, easygoing and half sly.

"My daddy came from farmers and the only thing he had was a farm, but he decided when he was thirty, not long married but already with two kids, me being one of them, that he'd make his fortune in pearl buttons. He went ahead and got the boat, dredges, and rakes to harvest the shells where they piled up at a bend in the river. That was back in fifty-one.

"He was cautioned by more than one to look into the laws about riparian rights, but he insisted the bottom and banks of rivers were free for anyone's use and profit, and went on mortgaging everything we owned to get into the button business.

"They were years so hard, my mother says, they could make your nose bleed, but I was a kid and what do kids know about hard times as long as they got a warm meal and shoes and Ma and Pa talking away at night over the kitchen table while they're under the covers of a warm bed? I look at my mother's hands now and I know what she means by hard times. She used to squat right down with my father and his hired help, shucking the meat out of the oysters.

"So for five, six years it was very hard, and then it looked like my daddy'd finally turned it around and the business was going to make a profit, and even maybe make us well-off a few years down the road. That was when a man named Martin Magpie—I'll never forget that name, even if it wasn't so foolish—comes visiting with a leather briefcase, wearing a four-hundred-dollar shearling coat in the dead of spring, and tells us the right to fish that stretch of river, to harvest the shells or prospect for minerals, belonged to some people back east.

"To make a long story short, my daddy went to law and fought it. In the end, he had to accept a kind of settlement. He'd been kept from working the river while the case crept through the courts. The lawyers ate up all the cash he had. Tough as he was, he was just plumb wore out. He lost the business, and sold the machinery and dredges to the enemy for pocket change, and went back to the few acres he had left in Bunt along the Skunk.

"It didn't really much mean a damn. Like I said, plastics came in, so my daddy, that Magpie, and every damn body else in the shell trade ended up losers."

"So he farmed what was left?"

She laughed through her nose, snorting out the bitter memories. "Did you know that Iowa raises several million dollars' worth of popcorn every year?" she asked.

"Well, no, I didn't know that," Whistler said.

"The next grand scheme my daddy had was about popcorn. He decided he'd raise popcorn that puffed up in technicolor."

"I've seen it."

"Oh, no, you haven't. What you've seen is popcorn that's been dyed with vegetable coloring. Jessie Reinbeck would have none

of that. His popcorn would come from a rainbow grown naturally. I even liked the idea. But then, I was twelve and what the hell
did I know? It took him only three years to go really broke on that
one, but I was long gone by then.''

"Did he go back to farming?"

"There was hardly anything left to farm. He was fifty and
looked ninety. It's not that he wasn't willing to work his ass off.
He was never lazy. Just hard-nosed. Hard-nosed and soft-headed.
A dreamer with dreams that were really of no use. He sold the
land. My mother and him lived in a tenant house until the last of
my brothers and sisters left. Then she left for the city. Cedar
Rapids. That was her idea of a city. He went after her that time,
too. Tried to get work. They make furniture in Cedar Rapids. He
didn't know a thing about making furniture. After a little of that,
my mother came out to find me, or so she said. We made like it
was fun hanging out together. It's no fun going to bars with your
mother. When my father came out after her, I took the chance
and moved to Hollywood.''

There were all kinds of deep pits filled with dark water in the
way she stopped talking as though her tongue had been cut. All
kinds of things floated face down in the silence, drowned but not
quite dead.

"When *was* the last time you saw them?" Whistler asked.

She looked at him with eyes struck by something like regret.
"It's been four years, Whistler. I'm afraid to look."

He turned off on Adams. They rode in silence over to Washington and all the way down Washington to Speedway and
Dudley Court. Whistler started looking for a place to park.

Venice is a twelve-year-old anarchist's dream of heaven.

Dark-skinned clowns in white-face and half-naked witches in
bikinis and Day-Glo kneepads skate by winos, freshly mugged
and beaten just the night before, left lying in the sand.

Hookers ply their trade sitting on the pavement along Ocean
Front Walk, improving their tans with aluminum reflectors stuck
under their chins, while roosting pigeons on crumbling cornices
crap all around them.

Old Jewish men and women air themselves on wooden
benches under wooden parasols shielding them from the sun
they came three thousand miles from Brooklyn and the Bronx to

find. Their loyalty and affection for Venice, since muggings and
robberies after dusk are so commonplace that the orthodox
among them hold the traditional Sabbath sunset service in the
afternoon, surprises everyone but themselves. If you asked them
would they like to go back east, they'd tell you only if you could
make them young again.

Gonifs, muscle builders, bathing beauties, nuns in short-
sleeved habits, rabbis with flat hats and side curls, roller skaters,
and casual killers all sport the same sunburns, peeling noses, or
oil-slick tans.

Artists, living on paste and promises, are still fighting the
losing battle against the entrepreneurs who mean to fill every
cubicle with fugitive stockbrokers from downtown L.A., turn
every canal-side cottage into a condominium and every shop
into a chic boutique selling llama-wool sweaters from Peru,
lizard-skin purses from Mexico, and crack from Colombia.

Practically every rooftop has a two-hundred-thousand-dollar
penthouse where some divorcee makes pots and jogs in the
early morning hours wondering if that will be the morning
when the odds against her will run out and she'll end up being
raped.

Whistler tooled the van around a spread of blocks four streets
wide and ten blocks long. If there was a spot for a bird to park
along the curb, he couldn't find it.

Just around the corner from Pacific, on Paloma, was a hand-
printed sign pasted to the wall beside an empty lot. It announced
all-day parking for ten dollars. There was an empty spot big
enough for the van but no driveway access. Whistler drove over
the curb and backed it in.

"Lock it up," he said, getting out his side. "Hit the button and
hold the handle."

A tall, skinny kid, who looked to be a stoned-out twenty, came
slouching over, rubbing his leaky nose off on his bare arm.

"You shouldn't have jumped the curb," he said. "That space is
reserved anyways."

"For who?"

The kid stared at the ground under the van as though there was
sure to be gold nuggets lying there. "That's probably the last
parking spot left in Venice."

"You own this lot?"

"Oh, no. I work it for the guy what does."

"What's the cut?"

"Cut?"

"You working the concession on commission? How's it work?"

"He lets me sleep over there against the wall nights."

"And throws you a bone now and then?"

"Something like that," the kid said, as though it were all Whistler's fault that he should have fallen so low.

"This is your lucky day," Whistler said.

"How's that?" the kid asked, brightening up a little.

Whistler handed him a twenty.

"Ah?" the kid said.

"I got you." Whistler retrieved the twenty and gave the kid two tens.

The kid managed a smile. He thought about saying thanks, but then turned away, in a terrible hurry to find his dealer and buy a two-cube tube of crack.

Nell matched Whistler's stride and put her arm through his as they walked back to Dudley Court.

"Remind me, if I ever want to work a game for the price of room and board, to come to you first."

"You think he worked me?"

"You worked yourself. Probably nobody owns that lot. It's waiting for somebody to build on it."

"You're a cynic," Whistler said, smiling.

"And you're every hustler's patsy."

"Present company excepted?"

Her arm grew rigid. He grabbed her hand and pressed her forearm to his side as she tried to pull away. Her face was twisted up and mean, her eyes bare as knucklebones. It was only a flash, one part of a second split in two.

"Don't pull my leg, for God's sake," she said. "I just got away from a man who likes to pull wings off flies."

The Dugout was a bar for all reasons. It was on Santa Monica Boulevard, just over the border of the beach city, on a stretch that was, comparatively speaking, in the low-rent district. It had seventeen different brands of beer on tap and was said to have the best steaks available anywhere for miles around.

It drew a lot of celebrities for lunch and dinner because there was a short book of unwritten law that had grown up over the years. Customers were not to go up to any famous person and bother him or her for an autograph. You could gossip afterward all you liked, but you were not to eyeball a celebrity when he or she was groping someone, male or female, under the table. Especially if that someone was not the celebrity's mate or spouse. You were not to ask the piano player in the bar to sing "My Way" or "Days of Wine and Roses."

It was late for lunch and early for dinner when Roger Twelvetrees arrived with his band of nomads in tow. This tribe, except for Harry Klorn, was not his television tribe. This was his feature film tribe.

There'd come a time when Twelvetrees's salary could go no higher. Even he had admitted it was beginning to spoil his image as a simple small-town boy who'd made good, and "who the hell wanted to be the one to bring down the revolution?"

Free this and free that, cars and boats and planes and broads, didn't cut it. Deferred payment until he was a hundred and twenty didn't appeal.

When some junior ass-kisser came up with the idea of the network financing a three-feature production deal for his own production company—not his *television* production company but a *moving picture* production company—he'd been more than cool at first. After all, he'd said, every asshole in the business had production companies, one of each, television, music publishing, and features.

But the junior fart pointed out that he could star in every picture. "We'll have Swifty Lazar . . . is he still alive, God bless the man . . . offer you ten million dollars on the air. He only offered Carson a mil. Ten million to star in a Norman Mailer screenplay. Mailer don't even do screenplays except for himself, so it'll be a first. You'll refuse, of course. But now we got America thinking, maybe he can really act. Instant credibility. If Sinatra could get beat up and win an Oscar, you could get yourself punched in the mouth on the screen and cop one of them little golden pricks without straining a nut."

"I don't like it," Millie Bothwell had piped up. "There's no guaranteed money in it."

"Only a thirty-million-dollar finance package," the executive fart said. "And besides, money isn't everything, Roger. Fame on

the tube is fleeting. There's the permanence of film. There's the
record books. There's fucking posterity!''

So that's how come Millie Bothwell was not welcome in
Twelvetrees's feature film tribe, the junior executive with the
notion was a vice president, and John Bama was licking his lips
over his first hundred-thousand-dollar screenplay, less ten for
his agent, ten for a finder, five for his lawyer, five for his business
manager, one and a quarter percent for the Writer's Guild of
America, West, Inc., and ten in kickbacks without written
destination.

So the feature production team was composed of Red Akron,
the producer; Hicky Caddo, the director; Pip Pomeroy, a production supervisor; Chips Durham, who did budget breakdowns;
and John Bama, looking like a shaggy dog and making sad eyes at
Jenny who was there at her father's insistence, but didn't know
why.

The first four were aging has-beens and never-weres. They
were so grateful for this one more job, and the chance to steal a
little something for their golden years, that their biggest worry
was not to lose control and piss all over their master's leg.

Bama was twenty-seven and a comer. His foot was on the
ladder. All he had to worry about was that nobody should take
the notion to kneecap him and leave him for dead.

He had trouble knowing where to put his eyes. Whenever they
landed on Jenny's blouse, Twelvetrees gave him a look as though
he could read Bama's dirty thoughts. He noticed that Twelvetrees rubbed his wrist against his daughter's tit every chance he
got. The second time it happened he tossed a glance at the quiet,
blond character who'd been introduced as Spinneran to see if he
was the only one catching the action. Spinneran had flat-eyed
him, letting him know it was something he saw every day, and
anyway, who gave a damn if a father wanted to feel up his
daughter?

The look was also more than a little superior, as though
Spinneran was convinced he could have Jenny any time he
wanted her. Bama could drop his drawers and ask for a measure-
ment, but it wouldn't do any good. It was Spinneran's call.

Bama couldn't figure out what the hell Spinneran was doing
there in the first place. He walked a step or two behind everybody
else, as though he didn't want anyone making the mistake of

thinking that he was actually part of Twelvetrees's parade of
flunkies, but just an innocent bystander called in for consultation
about a matter too complicated to explain.

Walter Pulaski walked on one side of Twelvetrees. His brother,
Stan, was at his back. The brothers weren't twins, but they
looked so much alike that there were people who believed there
was one man named Pulaski who, like the legendary kiddie vice
cop, Isaac Canaan, never slept. There were ladies who talked
about this man, Pulaski, who left them in bed to go wring out his
sock a lot, but who had the staying power of a stallion.

The Pulaski brothers walked as though they were ready to
catch bullets in their teeth.

The party was shown to a pair of tables in the back that were
pushed together because Twelvetrees wanted them pushed together.

They all ordered something to drink, except Spinneran. Nobody seemed to notice. He might have been an alien from
another world.

Twelvetrees had started talking when they'd walked through
the door and kept on talking. He had five highballs in the time it
took the others to finish a pair of whatever they were having.

He kept on talking while he ordered his dinner and everybody
else ordered dinner. Almost everybody had steak, baked potato,
and salad because Twelvetrees had steak, baked potato, and
salad.

Jenny ordered otherwise. After making a face of mild disgust,
silently commenting about the way her father and these people
around her father stuffed themselves, she asked for a chef's
salad.

Spinneran sat back from the table, toying with a spoon. He
ordered nothing but coffee. It was another way of staying
separate, and Bama though he'd use the bit to define a character
in a screenplay some day.

The waitress did a good job picking up the orders in spite of
the background noise generated by Twelvetrees. Once he paused
to smile at her, as though he was giving her a thrill. When he
looked away she caught Bama's eye and raised one eyebrow a
half inch as if she were saying, what does he expect me to do, lay
down and spread my legs?

Spinneran could understand why she'd singled the writer out as a sympathetic soul. He looked the shabbiest.

Bama gave her a big reaction, which Spinneran thought was a stupid thing to do.

But Twelvetrees didn't catch it, and might not have known what it meant if he had. It was in his manner that, as far as he was concerned, she was a low-class broad already made and laid if it was his pleasure, which was a curious way that certain celebrities had when dealing with people. Curious because it made people feel like losers even though they hadn't asked to get in the game.

After the salads arrived Twelvetrees talked while the others ate.

Everybody knew when to nod, when to say uh-huh, and when to roll over and die with laughter. It was an art that very quickly got to be second nature, otherwise hope for survival became very small.

Twelvetrees knew all about it. He didn't really give a rat's ass if nobody responded. He wasn't looking for conversation. He didn't really care if anybody even listened. In fact, knowing that people were bored spitless with his nonstop monologues and twice-told jokes, yet kept on nodding and saying uh-huh and laughing fit to bust a gut, gave him a lot of pleasure. Made him feel like a king, smarter than all the assholes surrounding him who thought they were smarter than he, but who were afraid not to pretend to listen to every goddamn word he spoke as though he were dropping pearls.

"And the green grass grew all around, all around," he said, "and the green grass grew all around."

He paused to see if anyone would comment, his eyes flickering to Spinneran.

"You said it," Akron mumbled.

"Gotcha, babe," Caddo growled.

Somebody let loose a sneaker. Spinneran thought that was the best comment of all. Then he saw Jenny was looking at him with a little smile on her mouth and her eyes slightly crossed.

"Who the fuck's the pig did that?" Twelvetrees said. "Fachrissakes, you're disgusting."

Then he grinned like a gargoyle and dropped his head in his plate, playing the clown. "Roggie do poopie, Mommy," he said.

When he lifted his eyes he looked at Spinneran in a calculating way.

Spinneran wondered when Twelvetrees would make up his mind and make the approach.

Twelvetrees was still running off at the mouth like a loose cannon when the waitress came around to pick up. Everybody was finished with the salad except Twelvetrees. The waitress hovered at his shoulder, not sure whether she should or shouldn't pick up his plate. He looked up at her as though she'd stepped on his punch line.

"You want to keep your salad off to the side?" she asked.

"What do you think?"

"I don't know, sir. That's why I'm asking. You can have it either way."

"Sonofabitch. You hear what she said? I can have it either way. Wha-wha-what does she mean by that?"

Everybody but Jenny and Spinneran broke up. Caddo slapped his knee. When Twelvetrees's eyes fell on him, Bama even managed a grunt that could be called a chuckle. Spinneran could see it made the writer feel like a coward and a fool, but was figuring what was a little humiliation when there were millions to be made.

"Okay, okay, honey. Just havin' a little fun. You can take it away," Twelvetrees said.

The waitress smiled, though the look behind her eyes told Spinneran she'd like to cut Twelvetrees's throat, and removed the salad. She laid out the platters of steak and potatoes quickly and efficiently, following right up on requests for sour cream and chives.

They picked up their knives and forks, except for Twelvetrees, who started talking again. And kept on talking while they cut their meat and forked their potatoes and wiped their mouths and settled back to wait for coffee. Kept on talking while his own plate went untouched and the food grew cold. Kept on talking while the waitress gathered up the dirty dishes and ended up at his shoulder again, not knowing what the hell to do with a man who ordered food and then didn't even touch it.

He reached into his pocket and pulled out a piece of paper. "Are you listening to me, Bama?"

"Sir?"

Twelvetrees unfolded the yellow piece of paper, pushed his uneaten meal aside, and pointed to the diagram on the page.

"I want you to write in a scene in a wine cellar."

"What?"

"A wine cellar. Here's a floor plan you can use. Make copies for the set designer and the carpenters. You look at this, Red. I don't want to chew my cabbage twice."

"This picture takes place in back alleys and shooting galleries, Roger," Bama said.

"You're not listening to me. I'm saying I want this set built. No false fronts. A practical wine cellar. I don't care if we never shoot a foot of film on it. I want this set built and furnished . . ."

"If you got in mind what I think you've got in mind," Akron said, "don't worry your head about it."

Twelvetrees ignored him. He was staring at Bama, leaning forward, boxing him in. "Write me a flashback. Write me a dream sequence. Use your imagination. I can't do everything. Just put it in the script. Anybody asks did we have a wine cellar in the story, there it is. You understand what I'm saying? I tell you what I want, you go write it in. If I had the time, I'd write it myself. I haven't got the time. You think I should make the time?"

"No, of course not. That's not what I think, Roger."

"Do I know you that good, kid? I mean, I'm nearly old enough to be your father. We meet once, twice, and you're calling me Roger?"

"Everybody in town goes first names," Caddo growled, the only one to move a finger in Bama's defense, the others busy sugaring, creaming, and stirring their coffees.

"What are you, a sociologist? What are you Miss Manners? Are you the protocol maven here?" Twelvetrees asked, glaring at Caddo.

"Mr. Twelvetrees . . ." Bama began.

"I'm listening."

"I don't see why . . ."

The waitress, seeing Twelvetrees's plate pushed aside, started reaching in like a monkey pulling a chestnut out of the fire.

Twelvetrees spun around and looked up at her.

"What the fuck are you doing?"

"You pushed your plate aside. I thought . . ." She choked up, afraid in spite of herself, and hating herself for it.

"What did you think?"

"I thought you were finished."

"So you think I'm finished?"

"It looked like you were finished."

"Well, you say I'm finished, then I guess I'm finished."

"Please, sir, if you—"

"You say I'm fucking finished, then I'm fucking finished."
Twelvetrees separated each word and coated it with venom.

The waitress took the plate and added it to the pile on the
trolley. She wheeled it away. Spinneran could see her jaw
trembling with rage and distress. He took a sip of cold coffee.

"Cunt," Twelvetrees said. "That cunt just lost her job, but she
don't know it yet."

Jenny was looking at the men gathered around the table,
weighing them, judging them. She even looked at Spinneran,
who had the flat, pale look of a hangman, as though none of this
had anything to do with him. Make your move, her look said, or
get down and lick my father's shoe like the rest of these
assholes.

Spinneran leaned forward and, keeping his voice low and
confidential, said, "Mr. Twelvetrees, here's this girl, probably
from Newark, New Jersey, Cleveland Heights, Ohio—who knows
where—and she gets a job in this restaurant. Who comes waltzing
in one afternoon with some friends but Roger Twelvetrees, Mr.
Midnight America. Oh, my God! She's scared to death." Twelvetrees started to smile. "She's afraid she's going to make a
mistake, drop the salad in his lap, bring his steak out when it's
not hot enough. Who knows what terrible things could happen?"
Twelvetrees allowed his expression to go soft. "I mean, she just
knows she's going to ruin the biggest day of her life, and,
goddamn it, that's just what she does."

"No, no," Twelvetrees murmured as though reassuring a
condemned man's lawyer that he didn't mean to burn his client.
He looked at Akron, then at Caddo, and finally at Bama. "Maybe
we should give this kid a job writing. He's got a way with words.
Has this kid got a way with words?"

"I think that's what's going through that poor girl's mind right
now," Spinneran said with gold-plated sincerity.

"I really like the way you think, kid."

"If you want, I'll sign Connie to a writer's contract," Akron
said.

"What does he need with a writer's contract? Would you

believe it? This kid, looks like a girl, is a private eye. A shamus. A gum shoe. Where's the check?"

Akron lifted a hand and the waitress sneaked the check in under his arm. Akron signed the meal off against a company credit card.

"You want a wine cellar scene, I'll write you a wine cellar scene, Mr. Twelvetrees," Bama said.

"What's all this Mr. Twelvetrees crap, Johnny? We're going to make a picture together. You call me Roger, just like everybody else." He took a hundred-dollar bill from his money clip and put it under his coffee cup, letting the waitress know it was a personal tribute from Roger Twelvetrees. "Just make sure it's a hell of a wine cellar that will look good in my house."

When they were all outside in the heat, Twelvetrees took Spinneran's elbow and led him off to the side.

"You got anything occupying your time at the moment?"

"Nothing that can't be put aside."

"How much?"

"Fifty."

"Jesus Christ!"

Spinneran started to walk around him.

Twelvetrees grabbed his arm, looking over his shoulder to make sure nobody was going to interrupt. "This service you offer . . ."

"Nothing will ever come back to you."

"You'll make it look like an accident?"

"That's in books and sometimes in political assassinations. Ordinary jobs are very straightforward. With all the crazies out there killing anybody who makes the news, all you have to do is make sure the weapon isn't traced to you and that you've got an alibi."

"Suppose it's traced to you?"

"There's no sheet on me or the weapon I'll use."

There was a film of sweat on Twelvetrees's upper lip and the hand that pulled at the skin of his throat was trembling.

"You don't have to worry, Mr. Twelvetrees. I know that simple is best. I have no intention of putting my *girlish* ass in a sling. Now, about my fee."

"You'll want cash?"

"Yes, cash. If I were you I'd collect it tomorrow. I'll be coming for it when the job's done."

"So soon?"

"The sooner the better. It doesn't have to be fancy."

"I know, simple is best."

"That's right. I'll do it, then come for the money. I don't want any witnesses to that."

"I can meet you—"

"You've got a beach house in Malibu, haven't you? Arrange to be there alone at night for the next day or two."

"Without anybody around? Where's my alibi?"

"The guard at the gate has to check you in. That's your alibi."

TWENTY

WHISTLER AND NELL came up on the broken-down Hotel Beau Rivage from the ocean side, having gone down Paloma and Ocean Front Walk.

Somebody with the idea of dressing up the old building had turned her into a painted trollop. Every separate architectural detail on the facade had been painted a different color. The entrance, cut into the corner, had two steps leading up to the double door with glass insets so dirty they looked as if they were painted too.

At first, Whistler thought Nell had placed a foot wrong. He caught her elbow and steadied her. Then he realized she'd recognized the man who sat on a folding chair down at the end of Dudley Court. He looked like an old pile of clothes sitting there staring at a naked woman somebody had spray-painted on the brick wall of the building on the other side of the alley.

Whistler had seen old actors and writers who'd lost their best chance. Had coffee with them and listened to how close they'd come to the big break when this famous director, that big-time star, or that successful producer called them by name and shook their hand. Or how their big opportunity had been clowned away by fate, pissed away by drink, stolen away by villains even now living the high life in Beverly Hills, Bel-Air, and Malibu. He got enough of losers on the four corners and in Gentry's. He didn't have to travel all the way to the seashore to meet another.

The bag of rags turned its head and looked their way. The eyes flashed milky blue and for a moment Whistler thought the old man was blind with cataract. But the eyes were just clouded over with defeat.

Whistler could see the storefront behind the old man had lost its plate-glass window. The huge hole had been filled up with flattened cartons and pieces of discarded lumber.

"Pa?" he heard Nell scarcely murmur, then loudly, "Pa, its me."

The old man stood up, his jeans falling around his feet as though he were a small man living in a big man's clothes.

"Nell?" he said. "Come to see your mother, have you, Nell?" The voice was hard-centered but soft around the edges, a dreamer's voice trying to sound severe and failing at it.

Another voice, light and fuzzy, spoke from inside the shadows where the sunlight couldn't reach.

"Honey, honey, honey, honey," it said.

A disorderly looking woman stepped out into the light. She was wearing a two-piece bathing suit, showing rail-thin neck, shoulders, and arms. Her breasts should have been those of a much larger woman. They thrust out with surprising vigor for one her age. Her hipbones anchored a tired belly and supported legs that would have been the envy of many a young girl, even soiled as they were with splashes of dirty water. She had the kind of body that looked more naked clothed than other women looked naked.

Her hair had once been the red of Nell's, but, trying to help it when it began to fade, she'd ruined it. It looked like crepe paper that had been caught in the rain. Strands of it clung to her cheeks and around her neck.

She had a water glass half full of red wine in one hand. With the other hand she combed back one side of her hair and caught it behind her ear.

Nell walked past her father, who half-turned away from her.

She touched her mother's arm, feeling along its fragile bones as though testing their fitness, until her hand lay on her mother's shoulder, resting there as if seeking support instead of giving it. Her mother reached out and touched Nell's cheek. For a second they looked like sisters, both very young, in spite of the fact that one's face was as brown and lined as crushed leather and the other's looked half made, with only traces of paint left on the eyes and mouth.

They hugged. When they disengaged, they held each other around the waist as they turned to face Whistler and the old man.

"This is my mother, Florence Reinbeck," Nell said.

"Flo," her mother said.

"And this is my father, Jessie Reinbeck."

Whistler turned toward Jessie Reinbeck and held out his hand. He saw tears in the man's eyes. Reinbeck squinted and jerked his head toward the ocean, knowing that he'd been found out. "Sharp wind off the water," he said though there wasn't any.

"So you got anything interesting to tell me?" Mocky asked.

"How would I know do I got anything interesting to tell you when I don't know what you want to know?"

"So just tell me what you found out, if you found out anything."

"Your boy has a very nice social life."

"How's that?"

"He was at the big party Roger Twelvetrees threw for his daughter's twenty-first."

"Well, he's a very presentable young man. Maybe he met the girl someplace. He's entitled."

"Maybe he did. Was the rent-a-cop at the gate your rent-a-cop?"

"I'm sorry to say we don't have Twelvetrees for a customer."

"Spinneran didn't stay long. He was like in and out."

"So he wasn't working."

"For a minute there you thought he might have been guarding a body?"

"It crossed my mind."

"He left early because he had to pick up his roomie."

"Does he have a roomie?"

"Don't you know?"

"He's a very private person and we never had reason to inquire into his domestic arrangements."

"Until now."

"Well, we got curious."

"You want to know is he going into business for hisself."

"What makes you say that?"

"It's not hard to figure."

"He was very anxious for us to pay him for a job on which we hadn't made collection. Whenever you got an employee looks for an advance on his salary, you've got cause to wonder in this business."

"In practically any business," Rialto said. "You want to know who this roomie is."

"Is it significant?"

"You know a she by the name of Jan Savoda?"

"I ain't been running a stable for some time, Mike. I've got no reason to keep a list anymore."

"Well, this trick rider pikes his pecker up his crack and takes it between the legs like a woman."

"Operation," Mocky said. She wasn't talking to Rialto. It had just popped out.

"How's that?"

"Spinneran said he wanted the money because a friend needed an operation."

"So that's cleared up," Rialto said.

"You've been very helpful, Mike."

"Glad to be of service."

"I paid you for three days."

"No refunds."

"That don't seem very fair."

"Well, what's fair, Mocky?"

"Fair is you give me two more days."

"Doing what?"

"Tailing Spinneran. What the hell. You might come up with something else."

"You just hate getting beat, Mocky."

"Nobody's ever beats me, Mike."

Somebody had started turning the storefront into one of those artist's studios they write up in the magazines. The floor had been painted battleship gray. There were big patches where paint had dripped and spattered. You could have jack-hammered out chunks of it and sold it as art.

There was a wooden counter that blocked off a little kitchen area. The sink was a grainy-white where it wasn't paint-stained. A ladder climbed up to a sleeping loft.

A dozen huge pillows were tossed up against one wall and two or three doors had been turned into tables of various heights on homemade sawhorses.

"You want a drink?" Flo asked. She was looking right at Whistler with a certain speculation in her eyes.

"I don't," Whistler said.

"Whattaya mean you don't? A big boy like you?"

"I don't because I did," Whistler said.

"Oh, one of them," Flo said.

"What are you doing living in here?" Nell asked.

"Somebody threw a concrete block through the window," Flo said.

"Hetty was going to leave," Jessie said.

Flo smiled at him like he was a dog she wasn't very fond of but didn't want anybody else to pet. "Jessie didn't want Hetty to leave, did you Jessie?"

All of a sudden there was a cruelty in the room. Whistler wanted to leave but he was stuck where he was, standing in the middle of the floor.

Jessie turned on his heel and walked out of the studio into the sunshine.

"He wouldn't have nothing to peek at," Flo said, lifting her chin and raising her voice.

"What's going on, Ma?" Nell asked softly.

"What do you mean what's going on? You want a glass of wine?"

"All right. What I mean is how come you're living here instead of the super's apartment?"

"I just told you. Somebody threw a building block through the plate glass, gave Hetty the screaming meemies. She was going to leave, but Jessie told her we'd switch apartments until we got the window fixed."

"When are you going to fix it?"

"Well . . ." Flo said, and smiled.

"Well, what?"

"Well, the insurance adjuster came the next day. We had a talk, him and me. No arguments. He gave me a check for the damage."

"So?"

"I spent the money." She went over to a twenty-five-inch color television set and stroked its flank.

"You spent the money on that?"

"Well, we didn't have one."

"What happened to the one I sent you the money for last year?"

"Well, you know. Money got short. You going to stay for supper?"

Nell looked at Whistler. Something fell from the ceiling and landed near his foot.

Flo walked over and stepped on the cockroach with her bare foot. "It won't bite you," she said.

Whistler knew the type. Every other remark had a double meaning. She fed herself on sexual innuendo. It was second nature, not to be condemned.

He looked up. Somebody in an excess of ingenuity had spray-painted cardboard egg cartons and stapled them all over the ceiling.

"What happens is, somebody sprays for roaches on the third floor, the roaches move to the second. Spray on the second they move down here. Spray here and they go back upstairs. Some things you learn not to fight," Flo said. She looked at Nell. Every remark wasn't sexual, but they all had double meanings. She was always at war with what she wanted people to think she was and what she was afraid they thought she was.

"So you'll stay for supper. I'll make spaghetti."

"Well, don't you like it?" Twelvetrees asked.

Jenny just stood there, feeling oddly uncomfortable.

"Well for chrissakes, you could say if you like it."

She didn't know what to say. She didn't know how it was meant or when he'd had it done. Looking at the bedroom made her nervous like it had made her nervous when he'd stood there looking at her in the bath.

"I'm just so surprised," she said.

The bedroom was huge. Light pouring in from a walled garden washed over a rug the color of sand. A gate led out to the swimming pool, but it couldn't be seen.

The bed was shaped like a shell. The satin sheets were appliquéd to look like waves lapping at the beach. The furniture was pale tortoiseshell veneer. Every accessory in the room was made out of shell, real or fake. Even the telephone was a clever arrangement of small conches.

Twelvetrees went over to the night table and pulled out a drawer that contained a control panel dotted with buttons of mother-of-pearl. He pushed a button and a television rose from a credenza in the corner. Another caused a panel to slide back to reveal a stereo. Others worked the closet door and the drapes. As they swished grandly closed and then opened again, he said, "Come over here. This you got to see."

He opened the door to the bathroom.

Jenny walked over and stood in the doorway. It was all sea-green marble. Twelvetrees pushed a button. Water started pouring into the tub.

"You can run your bath without even getting out of bed," Twelvetrees said.

"I don' know what to say." She wanted to say What's this for?

"That other bedroom was okay for a kid. But you're a grown woman now."

She turned around and saw herself in a huge mirror on the wall facing the bed. She was standing there with her eyebrows arched, her lips puckered, one hip sprung.

"It cost a bundle," he said.

I look like a hooker in a harem, Jenny thought. It scared her.

Flo drained the spaghetti in a colander. She'd put on a housedress over her bathing suit. The breeze had kicked up with the setting of the sun. It was cooler than it had been but still gusted hot with the Santa Anas.

"This is going to be a night like a summer night back in Iowa," Flo said, then picked up her glass and took another swallow of wine. "I can't get used to the way things cool off nights here in California."

"People brag about it," Whistler said.

She lowered her eyelids at him. "What do people know."

Whistler hoped this sentimental journey would hurry up and end.

"Go get your father, will you?" Flo said.

"Where will I find him?"

"Down on the bench at the end of the alley looking at the young girls in their bathing suits."

Nell went out.

"What are you to Nell?" Flo asked abruptly.

"A friend."

"I don't believe that."

"Why don't you believe it?"

"You haven't touched her once since you've been here. I may look something like a raisin but my brains ain't dried up. A man like you and a woman like Nell would touch."

"Well, if I'm not her friend, what am I?"

"What's this, twenty questions? I'm not trying to play games. I want to know."

"We're friends that don't touch."

"You're watching out for her, ain't you?"

"All right, yes, I am. How did you figure it out?"

"You look over your shoulder every time a shadow passes by on the pavement outside."

"That's just a habit."

"Has that sonofabitch threatened her?"

"He's said some things. You know how that goes."

"Yeah, I know how that goes. Some men threaten to hurt a woman, it's only a threat. Some men do it."

Jessie and Nell walked in the door just then.

"Some don't do nothing," Flo said. It was like a sigh.

TWENTY-ONE

EVER SINCE CHILDHOOD there'd been the desire to take every chance, dare every danger, learn how to survive any trap, never asking for help or favor, always self-sufficient and unafraid.

To be unafraid you had to invent yourself. That was the trick. To be unafraid you did what you had to do to save yourself. Being tossed from hand to hand taught a person that lesson.

What were you supposed to do when you were twelve and a drunken man you'd been told to call uncle got into bed beside you and started fumbling at your ass and crotch? Just what the hell were you supposed to do when you had no place, no home, no power to persuade anybody of the truth?

What you did was wait for a night when the uncle fell asleep at the kitchen table, full of gin, sweating on the front page of the news, head twisted to the side, mouth open and drooling. You put out the pilot light on the gas stove. You turned on the jet and went back to your room, pulling the cot and mattress over on their side and pushing back into the corner away from the window and the danger of exploding glass. You waited until the gas built up in the filthy kitchen and finally reached the lighted pilot on the water heater at the very end of the room beside the laundry tub.

When the explosion came it had thrown the uncle against the wall and broke his neck. Neighbors later said he probably never knew what hit him. That was the only unfortunate thing about it.

It would've been better if the bastard had seen it coming, had known he was getting it. From where and for why.

The explosion hadn't done much to the bedroom except blow out the window.

There'd been some cuts and bruises, and a dead uncle, and no place to go but a foster home. That had lasted a week.

"What are you thinking about?" Savoda asked. He was standing there without his wig or makeup, the half-stocking holding down his hair, a flowered silk robe belted around his waist. It was gaping open in the front. Not an enticement, because Spinneran clearly had no interest, just a pleasure for himself every time he walked past a mirror and saw the hormone-induced swelling of his breasts.

"I've got to make a call," Spinneran said.

"When you're finished come into my room. That book you wanted came in."

He walked down the hallway but paused when he was just out of sight. He heard Spinneran make the call.

"This is Spinneran. I've been hired. Yes. No date for delivery was set. Soonest, I'd say. Where? Will you repeat that? No, I'm not writing it down. What the hell do you think, I don't know my business? I want to hear it twice so I'll remember it." He hung up.

When Spinneran walked into Savoda's bedroom, Savoda was bent over emptying his scrotum by pushing his testicles up into his abdomen.

"What the hell are you doing?" Spinneran asked.

"I'm going out on the stroll." Savoda wrapped his penis in tissue paper, then tied a string around and around the package, leaving two very long ends dangling on either side of the knot.

"How can you put up with that?"

"We all have to make sacrifices. If you want to stay in . . . ?"

"I've got business."

"So I don't want to stay by myself, just me and the tube."

"I'm not going to drive you over to the corners."

"Who cares, I'll take a cab." Savoda stood up and hauled his wrapped penis back and up, settling it into the crack of his ass. He took the long ends and tied them around his waist.

"Why do you pike?" Spinneran asked. "Don't most of your customers just want you to go down on them?"

"Most of them do, but every once in a while you get one wants to stick it in. You know, some fucking straight arrow."

"And it fools them?"

"Hell, in the front seat of the car, in some dark alley, scared half to death, they stick it between the folds of my scrotum, they can't tell the difference. It's all in the head anyway. Don't you know that, love?"

"Don't call me love."

"Oh, my, aren't we touchy?"

"That must hurt like hell."

"You get used to this kind of pain. It's the other kind of pain that's hard to get used to."

"Yes," Spinneran said.

"Oh, Christ, sometimes I'm nothing but a selfish bitch," Savoda said. He hurried over to Spinneran and hugged him in an excess of contrition. "Don't be mad at Jan."

"I'm not," Spinneran said and kissed Savoda on the cheek, a thing he'd never done before.

Savoda backed up and let him go. Now that would be something, he thought, Spinneran and me.

Spinneran picked up the book that was lying face up on the bed cover.

The title was The Female Transsexual.

After reporting in to Mocky Hush, Rialto had spent the whole day trying to make contact with Spinneran again. It's why he hated tailing anybody who wasn't tied to a job in an office or a shop, and wasn't tied to a house or an apartment by family either. He wasted part of the day watching the ugly entrance to the building where Mocky had her office, but the maroon BMW never showed.

He didn't feel any great urgency about this assignment anymore anyway. All he was doing was going through the motions because Mocky wanted her nickel's worth. After short-changing him, too. If he had any balls, what he'd do is go over to one of the card rooms in Gardena and have a little play. Make out that was where Spinneran led him. What's she going to do, ask the kid?

What was she doing with a skinny, greenhorn faggot like that baby-faced schmuck anyhow? What kind of a fancy organization was it? He didn't care about her fucking rings, there wasn't even a decent carpet on the floor. She had an organization like a sieve.

That's what she got for taking up with that guinea Mafia soldier
from New Jersey. Setting up in business with him. A goddamn
detective agency that hired a faggot what lived with a drag
queen. Probably peddled his tender ass on the side. That's how
he was going into business for hisself, anybody wanted to know
was he going into business for hisself.

Rialto had cruised the Twelvetrees mansion on the hill once or
twice thinking maybe Spinneran would be up there sniffing
around the daughter. No telling what kind of action was going
down in that department either.

So now it was getting on toward dark and he was camped out
at the back of the apartment complex where Spinneran lived,
right by a pair of big green dumpsters. The wine-colored BMW
was sitting in its bay, it's hood ticking away as it cooled off.

He slept for half an hour, figuring it would take Spinneran that
long even if all he did was change his socks. Rialto had trained
himself to sleep a half hour here and a half hour there. He
remembered reading once that Thomas Edison got his rest that
way. He often said he was very much like Thomas Edison—
who'd invented the electric light, God bless him.

He had his car parked with the back end toward the side door
of the apartment house. Every couple of minutes or so he took a
peek in the rearview mirror, which he'd adjusted for that
purpose. Every time the door opened and somebody came out to
get into a car, he sat still, knowing any movement would draw
their eyes.

He had no intention of losing this fox. He was going to follow
him everywhere he went until he had the rest of his action taped.
Then he was going to stick it under Mocky's nose and show her
that he could do better than she could do checking out her own
employees, even when he was doing better just so she could get
her nickel's worth.

When Spinneran came out, he didn't even glance Rialto's way.
He backed the BMW out of the stall and went down the broad
alley between buildings leading out to Ventura Boulevard.

Rialto pulled out into the street, turned right and right again.
The BMW was going west along Ventura toward the San Diego
freeway. Rialto was six cars behind, in good shape, when the
BMW got off at Wilshire, then turned west toward Santa Monica.

The traffic got thicker and thicker by the block. Rialto took
every opportunity and moved up three cars by the time they got

to Lincoln. There was plenty of beach-bound traffic, all the thousands who worked their asses off in the sweltering town and made the long, slow trek down to the sea every night just so they could breathe a breath of halfway clean air. He chased him all the way down to the mall, where Spinneran pulled his car into a municipal garage.

Municipal garages were lovely places for people wanting to see if they had a tail. You went right up to the roof level, ignoring all the empty spots, and parked the car. At the very least, you got a very clear gander at anybody who drove up to the top to see what you were up to, if the gazoony was dumb enough to do that. It was a reasonable assumption that anybody coming all the way up to the roof when there were slots available under cover was not looking to bake the finish on his car.

Once you had an idea there actually was a tail, you had at least two ways out. Usually more. Down the elevators, down the stairs, out a half a dozen doors.

Also bad for the tailer was the fact that the tailee could have another car stashed waiting for the switch. Or, if you waited on the street and didn't get sucked into the garage, the tailee could drive back down again and out a different exit if there was one, like there was in this municipal on the corner. Or the tailee could walk out and hoof it around the corner faster than a car could follow if there was any traffic at all.

Rialto drove into the garage, pulled a ticket and parked in the first slot he found. He hurried back down to the street faster than a man his size should be able to move and flagged a cruising cab.

"Back into that driveway and wait," Rialto told the cabbie.

"Suppose somebody wants to use it?"

"Then we worry about it. Just back the sucker in far enough so's we get the shade but can see across the street."

The cabbie did as he was told after Rialto plugged one of the holes drilled in the Plexiglas thieves barrier with a rolled up ten-dollar bill.

Rialto had picked a drive that had a view of both exits to the parking garage.

After a few minutes Spinneran strolled out dressed in black with a black canvas carryall slung over one shoulder. He stood on the corner until another empty cab came by and waved it down.

"Okay," Rialto said.

"Oh, boy, just like the movies."

"Never mind the fucking editorial remarks."

"Twenty bucks if I don't lose him?"

"A kick in the ass if you do. Don't let that sawbuck give you any grand ideas."

The cabbie looked in the rearview at the fat man leaning forward in the back and decided not to push it any further.

When Spinneran's cab pulled up to the curb at Speedway and Paloma, Rialto told his cabbie to make the turn at Dudley Court.

He almost broke a kneecap ducking back into the cab when he saw Whistler walk into the storefront with the boarded-up window, an old bum and some familiar-looking woman at his side. He'd just seen that face sometime today. In a photograph. "Fachrissakes," he said aloud. It was Nell Twelvetrees.

TWENTY-TWO

THE SPAGHETTI WAS overcooked, the tomato sauce too acid. Even the Parmesan cheese had been in the refrigerator so long it had lost any flavor it once might have had. There'd been no Italian bread to go with it, just half a loaf of commercial crap so full of stuff to keep it from getting stale that it tasted like paste. There was plenty of wine. Whistler knew there'd always be plenty of wine.

Jessie went at the food as though he found it really tasty. Nell picked at hers and drank more than she should have. Flo was at the stage where she had no taste for food. The wine was all she wanted. Later on she'd want something stronger. She probably had a bottle stashed somewhere. He didn't know what to do about the supper except sit and wish himself the hell out of there.

The door was open. He'd been put at the table with his back to it. Every time he heard somebody go by he tensed, just like Flo had said he did. Finally he got up and closed it.

"Hot night," Jessie said.

"The mosquitoes'll start coming in," Flo said. "You did good, Whistler." She smiled at him as though closing the door had been something hard to do.

"No mosquitoes in California," Jessie said.

Flo showed her arms, marked with bites and the tracks of her nails. "Where you been?"

"There's no breeze anyway," Nell said.

"Where's your car parked?" Flo asked.

"Down in the empty lot at Paloma," Whistler told her.

"Itzie's living," she said. "He'll be in his toilet paper carton by now, stoned out of his head."

"Isn't he afraid of getting robbed?" Whistler asked.

"Oh, he won't have any money on him. Canada Blue will've come and taken it away from him and given him a few lumps of crack. These damn fool kids don't understand the harm they're doing to themselves with that dope."

She took another swallow of wine, then looked into the empty glass as though wondering how it had fallen into that sorry condition. Jessie raised his head and watched her. Nell watched her, too. So did Whistler. Three people watching a drunk decide whether she was going to pour another glass of red.

How many years of that had Nell put up with before leaving home, Whistler wondered. He looked sidelong at Jessie. Had Nell had to put up with anything else?

"You better move your car . . ."

"It's a van, actually."

"Whatever it is, you better move it, or it won't be there in the morning."

"We're not staying all night," Nell said.

"Why not? We could find you a place to sleep."

"No. I've got a place. Whistler has a place."

"Oh, do you?" Flo said, letting what she meant show in her voice and face.

Jessie went red and glared at Whistler.

"Maybe we should get going," Whistler said.

"Oh, fagod's sake, lemme have an hour with my daughter. I don't see her but once every four or five years." Flo acted like she was going to cry or fight.

Nell patted her hand. "Where can we put the van for an hour?"

"Where can you put it? Why you can put it right out there in the alley in front of the storefront, can't you?"

"It says no parking."

"Oh, well, I know the beat cops, don't I?" She smiled the same smile she'd smiled when she'd mentioned the insurance man.

She could be paying off half the tradesman, half the service reps, with whatever she had left, Whistler thought. Jessie must have had one hell of a time trying to keep her down on the farm. Well, he hadn't managed to do that, had he?

Nell said, "Is that all right?" as though it would have made any difference what he said. He was still the hired hand. He'd do what he was told. Even act like they were just friends and he had a choice. She didn't know that Flo had surmised rightly that he was there to watch out for her.

He pushed back his chair.

"You're not going, are you? You're not going?" Flo asked in real panic. "Here, I won't even have any more wine, you don't go."

"I'll just walk down to Paloma with Whistler. We'll be right back with the van," Nell said.

"Now don't run out on me. See? My glass is empty."

"I see."

Nell followed Whistler to the door.

There was still some light in the sky. It would be another forty minutes before any stars, except for the brightest, would be visible. Spinneran had on a pair of sunglasses.

He stood on the walk by the wooden benches where the old Jews sat, braving the chance of robbery or attack because the night was so warm and it reminded them of Brooklyn.

The skaters were still at it. A line of them used him for a pylon, coming close. He didn't move a muscle, just stood there looking up and down the buildings, up and down the concrete path, up and down the wide beach that was starting to empty.

Rialto sat outside a cafe behind an open railing sipping beer out of a bottle, thinking if he'd ever seen somebody looking for a shooting blind he was seeing one right then and there.

Spinneran started into Dudley Court. Rialto didn't move. He didn't think Spinneran was going anywhere, knew he'd be back.

Spinneran saw Whistler and Nell leave the storefront and walk into the circle of light cast by the street lamp. He heard her say, "We'll be right back, Ma. Only take five minutes."

"You see, there's nothing in my glass," a woman's piercing voice replied, the sound carrying down the alley.

Spinneran went back the way he'd come.

Rialto smiled in satisfaction.

Spinneran walked past him, saw the door leading into the building occupied by the cafe, and went inside.

Rialto pictured him climbing the stairs, going for the roof.

*   *   *

Nell was talking more to herself than to Whistler.

"My God, Pa looks old, doesn't he?"

"Well, how old is old?"

"My mother wasn't always a drunk, you know?"

"Maybe you shouldn't talk about her that way."

"Who's around to hear me say it?"

"You are."

"When I hugged her, she sagged she was so drunk. There's nothing to her but bones."

"Maybe she's just tired."

"You know her whole body used to be as beautiful as her legs. You see her legs? Her whole body used to be like that before life sucked the juice out of her. With legs like that—"

"She could have been in the chorus of *Guys and Dolls*," he finished for her.

"And ended up being a hooker?" Nell snapped back.

"Hey, who said chorus girls have to end up being hookers?"

"I'm letting it all hang out, aren't I? That's my father talking. That's what I was told would happen to me if I left home."

"So it didn't happen."

"I just fell down the rabbit hole and found Wonderland, right?"

"La-La Land. Wonderland. Maybe they're the same thing."

"Not real?"

"Maybe not even rational. Even sane."

"My mother wanted me to do it. She wanted me to try for it."

"Like she wanted to try for it?"

"Oh, sure, once upon a time. But Wonderland was a lot farther away and harder to get to back then when she was a girl. She used to spend money on movie magazines and that made Pa mad as hell."

Nell slapped herself on the neck. She grinned. "No mosquitoes."

"Don't tell Jessie."

"It's not his fault, you know."

They reached the lot on Paloma. Itzie wasn't there. There were two kids, sixteen maybe seventeen, jacking up a car.

"You got troubles?" Whistler asked them.

They laughed at him and went on with what they were doing.

He checked the tires all the way around the van.

"Either they were saving these until later or they figured they weren't worth taking," Whistler said, as he unlocked the door on the passenger side and opened it for Nell.

"Is that what they're doing, stealing tires?"

"Well, I don't believe they could afford that Cadillac."

He shut the door, walked around, and got in after Nell reached across and opened the door for him. He started the engine and turned on the headlights. The kids grinned at them, their teeth and eyes shining in the white glare.

"Nothing worries you when you're young," Nell said. "You'll take all kinds of chances."

"Pretty soon they'll get caught doing something heavy. They'll pull heavy time and they won't be young anymore."

"You don't sound as though it bothers you."

"You want me to go over there and give them the lecture on good citizenship?"

"Would they listen?"

"You got it. I won't lose any sleep."

He drove around to Dudley Court and parked alongside the cardboard window.

"You shouldn't blame yourself either," he said.

Anybody might think he was talking about Nell not worrying about what would happen to the two young thieves, but she knew he meant about Jessie and Flo. About leaving home. About not seeing much of them even though they lived just down the road the way distances were measured in La-La Land.

"All the children left," she said. "I wasn't the only one. None of the others come to see them either. None of them even write. I don't even know where my brothers and sisters are right now."

"So then don't take it all on yourself."

"He blames me more than the others. I was his pet. Once, before I married Roger, I asked them to come live with me in West Hollywood. He wouldn't have it."

"How's that?"

"I don't know. He blames himself for failing. That's why she does what she does, drinks like she drinks. She tells him that's why. He didn't want me to see how she treats him like he was nothing."

Everybody built their lives on a pile of lies, Whistler thought. He was beginning to have ideas about how fourteen-year-old

Nell survived the relocation from Iowa. Ideas about what mother and daughter did when Flo had run away from home, too, and came to see how Nell was doing.

"He's got his pride," Whistler said. "That's good."

"You're a soft man, Whistler. That's good, too."

She started moving toward him across the width of the van, her eyes fixed on his mouth. She reached out and crossed her hands behind his neck. The moonlight coming through the back window struck off the rearview mirror and into her eyes. She gave a little gasp and turned her head, looking back over her shoulder.

"Oh, God, look at the moon. Let's go down to the beach."

"If we don't go inside your mother will think we left."

"She'll see the van. She'll know we went down to see the moon on the ocean. It was the only thing I thought about when I ran away from Bunt when I was a kid."

She moved across the seat, pushing past the gear shift and shoving at Whistler's body with her hip. He practically tumbled out of the van. She was laughing softly. She rushed down the alley toward the sand and he went after her.

Rialto was sitting on the darkest bench along the walk where the moon was blocked by the wooden umbrella overhead, and no street or shop light disturbed the shadows.

He saw Nell and Whistler rush out of Dudley Court and onto the sands. He turned his head as she kicked her way halfway down the beach toward the shushing surf with Whistler plodding after her like a patient father after a child.

He faced front and raised his eyes to the roof of the three-story building above the cafe.

Spinneran squatted on the roof behind the parapet. He put together the breakaway rifle and screwed on the scope, then hesitated a minute before gingerly lying belly down on the filthy tar and gravel. He removed the sunglasses and laid them down beside him.

The picture in the eyepiece was pearly with the last lingering light rising from the sand and sea. The figures of Whistler and Nell were dark, but when he brought up the magnification and fixed the sights on her cheek, he could even see the glisten of her lips.

*   *   *

She tucked herself underneath Whistler's armpit so that her cheek was up against his shirt.

Whistler thought of all the girls who hadn't known how to stir a man, and the few who did. He remembered dancing with a pale, teenaged, practicing vamp who'd placed her hand on the back of his neck while doing the foxtrot. She hadn't even been all that pretty, but she'd known just what to do. Little moves. The way a woman tucked her body around a man's thigh and hip. The way a woman made herself seem fragile and so much smaller than the man, ducking under his chin, looking up at him from beneath her lashes. All the tricks learned from the movies. A million directors and actresses making up the myths, so that life could never match the make-believe.

It was different now. The ladies sweat and fired Uzis and sometimes raped the men.

Nell stirred. Whistler looked down at her upturned face. She was working him. My God, how she was working him. You had to wonder why. He started to reach down with his mouth.

The first splat in the sand sounded like a heavy raindrop.

They both looked up at the sky.

"Rain?" Nell asked.

The second splat kicked up a puff of sand.

Whistler knocked her down, and quickly dug them in behind a furrow made by the wind.

TWENTY-THREE

"MY GOD, I don't want to scare them," Nell said.

"I don't want to do that either," Whistler replied, "but that van's the easiest thing I know to follow. I could take off and hope that whoever fired those shots will tail me, though we'd have to fake somebody in the passenger seat some way, and that kind of thing almost never works."

"I could stay right here with my mother and father until you came back for me."

"No, we couldn't do that. All that shooter has to do is walk up and knock down that cardboard without any noise and fuss, and see all he wants to see. We just don't know what he'll do after he sees me leave. He could do that and still have time to pick up the van because he's got a fair idea of where we'd be heading."

"Then you think it's the same person that took the pictures?"

"Well, no, I don't really think that. I don't know. But you've made a believer out of me. Somebody's out to do you, and unless there's more than one person wants you dead, I don't know how many people he'd be letting in on the news."

They arrived back at the storefront, having run across the beach and then the concrete walk, pussyfooting their way along the shadowed side of the building. Half expecting to feel a rifle bullet slam into them, pinning them momentarily to the stone wall before they died.

"We've got to split up. I don't like to do it, but we've got to split up."

She grabbed his arm. "Oh, no, I don't want to do that."

"We haven't got a clue if this shooter is still around here or if he already split. We don't know where he's going to be hanging out waiting for a chance to try again. We don't—"

"I hired you to guard me. I don't see how the hell you're going to be guarding me if you're in one place and I'm in another."

The door opened up and Flo stood there half frowning, half smiling. "What's the matter?" she asked. "What's going on? It took you long enough to park the goddamn van."

"Well, see," Whistler said, improvising on the spot, "we got it here and the damned thing died on us."

Jessie appeared in the doorway. "What's wrong with it?"

"Won't turn over."

"Flooded."

"Won't turn over at all. Something wrong with the starter."

"Lemme have a look," Jessie said, reaching out for the keys.

Whistler quickly got into the van. "Well, you can see for yourself." He hooked a finger around a wire and broke the connection from key switch to battery. "Just won't turn over." He turned the key and tramped down on the accelerator. Nothing happened.

Jessie came around and stood there. "Well, move over, move over. Lemme have a look. I'm pretty good with machinery."

Whistler moved over and let Jessie get behind the wheel, hoping he wasn't good with machinery at all. Jessie tramped on the starter and turned the key hard, but nothing happened for him either. He peered at the ignition lock as though he expected it to speak to him.

"Starter's broke," he said.

"So you got to stay the night after all," Flo said. "We can have ourselves a little party."

"I don't think so," Whistler said, wishing they'd all just get inside, uncomfortably aware that the shooter could be looking down a scope even as they stood out there like a bunch of neighbors discussing a busted vehicle. "I've got to get back into Hollywood one way or another."

"Me, too," Nell said, taking a step closer to him.

"Do you have a car we could borrow?" Whistler asked.

"We've got no car," Jessie told him. "Don't go anywhere much. It'd only get busted up or stole around here, sooner or later."

"Any chance we might catch a cab?" Nell said.

"No cruisers down around here," Flo said. "Not often."

"Billy," Jessie said.

"What's that?" Whistler asked.

"Billy lives in the hotel. He's got an old car and does some gypsy driving. Takes the old Jews where they want to go. Up to Fairfax. Here and there."

"Could you call Billy and tell him we'd pay him pretty good to take us into Hollywood?"

They went inside, and Whistler felt relieved.

"Well, you don't have to call Billy right away," Flo said. "Sit down. Sit down." She went over to pour herself a glass of wine, forgetting all about the deal she'd offered. "You promised to stay an hour."

Rialto sat through the shooting, watching the muzzle explosions get eaten up by the baffles of the brake that killed a lot of the bang. The marksman had pulled off three shots, one then a pair. Whistler and Nell had fallen to the beach, but Rialto could tell they hadn't been hit. He saw them knee and elbow their way through the sand behind a long furrow made by the wind until they found cover behind a trash bin. They'd waited a while, then Whistler had shown himself. After a minute or two, he'd taken Nell's hand and, crouching over, they'd made it onto the concrete, passing twenty yards away from where he was sitting.

Rialto didn't wait to see what Whistler intended to do next. He was on his feet and down Paloma hoping to see what Spinneran was going to do next, but Spinneran was nowhere to be seen.

Rialto went looking for a cab in the lousiest cab town in the world, and got lucky. As he rode back to Santa Monica to get his parked Cadillac, he made a note in his expense book. Maybe this extra two days working for Mocky wouldn't end up a total loss.

The stew was getting thicker and thicker, he thought. Here's this kid, friendly with the daughter of Roger Twelvetrees, a well-known first-class sonofabitch about to have his nuts squeezed by a wife leaving his bed and board but no doubt ready to hijack his assets before dumping him altogether, goes to a party and not twenty-four hours later is taking a shot at the wife.

You read about it. But you didn't read about it as much as you would if contract killings didn't go unsolved most of the time.

People weren't generally aware, but such murders were common and getting more so.

He got his car and drove around the garage checking the stalls for Spinneran's BMW. It was already gone.

Well, he could go running around looking, but he figured he'd already put in better than a good day's work. He paid his parking fee going out, not forgetting to mark it down under expenses, and drove out to Gardena to play a little cards.

Billy brought his dirty Pontiac around to the front of the Beau Rivage Hotel forty minutes after Whistler and Nell had been shot at.

By that time Whistler had come to believe that the delay, sitting there watching Flo get drunker and drunker, and sorrier and sorrier for getting drunk, wasn't a total loss. Every minute that went by made it a better bet that the shooter hadn't hung around, but was gone, perhaps to try another time, but at least gone for right now.

Billy wasn't interested in anything about his passengers. He was a thin man of indeterminate age, with a thin mouth, hidden eyes, and the manner of somebody who believed he was ferrying people to their doom. After he'd made the price for taking them to the Bel-Air Hotel, he didn't speak another word.

Nell sat in back with Whistler, pushed in close against his shoulder, playing the frightened woman depending on the strong man. It wasn't long ago she'd stood out under the light of the street lamp and the light coming out of the storefront apparently unconcerned, though there was every reason to believe that they might still be targets.

"Why the Bel-Air?" she wanted to know as Billy pulled the Pontiac up to the door.

"I know the people here. I'll get you a room that's as safe as Sunday—"

"Oh, no," she said, pulling away from him and practically crouching in the corner.

"—with somebody I'd trust with my life to sit right outside your door."

"You're working for me, don't you forget," she said fiercely.

"The three days are up. You spent your money."

"You said you'd wait and I said I'd get you more."

"I changed my mind. So give."

Billy finally raised his eyes to the rearview mirror and took some interest in the negotiations. He was trying to sort out who was buying who and for what purpose.

Nell held out her hands, showing them empty.

"And I don't take plastic," Whistler said.

Her face started to work itself into a fist, her mouth going ugly and her eyes closing. He waited for the tears. When they came, they were thin. "My God, you're walking out on me," she said.

He put his mouth close to her ear, keeping his voice very low. "I'm not walking out on you, Nell. I've got some things I've got to do if I'm going to keep you safe and I can't do it dragging you around with me."

"Leave me with Canaan and Bosco, then."

"Or some other familiar place? For God's sake, use your head. Nobody's going to expect you to be in the Bel-Air." He reached across the back of the front seat and tapped Billy on the shoulder. "Wait for me. I've got another trip for you."

"Extra," Billy said.

"Naturally."

For a minute there Whistler thought Nell was going to throw a fit and refuse to leave the Pontiac. "You can do it the way you want," Whistler said, "but I'm going to leave you here one way or another. You want the use of Billy's car, I can take a walk. But if I take a walk, I don't come back in the morning."

She got out of the car. They went inside while Billy waited. Whistler talked first to his friend Marvin Dwyer, who worked the night desk, and got Nell a room in the front, closest to the lobby, that had no sliding doors leading from a patio. Then he spoke with Frank Patch, the hotel security man, moving him over to a corner so he could tell him what he wanted Patch to do without Nell hearing.

"Ain't that . . ." Patch started to say.

"Forget you recognized my friend," Whistler said.

"For Christ's sake, Whistler, you're not playing with dynamite here, are you?"

"I'm not even staying in the room. That's why I want you to watch her."

"I'll keep an eye out."

"I don't mean keep an eye out. I mean make goddamn sure nobody comes to call."

"What am I looking at here, Whistler?"

"You're looking at somebody tried to do her."

"Now, wait a minute—"

"But I don't know how seriously it was meant."

"How's that?"

"He could have just been a lousy shot. But if you can't hit a silhouette standing out against a light background, I don't know if you should be in the trade."

"A scare?"

"That's what I figure. If I thought there was a real chance this gazoony was stalking her all the way up from Venice without me seeing I wouldn't be asking you to do what I'd be doing. I'll pay."

Patch waved his hand in front of his shirtfront.

"I appreciate that, Frank. You've got a big one coming from me. All you got to do is ask."

"Which I'll be glad to do if I'm still around to ask," Patch said.

"One more thing," Whistler said. "You ask Marvin to let you listen in on any calls she makes."

"That's illegal."

"I know. So I owe you two very big ones."

TWENTY-FOUR

GARDENA IS A community south of Hawthorne, north of Torrance, east of Lawndale, and west of Compton. Gardena is not the fun capital of the Los Angeles basin, but it does the trick for card players of every description. A glitch in the local ordinances makes it legal to play certain games of chance involving cards.

There were card clubs all over town and Rialto knew every one of them.

The way they work is that the management makes up tables, first come first served, so everybody gets a game. Plenty of regulars play with the same people day in day out, but if there's an empty chair and a stray walks in, he can sit down and take a hand. After all, everybody's money is just as good as everybody else's money.

The management also has floormen who walk around and make sure that the house cut is deducted from every pot, there's no fights, and fair play all around.

Rialto was a regular and highly valued patron. Sometimes, if you took his marker and he lost the bet, he'd try to pay you off with a choice bit of ass, but that was all right, too.

There were half a dozen thirteen-inch black-and-white television sets sitting on shelves high up on the walls. Mostly they were there to get the race results, bets being wagered on a steady basis but wires being illegal. But now they were all fixed on the "Midnight America" channel.

"We got a great show for you tonight," a black-and-white Roger Twelvetrees squeaked from six speakers. "We got Ba-Ba Lupescu, the world's most married Yugoslavian. We got Marvin Shuffler, the man who took responsibility for his own safety, and put down those hoods who tried to hold up that diner in Torrance. We got . . ."

"It was a card club in Gardena, asshole," Rialto said. "Get it right. And they wasn't holding nobody up, they was hustling him for a handout. Jesus!"

Rialto was already losing a bundle and was very irritable.

"We got Snitsy Finchley, the cockney juggler . . ."

"Let's hear it for the juggler," Willy Keep said.

"Here, juggle these," Abe Forstman added.

"Could we have a little more silence, a few less jokes," Rialto said. "Let the man what is being paid an obscene amount of money for being funny be funny."

"So who's making jokes?" Dewy Messina murmured. "Can you open, Rialto, or are you counting on your toes?"

The floorman paused behind Rialto's chair.

"Soooooooo, are you ready for the show?" Twelvetrees caroled.

Rialto held his cards against his belly and wouldn't look at them. Instead, he gave the floorman the stare with his good eye.

"Yeeeees!" shouted the studio audience.

"So much for that crap," Chuck Wissy said.

"Now we can relax with fifteen minutes of some good commercials," Keep said. "Come on, Rialto, do you open or do you don't?"

"I'll open when certain persons take a walk," Rialto said.

"For Christ's sake, Charlie's the floorman, don't you know?" Messina said. "Look at your cards and make your play, you're holding up the game."

"When this gazoony takes a stroll," Rialto said, placing his cards face down on the table, stubborn as a rock.

Charlie, the floorman, decided to be just as stubborn.

"I got a right to stand anywhere I please," he said.

The other players were getting annoyed.

"You don't want to play your cards, we'll go on without you, Rialto. We'll pass you by."

"Oh, the hell with it," said Rialto, "have it your way."

He pulled the cards past the edge of the table by his belly, took the glass eye out of his head, held it under the cards and said, "I pass."

They started to argue about whether Rialto taking his eye out made it a misdeal. Rialto popped his eye back and, feeling better after causing a little trouble, looked up to watch the commercials until Twelvetrees came back on.

"Let me introduce Big Ben Bova who'll soon be defending his World Heavyweight Boxing crown down in Vegas," Twelvetrees said.

"Light heavyweight International Boxing Club crown, schmuck," Rialto said. "Why can't you get it right?"

Rialto was mad at Twelvetrees. Mr. Midnight America had once done a lot of business with Rialto. That was some time ago. His services had not been called upon by Twelvetrees for at least two, maybe three years.

It wasn't that he regretted so much the loss of revenue, though that was a not inconsiderable consideration, it was more that he couldn't brag in the right places that he supplied Mr. Midnight America with choice merchandise. It was a matter of business reputation, like the English vendors liked to put "Purveyors to the Queen" on their goods. It was, when he thought about it, probably Twelvetrees's fault that his referral business had fallen off.

You do favors for a person, and what does it get you? They forget the favors and shit on your shoe.

Here was Mocky Hush, who used to be one of the better fucks around, out of the business and . . . doing what? Whatever she was doing in partners with the Mafia asshole, who was not even a made man, she calls on him to do a job and treats him like a turd. Knocks him down from his regular rate and pays him off with chump change. And don't she know it. What was he doing at his age trailing people, anyhow? He wasn't as young as he used to be and, he had to admit, carrying his belly around wasn't all that comfortable anymore. Especially when you had to stay up late looking for a skinny asshole with brassy hair who lived way the hell out in Sherman Oaks with a drag queen, and who couldn't hit a fucking standing target against a light background at a hundred yards.

He had the suden notion that there might be a lot more in it for him if he went and told Whistler who the gazoony was what took the shots at him. Anybody would be grateful to know a thing like that, wouldn't they? Except Whistler was almost always broke, and it was all right to do a large favor for a friend, but first you had to figure out where the biggest profit was hiding.

"This time, Rialto," Wissy said, as he dealt out the cards, "keep your goddamn eye in your head, I shouldn't throw up on my full house."

Rialto ignored him and flicked a glance at one of the screens. "I think I saw this fucking show," he said.

"You did, it's another repeat."

"Don't that sonofabitch ever work?"

Twelvetrees was into an interview with a little girl, maybe ten or eleven, who looked eight one minute and eighteen the next. She had legs that were pretty long, shaped almost like a woman's, with little Mary Jane shoes and white socks on her feet, and a short skirt halfway up her slightly chubby thighs.

Twelvetrees was doing his best to look up the kid's dress without anybody noticing he was looking up the kid's dress.

The child was the latest sexy little bit out selling tight jeans, training bras, gourmet ice cream, and kiddie cosmetics.

"Oh, yes, Mr. Twelvetrees," the kid said.

"Call me Roger. You're beautiful. Do you know you're beautiful?"

"Well, maybe I'm pretty," the kid said.

The audience laughed and applauded. The kid was showing her ass and vamping a man old enough to be her grandfather, and the fucking audience was applauding, Rialto thought. They'd probably applaud if he tossed the kid down on the rug and screwed her. They'd think it was part of the show, like Twelvetrees working out with a gymnast and almost breaking his ass on a trampoline.

"It's a complete line," the kid went on, picking up her spiel without missing a beat. "Rouge, blush, face powder, mascara, eyeliner. . . . It's such fun, and a blessing for mothers, too."

"Their kids won't be stealing their makeup anymore, right?"

Laughter. Now what was so funny about that, Rialto wondered.

"Oh, you," she said, dipping her head and blushing on cue—film producers take note she could probably cry on a nickel—and reaching out to slap Twelvetrees's hand.

She never expected the old fart to be fast enough to capture her little pudgy fingers with the coral polish on the nails. You could see that in her eyes. She didn't like it. Twelvetrees had probably tried to pat her little buns in the green room, Rialto thought. But, on second thought, she was probably used to slipping and sliding from pats and pinches. What was frosting her ass was the fact that he was queering her pitch. She wanted to run through this goddamn product line she was hawking and get the hell out of there.

"Oh, it's only just for fun," she said, letting him hold on, too smart to make a thing out of it. "Makeup is fun, but ice cream is better."

She was warning Twelvetrees it was time for the ice cream clip. He picked it right up and told the projectionist to roll it.

The child-woman did a job on a suspiciously long and conical dip of what she said was raspberry, while a French-accented voice praised the virtues of this frozen confection, which was, the voice suggested, not ice cream but the frozen juices of a child ripe for plucking.

"Can you believe that sonofabitch eyeing that little broad the way he's doing?" Rialto said. "Somebody has got to do something about this commercial pornography on TV."

"For chrissakes, can you open?" Wissy asked impatiently. "Do I got to sit here and listen to a sermon when I'm eighty bucks in the toilet?"

The floorman came over and grudgingly told Rialto he was wanted on the phone.

"You tell them I was otherwise engaged?"

"He said you'd want to talk to him, it was business."

Whistler called La Costa and found out that Mary Beth Jones was staying there. She was plainly a lady that didn't pinch pennies and liked to be as close to the expensive action as she could get.

It was odds on she'd be in the lounge at the hotel or at the bar in the clubhouse at La Costa, where, during tournament time, the wheeler-dealers bellied up until the small hours of the morning. If he wanted to do it the easy way, he'd just get her on the phone and ask his questions. But he'd learned a long time ago that you didn't get answers that way. People didn't like to answer

questions from a stranger anyway, and refusing on the phone
was an easy brush.

If you've been around any time at all, you soon learn that you
can find out more by reading eyes than listening to what lips
have to say. Besides, Nell said the lady claimed to know him,
had recommended him. If that were true he might as well give
her back the kiss she'd sent him and see if he could trade on old
acquaintance.

Another call told him that Bosco had gone home from Gentry's
at a decent hour for a change. He had Billy take him over to
Bosco's apartment to get the keys to the Chevy. When he paid
him off, Billy said, "A matter of curiosity?"

"Sure."

"Who was buying who and what back there?"

"Let me tell you, it's tough being as pretty as I am," Whistler
said.

He knocked on Bosco's door and told him he'd come for his
keys to the Chevy.

"You put the van back in my slot?" Bosco asked.

"Well, I got to tell you, the van isn't downstairs."

"You didn't do any damage to her?" Bosco asked, immediately
sounding affectionate about a machine he scarcely ever washed.

"She's sitting down in Venice with someone keeping an eye
out."

"Venice? For chrissakes, it's lucky if it's still got an engine."

"Anything happens to it, I'll make it good."

"How can you make good a treasure like that van?" Bosco
asked. "And how come you didn't drive it back anyhow?"

"All of that would take too long for me to explain," Whistler
said. "If you'll just give me my keys, I'll be on my way."

"Now just a second . . ." Bosco started to say, but Whistler
plucked his car keys out of Bosco's fingers and was out the door.

Whistler took the Hollywood Freeway to the Santa Ana
Freeway. It would be Interstate 5 all the way.

It's about sixty-eight miles to Carlsbad from Redondo Beach,
give or take a few. An easy hour and a half down, hour and a half
back. Nell wouldn't be on her own too long.

He settled behind the wheel and rode in the wake of a semi
with aluminum sides that shattered the air along the roadside as

the Chevy drifted in an eye of calm. If the semi didn't slam on its brakes when Whistler's attention was elsewhere, and some highway patrolman didn't flag him down, he'd be in the bar at La Costa when the action was hottest.

He thought about what was bothering him. And it wasn't that some gazoony had snapped his picture in the buff or that somebody had taken a couple of shots at Nell. Those were big things and they didn't bother him so much as little things.

What bothered him was how come on the first night he ever met Nell she didn't lock her bedroom door? Not that a woman hired a bodyguard expecting he was going to come in and try to molest her, but wasn't it a fair rule of thumb that a nervous woman locked her door? Especially since the second night, *after* she knew he'd take no when she gave no and there was a hell of a lot more reason to leave it unlocked so he'd have access to the room, she *did* lock her door.

And how come the neighbor's little dog barked at the prowler, but the two bull terriers didn't bother? They were drugged, but that didn't explain why they hadn't barked before they ate the meat. And how come they wouldn't take any food from him in the morning when they at least knew him? Had they taken meat from the hand of a perfect stranger or meat that had been tossed over the fence?

Nell had said that she had Twelvetrees by the balls. Was the little package she'd given him at the party, just about the size of an audiotape, the pliers she was using and was she putting on the squeeze?

And how come he had this feeling that Nell was working him like a fish, pulling him in, letting him run, then pulling him in a little again.

Playing kissy face with him the way she was doing was a game for someone considerably younger. At her age either you did it or you didn't do it. You didn't keep coming on and backing away like Jimmy Durante putting on his coat then taking it off.

It had become goddamn lonely down in the beach house all by himself. Twelvetrees suddenly realized that he was always surrounded by people. Even when he was sleeping he was aware that somebody was prowling the grounds making sure he didn't get kidnapped or blown away by some fan who loved and admired him so much he wanted to send his favorite television personality to join the angels.

Even watching himself on the tube was no comfort. In fact, it just aroused him really strong watching that little pussy squirming around in the guest's chair.

It had taken him an hour of calling around, without giving his name, to run Rialto down in the card room over in Gardena.

"Where do you hide yourself?" he complained, when Rialto came on the phone.

"Who wants to know?"

"This is Twelvetrees."

"So go find a dog to piss on you."

"Twelvetrees. Roger Twelvetrees, goddamn it."

"Jesus Christ, Mr. Twelvetrees, how the hell am I supposed to recognize your voice? I don't hear from you much anymore."

"Don't you ever watch the show?"

"Well, of couse I do. Religiously. But your voice sounds different over the phone."

"I got an urgency."

"An urgency?"

"A need for companionship."

"I gotcha."

"Something young."

"How young? Eleven, twelve?"

"Nothing that goddamn young. I've got to be careful."

"Fifteen, sixteen?"

"I didn't say ancient."

"So, fourteen."

"But looks younger."

"I hope you ain't wearing your glasses."

"What's that."

"A little hooker humor. You don't want a girl that allows a person to bounce her? I don't mean on your knee, I mean like against the wall?"

"Nothing like that."

"I can guarantee it?"

"Of course you can guarantee it."

"How soon you want delivery?"

"The soonest."

"Where?"

"You remember the beach house down to Malibu?"

"You want it quick, but you also want it far."

"You're not the only pimp in town, Rialto."

"I'm not a pimp, Mr. Twelvetrees. I'd appreciate it, you don't call me names."

"Well, sorry. I didn't know you were so sensitive."

"I'm not that sensitive but, you know?"

TWENTY-FIVE

THE GIMMICK HAD originated back in New York City at a club something-or-other. The idea was to make it very hard for customers to get inside the disco, because, as Canaan once remarked, the way human nature operates, the harder you make it to get in, the more people want to get in. People were slipping folded fifties to airheads with sneakers on their feet just to get past the door. Losers, east and west, were making small fortunes being doormen.

In La-La Land the premier hole in the wall was Nifty Shiftie's, at the top end of Hollywood, just out of the flesh market.

Spinneran and Jenny were smashed into the crowd out on the street, held back from the entrance by ropes illegally blocking the sidewalk and the curb.

Jenny was having a ball. Her eyes were hot, small-town girl getting it good, liking the rubbing, pushing, and small grab-assing.

Spinneran *wasn't* liking it, standing inside his sphere of quiet, his transparent, chromium-steel bubble. People sensed it, knew contact could draw electric fire. They instinctively tried not to touch the young man with the pale face and brassy, slicked-back hair. Sometimes, when collisions were unavoidable, a person, man or woman, would look at him as though startled, or afraid. Out on the fringe, a dyke in leather jeans and jacket, name picked out in small reflectors over the pocket, Dandy Jacque, was mouthing off, making threats.

"Who the fuck wants to fight? Any of you assholes think you got balls enough to take me on? I mean, shit, take a look, I got tits. I'm nothin' but a girl. How tough can I be? You want to find out how tough?"

The crowd on the edge closest to her pushed back away. What could you do with somebody like that? Stay away. Stay loose. Laugh. Whisper among yourselves. "Asshole!" Don't make eye contact. "For Christ's sake, don't look at her. At *it*. Don't encourage her. Encourage *it*." Curly lips. "Dandy Jacque. Jacqueline?"

"I heard you, asshole. Jacquenette. You don't know nothin'."

Spinneran looked at her without expression, without even seeing her, as if there was a hole in space where the little bulldyke strutted. Not trying to catch her eyes. Not trying not to.

"What the fuck you lookin' at you? Yeah, you, with the custard face."

Spinneran allowed his eyes to focus.

"Look away," Jenny whispered, putting her head in close, clutching Spinneran's arm.

The crowd thinned around them, left Jenny and Spinneran isolated and alone, nothing but empty street between them and the belligerent lesbian.

"Oh, goddamn, here's a gazoony that wants to fight." Dandy Jacque made like a prizefighter, dancing around on the toes of her cycle boots, hands made up into fists held high and moving around themselves as she bobbed and weaved, coming in, going on, grinning derisively. "Come on you faggot sonofabitch, stick up your hands."

Spinneran just stood there with Jenny dragging on his arm.

"Here you go, you two," the doorman, purple hair and rhinestones in his nose, yelled out, wanting to get Spinneran off the street, away from the front of the place before a fight broke out and brought trouble down. "Pass right on through. Always room for two skinnies like you." Jenny dragged on Spinneran's arm, but not too hard, her eyes brightening with expectation, smelling trouble, smelling violence.

He just stood there in a trance, staring at the little leathered lesbian as if she were a creature from outer space.

Dandy Jacque moved in closer. Lashed out a hand. Spinneran didn't move, let the blow catch him high on the cheekbone.

"I'm going to hurt you," Spinneran said softly.

"Oh, sheeeeit!" Dandy Jacque said, and flicked out a hand again, slapping Spinneran on the cheek, bringing color.

Not many saw it. Spinneran kicked out twice, once to each kneecap. When the first joint shattered, Dandy Jacque let out a grunt. When the second one got busted she let out a scream and fell. She lay there in the gutter flopping around like a fish dragged up on shore, her eyes popping out in pain and staring at Spinneran as though wondering why he would have done such a terrible thing.

Some of the spectators even complained. "No reason to do that."

"Christ, the little clown was only drunk or high."

"What happened? That guy get kicked in the balls?"

"Hasn't got any balls."

"What the hell you talking about? Did you say somebody got their balls cut off?"

"Didn't have no balls. She's a goddamn biker dyker."

"You don't have to get fucking nasty. What did the poor creep do to you?"

"Well, that's what she is, goddamn it."

"Is what?"

"A lesbian with two busted legs."

"Who let them two go in? Will you look at that?"

"That's the one what kicked that poor sonofabitch in the nuts."

"She ain't got no nuts."

"Never mind, Margie, let's not go through that again."

"I can't understand how somebody does violence they get to go inside Nifty Shiftie's."

"That's the way it goes. Who said things was fair."

"Fuck it."

"That's what I always say."

Inside the club, bodies were packed in tight, doing something like dancing, something like swapping sweat, something like grabbing free feels. A joker in front of Jenny and Spinneran put a hand in back of him, feeling for crotch. He looked over his shoulder, his eyes opening in something like surprise.

Jenny held onto Spinneran's arm, half repelled by such swift and vicious violence, half aroused by the kind of sex that it implied.

Spinneran was a pretty puzzle, all right, all right, Jenny thought, just the kind she liked to take apart.

Rialto drove over to the stockyard at Hollywood and Vine.

The street creatures were out in force, all but stripped naked, having the excuse, in case they needed one, of the hot Santa Ana winds that were starting to rub people raw, scraping the nerves, stealing sleep, giving people rashes on top of rashes.

Whores and twangie boys were strutting around in two sequins and a Dixie cup, showing the flesh, advertising the bulges and swellings, the slick shine along the bones, the tender bluing of the flesh at crotch and armpit. Hot merchandise for hot nights. Temperatures rising more ways than one.

Rialto drifted up and down the boulevard three times, casing the prostitutes, looking for something choice. Across the street from Gentry's someone caught his eye. He pulled over to the curb. Three ladies moved to the open window on the passenger side, draping arms and elbows on the hot metal, tits on display.

One was black, one was white, and one was somewhere in between.

They all had hair like theatrical constructions. The black girl wore a wig of silver metallic thread, the tan one a wig of copper that sprung out around her head like a scouring pad, and the white girl had long falls of black hair, pinned to her bleached blond hair, so dull they looked like they'd been dusted with charcoal.

"It be ol' One-Eyed Jack," the silver one said.

"You lookin' for cut-rate, Rialto?" copper-head asked.

"I'm lookin' for a special."

"Don' one of us look likely? This for you, lover? Take all three of us. A package. We melt you down to a size thirty-six."

"I'm not shopping for myself. None of you is a likely."

"You want a child," the silver one said with a knowing look.

"I want a child that ain't a child."

"Shirley," the copper-head suggested.

"Shirley went and got tits."

"How come?"

"Said she was tired of cotton panties and training bras."

"What did she get?"

"Forty dees."

"That's disgusting," said the one with silver hair. She had bra cups at least that size holding up her treasures. "I can't stan' what ain' natural."

"Then you should stop shavin' your pussy hair into a heart."

"Shit, it grow that way," she said, laughing and showing teeth as white as a shark bone dangling on a black chest.

"There's a likely over there," Rialto said. "Is it a girl?"

They turned to look.

"Oh, yeah, the schoolgirl. Don't you know her?" copper-head asked.

"You sure she's a girl and not some shit-chute poke acting fly?"

"Fachrissakes, man, I know somebody what ate that chile jus' las' night, don't you know," the black girl said.

"You lyin', sweet meat."

"I never lie to a honky prince."

"So ask her to step into my office."

The black whore raised her hand above her head. "We got a man wants a squab over here," she singsonged.

"Rooster or hen?" somebody called back in a strained falsetto.

The girl who looked to be about thirteen, dressed in a white middy blouse and pleated skirt, caught the sign.

She came chicken-trotting over. The blouse was opened half-way to her patent leather belt, even though there was nothing much to show. The pleated skirt, like the skirts girls in the Catholic schools wore, was a good deal more than halfway up her white thighs. She wore white socks and Mary Jane shoes.

When she got closer she didn't look quite so young, her war record showing on her face.

The three whores faded, strutting off to join the parade, a customer with special tastes handed off, letting the schoolgirl doxie cut her deal.

"Hello, Daddy. You want to give me some candy?"

"What would you do with it, if I did?"

"What kind of candy?"

"Say a lollipop."

"Well, you suck a lollipop, don't you?"

"How about a peppermint stick?"

"You lick a peppermint stick."

"How about a Life Saver?"

"I always stick my tongue into the little hole."

"You got a name?"

"Felitia."

"So how you doing, Felitia?"

"I'm doing it any way you want it, mister . . ."

"Rialto. Mike Rialto."

"Oh, I heard about you. What's your take?" she said, her voice losing it's little girl whine, taking on the snap of a sidewalk novelty salesman.

"Jesus, you get right down to it, don't you?"

"No reason to waste the act on you, is there? Let's talk business."

"Business good?"

"I won't lie to you. Look around. Times is hard. Every fucking twirler and cheerleader in the country rushed out here this year *willing* to be a movie star. Well, I mean, when they find out you can be a hooker instead, who wants to be a movie star?"

"I got a customer."

"From out of town?"

"Local. Malibu."

"That's a long trip."

"I give you limousine service."

"Door to door?"

"Well, I don't know I can wait around. I'm too old to sleep in my car."

"This an all-nighter?"

"I don't know. It could be."

"Well, for chrissake, you can't expect me to go all the fucking way to Malibu and take the chance this sucker goes pop, pop, pop, good night Miss Bliss."

"Tell you what, I'll hang around, you go in, talk to the customer, you come out and give me the wave. If it's a quick trick, I wait to drive you back. If it's an all-nighter, I cop a sneak, you get home in the morning any way you can."

She thought about it, rolling her eyes up toward the sky, pursing her pouty cherry lips, making a number out of thinking. "So maybe he wants an all-nighter I get him for the taxi, plus I get a little sun and pick up some buster to give me a ride back to town in the morning," she mumbled, working out the deal in the little double entry book in her mind.

"I like the way your head works," Rialto said.

"Okay. You know what he wants?"

Rialto shrugged.

"Nothing weird?"

"I don't think he'll want to lick whipped cream off your toes."

"Fuck, that would be my pleasure. Nothing rough?"

"A little spanking, maybe. You know the routine."

She knew the routine. The john says, "How come you're home from school so early?" "I've been bad," says the little girl. "If you've been bad, that means Daddy will have to spank you, isn't that right?" "Oh, yes, Daddy." "Well, you just come over here then, lift up your little skirt, take down your little panties—you're wearing cotton panties aren't you?—and lay across my knees. Because, Daddy's sorry, but he's going to have to spank your little bum until it's rosy red." "Oh, Daddy, I'm so glad I was a bad girl." Or variations thereof.

"That's all?"

"I guarantee."

"The last time I was guaranteed, I went to the hospital."

She glanced up and down the boulevard looking for vice cops, not because what she was about to do would lead to her arrest for soliciting, but because they could pick her up for causing a disturbance. Just two weeks ago a whore had dropped her pants and mooned a customer—he wanted to know if she had pimples on her ass—and caused a three-car collision. Cops have a sense of humor just like everybody else, but they draw the line at gags that cause the destruction of private property and the endangerment of civilian lives.

Seeing that everything seemed safe for the moment, she opened up her blouse the rest of the way and, pulling the tails out of her skirt, showed Rialto her chest with half a dozen scars crisscrossing her slightly mounded tits.

"He was a cutter," she said, shivering at the memory. "I had to kick him in the nuts to get out from under him."

"Sonofabitch. You lose your wages?"

"I'm not that dumb. It's strictly pay in advance."

"My client's a proud man. I don't think he'd like that."

"You mean he wants to kid himself he ain't paying for it?"

"Hey, babe," Rialto said with the soft assurance of a hundred-dollar-an-hour shrink, "ain't that what they're buying? Dreams and memories? Dreams of things that'll never be, and memories of things that never was?"

TWENTY-SIX

JUST BEFORE OCEANSIDE, Whistler lost the semi. It made him almost sad. An empty road is a lonely road.

He left the San Diego Freeway at La Costa Avenue and drove along Batiquitos Lagoon toward the course and clubhouse.

By this time it's pretty much forgotten, but twenty years ago there was a considerable scandal associated with the development of the resort complex, Mafia interests having tapped the huge pension fund of the Teamster's union for massive loans at very favorable interest rates.

When the threats of arrest and trial finally died down, depositions gathered in convenient bound volumes, and the last subpoena buried in the dead-case file, the managers of the golf course started on a ten-million-dollar restoration project, the greens and fairways having been laid down on ground so full of alkali salts that not an acre of it had ever been farmed because nothing would grow on the barren land.

But that was all behind them now. Condominiums and a grand hotel had sprung up to accommodate weekend players and big spenders alike. Mafia chieftains and lieutenants were still members, still shot a round now and then, or played endless hands of cards in the rooms set aside for the purpose. Mostly aging men with the oddly reptilian eyes of watchful doubters.

Neatly uniformed parking attendants waited at the door to the clubhouse. They held the door for Whistler and took the car away.

The clubhouse was decorated like the funny-money palaces of
Las Vegas and Atlantic City. An excess of glitz guaranteed to put
you in a mood to spend because nothing had much value, all was
merely the glitter of tin and the swank of crepe paper.

A maître d' approached, menu and reservation list in hand, as
though there were still reservations required at midnight.

"Party of one, or will you be having guests?"

"I just thought I'd have a drink at the bar before going to bed."

That seemed to be okay with the maître d', so Whistler walked
on through the broad entrance into the chemical chill of the bar
and restaurant.

He heard her voice before he saw her. They say that smells
bring back memories better and clearer than anything else. With
him it was sounds, particularly the sound of laughter. Everybody
laughed in a certain rhythm, everybody stopped laughing in a
recognizable way. This laughter he remembered was like a bell,
honest and clear, but with a strange sobbing note underneath.

She was standing at the bar between two middle-aged men on
stools and three more standing around like big fat birds, pushing
their beaks toward her, jostling for position. Whistler didn't
know how the hookers worked the golf and tennis tours, the
grand prix racing, and the soccer matches. Every sport drew a
different kind of man. He didn't know if they tricked during the
evening and then took an all-nighter. He didn't know if the smart
ones just made a connection and worked it through the entire
long weekend.

He stood there watching and remembering, and shivering a
little.

The first time he'd met Connie Ranger had been in the bar
across the street from the drugstore on the corner of Sunset and
Crescent Heights. He didn't want to even think of the name of the
place because it wasn't there anymore, and when he used to hang
out there under a ceiling made of crisscrossed clothesline hung
with Christmas tinsel he'd been just about ready to eat the world.

But it was easy to remember the soft purple gloom inside and
the staircase in the back that led upstairs to a pair of johns no
bigger than two broom closets.

If you had to use the facility, you sometimes had to wait
outside on the landing at the top of the stairs, where there was
also another exit.

One night he was standing there, holding his water and talking to this guy Vinko, a veterinarian over in Hollywood Park where Whistler often went to watch the ponies run, when this little blonde, this doll with china blue eyes and a mouth like a cherry, this doll like a Barbie, only smart, comes bouncing up the stairs on the way to have a tinkle. He asked himself a hundred times afterward where he ever got the nerve to do it. Those days he took chances he wouldn't take today. He reached out and took her by the wrist and pulled her over—she didn't offer much resistance—and gave her a kiss on the mouth. No tongues, just a kiss on those cherry lips as though they'd known each other all their lives. The way her mouth felt on his mouth was like he'd kissed her when they'd been five and ten and then fifteen. And now they were kissing again like grown-ups, but it was all so familiar.

You would have thought that would have been the start of something big right then and there. But that's not the way it happened.

That night she'd just looked at him like he was a puzzle and went in to do whatever, and when she came out he was still standing there reaching for her, and she'd said, "No seconds," and went on down the stairs. So after Vinko came out of the john and he got to take his leak, he didn't go downstairs again. He went out the upstairs exit to the parking lot and walked home, not wanting to take any chances. Breaking spells and things like that.

He might never have seen her again, Whistler thought, sad all over again for the youngster he was back then who'd had no way of knowing that he was going to lose that little blond cheerleader, once to drink and once to the life. He saw her after that, here and there, looking at him in the mirror over the fountain at the drugstore across Sunset, at the bus stop, or the all-night market over on Sweetzer. Here and there. Sometimes he'd smile at her, but he never went up to her. Never talked to her.

Then one night a friend of his called him at the little apartment he had over a garage and said that he was in the bar talking to a friend of Whistler's, and she wanted to come over. When his friend arrived fifteen minutes later, he had her in tow. Her name was Connie Ranger and she wanted to be a moving picture star.

His friend left, and they sat there for a while. Then, all of a sudden, she'd said, "Who am I kiddin'?" got up, went into the bathroom, and came out five minutes later without a stitch.

Her laughter lifted Whistler's heart again. He saw her straighten up, then turn around as though his memories had stirred her memories. She saw him. The wonderful part was she recognized him as easily as he'd recognized her.

She said something to the men she was working. They all looked around as she walked away, first at her ass, then at Whistler, like a bunch of dogs ready to pounce on the stranger.

She smiled, stared into his face, and blinked. It seemed to take a minute for her eyelids to go up and down, like pulling down the covers on a bed.

"Ah, Jesus, babe, you picked up a couple of years," Mary Beth said. There was a nice edge to the way she talked, like she was just barely holding back her laughter.

"What about the Jones?" Whistler asked.

"It's my real name. Ain't that a kick?" She patted Whistler on the cheek with her eyes. "You look bushed. What's the occasion?"

"Occasion for what?"

"You didn't come up here to play golf, did you?"

"I came up to talk to you."

A little frown popped up between her eyebrows.

"Oh. You want to sit down and have a drink?"

"I'm off the sauce, Connie."

"How long?"

"Fifteen years come September."

"Just about the time . . ." Mary Beth didn't finish the thought. Whistler did. "Just about the time you walked out on me."

"Did I walk out on you?"

"Was I so bad?"

"No, you were goddamn good. That's what was breaking my heart."

"I went looking for you."

"And I wasn't there," she said softly. "That's because Connie Ranger wasn't there anymore."

Whistler looked for something more to say. Mary Beth put two fingers on his lips, closing the book. It was just as well because Whistler knew he didn't have anything more to say about the past.

They found a table. The men at the bar turned away as though she'd made a choice. She'd have a hard time working them up again if they were still there when Whistler left. They'd think she'd tried to score and couldn't and was turning to them for second best. It was pitiful and ridiculous how men bought it and tried to convince themselves they'd won it, Whistler thought. Himself included.

"Did you recommend me to Nell Twelvetrees?" Whistler asked.

"Is that why you drove way the hell down here? To ask me that? You could have called me and saved yourself the trouble. Or did Nell tell you that Mary Beth Jones used to be Connie Ranger?"

"I'd like to say she did."

"Well, you should have anyway, just to make me feel good. I'd know it was just a great big lie. The fact is Nell doesn't know I ever called myself Connie Ranger."

"So did you?"

"I don't know that I exactly recommend you. I mean, she said she was feeling doubtful about Twelvetrees. He's got a temper and a reputation."

"So I've been told."

"I might have told Nell to look up a bodyguard if she was that worried. I might even have mentioned your name."

"But you're not sure?"

"I don't know if I should say I'm sure I told her or I'm sure I didn't."

"You mean you think the wrong answer could do your friend some harm."

"Will it?"

"I don't know."

She looked at him very carefully, cool, trying to be detached. "You're not going to say 'for old time's sake'?"

"I'm not going to pressure you. I'm not even going to ask a favor."

"Can you tell me what it is about Nell that you want me to verify or deny?"

"Was Nell a hooker?"

"Putting it bluntly?"

"I'm not passing judgment. I'm just asking."

"She came out here alone when she was fourteen," she said, as though that told the story. How many ways were there for a kid to survive on her own? What goods did she have to sell?

"Later on her mother came out and lived with her?"

"Her mother worked the street, too. When she was sober enough. That's what Nell told me. I didn't know either of them back then. I wasn't in the life yet."

"I know. What happened after her father came out to Venice and she went out on her own again?"

"She worked out of her apartment. She'd learned a lot by then. Educated herself. Developed a lot of style. Her clientele were strictly gentleman callers. She wouldn't even deliver. Didn't have to. Around town she was just a popular professional woman. In public relations."

"She worked without a pimp?"

"I couldn't swear."

"Did she have a boyfriend?"

"I think there was somebody. A cop. Plenty of hookers got a cop boyfriend. They maybe bust her and they get friendly. After all, that's what the life is, cops and criminals. Everybody else hasn't got a clue."

"I know."

"I'm not so sure you do. You're not really in the life, Whistler, so I don't think you really know. You're just a watcher."

"When did she leave the life?"

"When she met Twelvetrees."

"Was it love?"

"Call it an investment. Like the house she lets me live in."

"Oh, like that," he said, not giving away his surprise.

"I don't know what you mean, 'like that.' You men are funny creatures. You think it makes perfect sense that you want a woman because of her face and figure. But it makes no sense at all that we might want a man for his sense of humor . . ."

"His fame . . ."

". . . his conversation . . ."

"His power . . ."

". . . and his stock portfolio." She grinned. "Hey, babe, ain't you heard, everybody's looking for the golden handshake. You've got your way, I've got my way . . ."

"And Nell's got her way."

She reached over and placed her hand over his. "Which is not to say there isn't time for fairy tales and old photograph albums."

"I've got to get back."

"You can stay an hour. I've got a room. You can hear the ocean."

He stayed two.

TWENTY-SEVEN

SPINNERAN'S HAIR WAS shagged across his forehead. Jenny reached out and brushed it back with her fingertips. They were sitting at the smallest table in the darkest corner of the Club Armentières. It was a table in the corner closest to the door, the one where timid straights often perched to watch the freaks at play.

Potsie, a waitress with definitely mannish ways, stood there with dollar bills folded over every finger, ready to pop off change. Her attention was on Spinneran as he ordered, but her eyes were on Jenny.

When she went away to get the drinks, Jenny leaned forward. "You see the way she was lookin' at me?"

"I think she fancies you," Spinneran said.

"Oh, my God," Jenny said, pleasurably titillated. "I hope I don' have to go use the johnny."

"She'd be right in behind you ready to pat you on the ass," Spinneran said.

Jenny peered into his face. "You're different all of a sudden."

"Different?"

"Relaxed. I don' know how to describe it. Like you feel comfortable here."

"Why shouldn't I be comfortable here?"

"Well, I mean, these people are very strange."

"Not our sort."

"Don' get mad at me," Jenny said, backing off, wondering why he was offended.

The drinks came. Potsie stared at Jenny. Jenny fussed at the opening of her blouse. Potsie didn't bother looking, but just kept staring into her eyes, playing the hard stud above copping peeks.

"We can take it from here, thanks," Spinneran said.

When Potsie went away again, Jenny leaned in close to Spinneran, looking up into his face. "I never saw anybody move so fast the way you did."

"I can move very fast when I want to."

She took one of his hands and examined it like it was a piece of glass. "I never saw such small beautiful hands on a man. But cruel. Very cruel. You hurt that woman very bad, didn' you?"

"I broke her kneecaps."

"Oh, God."

"You enjoyed it."

"Did I?" Jenny said, as though it came as a genuine surprise to be told that.

"Yes, you enjoyed it."

"Why haven' you tried it?"

"Tried what?"

"You know."

"No, I don't."

"Why haven' you tried to feel me up?"

"Do they still talk like that down in Atlanta?"

"You people like to play like you're very hard out here, don' you? All right then, how come you haven' tried to fuck me?"

Color came flooding up out of Spinneran's collar, staining his cheeks. It startled Jenny.

"Hello, Detective Cortez," Esme called across the room, giving everybody fair warning.

Spinneran turned to look.

Cortez walked into the club with a package about the size of a cigar box under his arm, went over to the zinc-topped bar, and ordered a beer. Spinneran watched him.

"What is it?" Jenny asked.

"Nothing."

"You know that man?"

"No, I don't know him. Excuse me. I have to use the johnny." The way he said the word it was like a private joke between them.

"You be careful somebody don' pat you on the ass," Jenny said.

Spinneran walked across the room and down the dark corridor to the rest rooms.

Cortez followed him about a minute later.

Spinneran was standing beneath the window with his arms folded, being careful not to lean against the stained, sweating tile. Cortez went over to the urinal, placed the box on the porcelain, unzipped, and started to take a leak.

"One more play and you're off the hook," Cortez said.

"Off your hook?" Spinneran asked.

"You keep on going around knifing people like you do, I can't keep the heat off you. You slipped that last one past me. I'm not your shield."

"I don't expect you to keep it off me. I just don't expect you to put it on me."

Cortez jerked around to look at Spinneran and splashed his shoe. "Sonofabitch. What are you talking about?" He pulled a paper towel out of the dispenser and wiped the toe of his slip-on.

"Have you got somebody watching me?"

"Like who?"

"A fat man with a funny way of cocking his head, drives an old white Cadillac."

"The only fat man I can think of drives an old Cadillac is Mike Rialto."

"Not a friend of yours?"

"I know him. He's not a cop, that's what you mean."

"I meant a friend of yours, cop or no cop."

"He on you now?"

"Well, he's not outside."

"I'll see what I can do about Mike Rialto."

"I hope you do better about Rialto than you do about taking a pee."

Cortez showed all his teeth. "We're not friends, wise guy. Don't crack funny with me. You do this for me, I let you get the fuck out of town. Stay out of town forever." He reached for the box and handed it to Spinneran who backed off a pace.

Cortez laughed. "For Christ's sake, it won't hurt you."

"It's not my specialty. I don't know why I have to fool with it. Dead is dead."

"This is for special effects. You understand what I mean, special effects? This is an important piece of the story line. Take it."

Spinneran took the box in both hands.

"Tuck it under your arm like it was a book," Cortez said. "You could drop it and nothing would happen. Trust me. After you do them, you put the box down beside him and pull the string off to arm it. Then you got twenty minutes. All the time in the world. You want to leave first? I wonder are them freaks out there wondering who's copping who? It's a filthy-minded town, ain't it?"

Spinneran started to leave. Cortez touched his elbow.

"That the daughter out there?"

"Yes."

"I got to give it to you, sonny. You're very cool."

When Spinneran returned to the table Jenny said, "You were a long time."

Cortez appeared from the corridor and looked at Spinneran. Jenny saw the look.

"You sure you don' know that cop?" she asked.

"He's not a friend."

"But you know him. You got the package he was carrying."

"Finish your drink," Spinneran said. "I'll take you home."

"I don' want to go home."

"How about going down to your father's beach house? You said you had a key."

Her eyes changed. "Well, all right," she said.

TWENTY-EIGHT

THE MALIBU COLONY is an exclusive seaside pocket of an exclusive seaside community on the western rim of La-La Land. It's a stretch of sand where motion picture and television stars live in isolated grandeur, sharing lobster and champagne suppers and the dread suspicion that the mobs are gathering outside the gates. They make their own parades and carnivals, dressing up in costume and marching to the music of improvised bands because there are no parades or carnivals they can go to without getting surrounded.

New laws of access had, for a while, forced public thorough-fares between some of the houses outside the colony along Old Malibu Road. The public took that way to intrude on the Colony in spite of the chain-link fences that protected its flanks. They just waded around them. Crapped on the sand in front of actors making three million a flick, looked in the windows at actresses who charged a million dollars a peek on the big screen, fucked on the decks facing the sea even when the owners were at home.

So they built the fences farther out into the sea.

Rialto drove up to the gatehouse with his little cargo of kinky pleasure, a familiar run for a man who'd been in the flesh trade for twenty-five years.

The guard stepped out of the gatehouse, a half-smile on his face. He measured his smiles to suit the customer as carefully as a TV minister. Smiles were not to be wasted.

"Ho, Hankus," Rialto said.

The smile didn't go away, but it didn't grow any broader. Rialto was worth a nickel grin, corners lifted, but no teeth showing.

"Ho, your fucking self, Rialto. I don't see you around much anymore. Business slow?"

"Well, it's picking up."

Hankus looked across Rialto's stomach at Felitia. "This for Twelvetrees?"

"He leave my name at the gate? So don't ask. And forget you saw my niece."

"Is she a good girl?"

"What's the matter? You think I can't talk?" Felitia said. "I ain't a pair of shoes or a jug of guinea red."

"Have you been a good girl?" Hankus asked her.

"Gooder than you're ever going to get."

"She's got a mouth on her."

Rialto handed him a folded fiver. "Quit while you're ahead."

Rialto drove down along the beachfront road with all the expensive houses lined up in a row. He stopped at a white house with pillars on either side of a black door.

"This is very nice," Felitia said.

"So go on and ring the bell. He'll let you in."

"He got a name?"

"Call him Roggie. He likes that."

She started to get out, then looked back. "You're going to wait until I find out if this is a dawner?"

"I told you."

"Well, all right." She slid out of the car, her little skirt riding up and flashing the white cotton panties on her skinny ass. She flicked him a sidelong glance and a smile. She looked like a depraved ten-year-old. Just what Twelvetrees ordered.

TWENTY-NINE

SPINNERAN AND JENNY drove in silence for a long while. The BMW seemed to drift around the long sweeping curves down to the foot of Sunset Boulevard and north along the Pacific Coast Highway toward Malibu. Glimpses of the sea popped up like frames of a movie set between the houses that blocked the common people from the shore. On the other side of the road, houses built on water-soaked shale waited to give way in the next torrential rain or burn to cinders in the next brushfire sweeping through the chapparal and mesquite.

Spinneran had witnessed the Malibu hills in flame, the sap of the mesquite shooting fire like miniature flamethrowers, dragon spit arching across the night.

"My father came into the bathroom while I was takin' a bath an' stood there lookin' at me," Jenny said.

"That's no news," Spinneran said. "Some of these old men do worse than peek at a grown daughter. Some of them . . ." He didn't say any more.

"He fixed up a bedroom an' a bathroom for my birthday. That's what he said," Jenny went on. "It's right next door to his rooms. It made me feel very creepy, I can tell you. It looks like a real whorehouse bedroom with a bed shaped like a seashell with satin sheets."

Spinneran smiled dryly. "I don't think you've been in many whorehouses if you think that's what they look like."

"What do they look like?"

"A bed with used sheets and maybe a stuffed doll sitting on the pillows. A chair where the customer can hang his clothes. How would I know?"

"Well, the way you said it."

"I don't hang around whorehouses."

"You know anybody ever worked in a whorehouse?"

"Oh, yes."

"You know, I don' really like my daddy much. In fact, I think I hate him."

"You sure you've got the key?"

"Right here," Jenny said, patting her purse. "You're really gonna stay with me? I don' like bein' by myself in a lonely place like that," she said, trying to turn it around so that when it happened it would seem that he had hit on her.

"We'll see," Spinneran said.

"Well, you really are the funny one," Jenny said, wondering what kind of fellow it was acted so casual about what was practically a straight-out invitation to sleep with her. She put her hand on his knee.

"I can' tell a thing about what you're thinkin'. I don' know if you even like me."

"I like you, Jenny. I like you very much."

"Why's it takin' so long for you to show it?"

He looked at her. There was a softness in his eyes for a moment. "I wish I could tell you. I really do wish I could tell you."

She leaned against him. "These bucket seats are the pits," she said.

Twelvetrees was half drunk. He'd had one for his nerves and another for the wait, and the first thing he knew he was half drunk and on the phone calling up Rialto. If Spinneran had done the job and came to get his money tonight, he'd probably be pissed off when he saw the whore. So the hell with him. Dirty little killer.

While he waited some more, he had another couple. Thoughts came floating up out of a dark pool. He started thinking about what was happening. Spinneran had set it up so he'd be alone without his Polacks. So maybe Spinneran wouldn't even do the job, but just come back and rob him. The fifty thousand he'd withdrawn from half a dozen banks that day was sitting there on the sideboard in a plain paper sack.

The alcohol fought with his fear. He went into the bedroom and opened the closet. He rummaged around on the top shelf and found the gun he'd stashed there in case he was ever alone some night and some crazies came stalking movie stars, snorkling through the waves, swimming far out around the chain-link fences that thrust out into the sea, and crawling up onto the beach like a bunch of goddamn commandos. He put the gun under the pillow of the bed. Just in case.

He went back into the living room just as the bell rang. He put on the front lights and turned on the surveillance camera. The little screen beside the door glowed. A girl in a middy blouse and a short skirt was standing at the door. For a minute he thought it was some kid from down the beach locked out of the house by mistake. Then he remembered and opened the door.

Felitia said, "What can I do for you, Daddy?"

"Go down the hall into the bedroom and we'll talk about it."

In the bedroom she took a look at him and thought, this gazoony looks familiar. Then she thought, this asshole is very drunk, which could be a good thing or could be a bad thing.

"You want me to take off my skirt or you want me to play hard to get?"

"What is this? You got a menu like a Chinese restaurant? I get to choose one from column A and one from column B?"

"Whatever you want. With any three items you get egg roll."

"Fachrissakes, even the hookers are comedians. Everybody's a comedian. That's the trouble with the world. You wearing cotton panties?"

"Is the pope a Polack?"

"Enough with the goddamn jokes. Take off your skirt. Let me see are you wearing cotton panties. Stop being a comic."

"I got you. If everybody's comic, who's going to be left to laugh?" When Twelvetrees frowned, she said, "You want to play games?"

"Like what?" His voice sounded clogged.

"You want to spank me?"

"Have you been a bad girl? Have you been laying on your bedspread with your shoes on?"

*   *   *

It figured, Rialto thought. The hooker goes into the house, finds out the john is Roger Twelvetrees. Mr. Midnight fucking America, and she forgets all about him waiting outside in the car in the middle of the night.

He started the engine and made a U turn. He left the motor idling, thinking that maybe the throb of the engine in the silent street would wake her up to her obligations.

Celebrities. Everybody was a sucker for celebrities. There was this American appetite for famous. How could you figure it? Here was a little whore probably done a hundred-fifty celebrities—football players and other jocks, motion picture and television stars, politicians and police officers of considerable rank—and all it takes is for her to meet another famous asshole and she's thinking what a lucky whore she is getting to meet all the big-timers, and forgetting all about the man who got her the job.

The hell with her.

He pulled out, the tires grabbing and squealing like a stepped-on cat. He drove down to the bend and turned right for the exit gate. Another car was pulling up at the gatehouse. He pulled over into a lay-by and doused his lights. He got a pair of night glasses, which had cost him important money, out of the glove compartment. He focused them on the BMW and its passengers.

Fachrissakes, Rialto thought, it's that little prick, Spinneran. What the hell was he doing scooting around the countryside at such an hour, and so soon after taking shots at Nell Twelvetrees? And, unless he was very much mistaken, the person in the passenger seat of the BMW was Jenny Twelvetrees. How could you figure a thing like that? It was an act of destiny that he should have delivered a hooker for her old man's pleasure at the same time the daughter was bringing home a professional shooter for a little whatever.

Rialto turned his head and bent down as though he was getting something out of his glove compartment as Spinneran and Jenny went by.

Rialto pulled ahead and eased up to to the gatehouse.

"Never a dull moment, huh?" Hankus said.

"How's that?"

"You see that car just went by? That's Twelvetrees's daughter with some blond guy. And you just delivered that little twist to the old man. Surprise, surprise."

"Why didn't you tell the daughter her old man was having a party?"

"That would be exceeding my authority, wouldn't it?" Hankus said.

"Twelvetrees ain't going to be happy with you, Hankus."

"What'd I do? What'd I do? Nobody give me the word. Besides, all that Twelvetrees give me for Christmas was twenty bucks and a bottle of cheap bourbon."

Spinneran felt the tension rising. It hadn't been simple, but it was all worked out now. Nothing was simple. He wanted things to be simple, but nothing was ever simple.

"Here," Jenny said. "Right here."

He pulled over and parked the car. They got out.

"I think I see lights from the house shining out on the sand." he said.

"How can you tell with the moon?" Jenny asked.

"Well, it looks like it to me."

"Probably a night-light."

"Well, you go on in and see. If there's anybody in the house, there's no reason for them to see me is there?"

"Well, why not? We can say you drove me down here because I wanted to stay the night."

"With me?"

She smiled. "All right. I'll go have a look. If anybody's there I'll say I asked you to come down with me to look at the moon on the water and that you're gonna take me back into town."

"That's a good idea," Spinneran said. "Leave the door open. If you're not out in five minutes I'll know it's okay for me to come in."

Her eyes looked like the eyes of a cat, sleepy and calculating. Her tongue darted out and touched her upper lip.

"Okay," she said.

She went quietly to the door, used her key, and slipped inside, leaving the door open a crack.

Spinneran looked up and down the road. There was no sign of anybody. He took the cigar box out of the backseat and put it on the roof of the car. He opened the trunk and then the case where he kept the guns, and picked out a target pistol.

THIRTY

THE KEY HAD turned without a sound, not even a snick. A thief's entrance. She'd taught herself to be very good at letting herself in late at night without waking her mother and stepfather back in Atlanta.

She held the latch and closed the door with both hands. There was scarcely a rustle of air. From long experience, she stood unmoving, legs wide, back tensed, chin up, head moving slightly from side to side, checking the house out for signs of life. She slipped off her shoes.

Far off, down the corridor that led to the bedrooms, she heard a murmuring. It could have been the sea. If anyone was in the house, maybe she could get out without their knowing. Then she and Spinneran could spend the night somewhere else. She felt excited by the prospect. She had the expectation that she was going to learn something marvelous about him.

He was a puzzle and a wonder. Always under some secret restraint, under such tight control.

She sidestepped down the carpeted hallway.

"Now don't tell me you never spanked a girl," Felitia said, doing things with her eyes and mouth that were supposed to make her look like Madonna.

"Oh, I've slapped a few around," Twelvetrees said. "Take off your blouse."

She took off the blouse, turning sideways to make the most of her small, pointed breasts. He reached out and she moved two steps closer. He saw the scars. His face changed. His tongue flicked out.

Like a lizard she'd seen on television, she thought. Television.

"Jesus Christ, it's you," she said.

"Didn't Rialto tell you who you were coming to visit?"

"Oh, Jesus, you know how forgetful he is," Felitia said, backing off. Oh, yes, she knew this sonofabitch all right. He was very bad. Very violent. People had told her this man, this Mr. Midnight America, was the john who punched her mother until she was hurt so bad that she died not long after.

"What's the matter with you," Twelvetrees said, sitting down on the bed.

"I just can't believe it. Roger Twelvetrees."

"Where do you think you're going?"

"I just remembered, Mike's waiting to find out is this a trick or an all-nighter."

She turned toward the door.

Jenny heard the voices clearly, but not the words. She thought the one that rumbled was her father's voice. the other, thin and threatening to break, was a girl's.

She was almost at the bedroom door, drawn by a powerful curiosity.

"So I'll just go tell him he should wait for me, should I?" Felitia said.

Twelvetrees had his thing in his hand. His eyes were fixed on the scars that crisscrossed her boyish chest.

"You get your skinny ass over here. Rialto gets tired of waiting, so he gets tired of waiting."

He started up off the bed.

Felitia turned, grabbed the doorknob, and yanked the door open. She screamed and stepped back fast, nearly tripping over her skirt that was still down around her ankles.

Jenny was startled, but she didn't scream and she didn't back off. She stared at the girl wearing nothing but her white socks, Mary Jane shoes, and cotton panties. She saw her father crouching there with his thing in his hand. Felitia bent down and scooped up her skirt. She almost knocked Jenny over as she went through the door.

Jenny started to turn away in fear and disgust.

"Wait a minute, Jenny. Wait a minute," Twelvetrees said. He lunged forward and grabbed her by the wrist.

Felitia ran out of the house.

There was no Rialto waiting in his old Cadillac. There was a blond-haired man with a gun in his hand coming toward her.

"Felitia," Spinneran said. "What the hell are you doing here?"

She was terrified, confronted by a stranger with a gun who knew her. Then she saw who it was.

"My God. Alice?"

They stood there staring at one another. Spinneran tossed the target pistol through the window into the backseat.

"Get in the car," he said.

"I can't believe it. What in Christ's name are you doing dressed up like that?" Felitia asked.

He came around and grabbed her, opening the door with one hand and shoving her into the passenger's seat with the other Then he ran around to the driver's side. He stood there for a moment, looking at the house, uncertain about what to do.

There was the sound of a gunshot.

A dog barked.

He got behind the wheel and turned around in the middle of the road. The cigar box fell off the roof and went clattering and skittering to the side where it lay shattered among the weeds, sticks of dynamite, a battery, and clockwork.

The dog kept on barking.

The door of the beach house opened, but the BMW was already at the turn in the road that led toward the gate. Spinneran and Felitia didn't see Jenny standing there screaming, blood all over her torn dress.

THIRTY-ONE

SPINNERAN'S UNASSAILABLE COMPOSURE had deserted him. He drove past the gatehouse at speed.

Hankus wondered what the little whore was doing in the BMW. He could understand that Twelvetrees's daughter had walked in on her old man doing the dirty with the make-believe schoolgirl hooker, but what was the half-naked whore doing with the daughter's boyfriend, scrambling into her skirt with her tits hanging out?

Spinneran hit the brakes where the feeder road met the highway, spraying gravel as he made his turn onto the Pacific Coast Highway. He raced by the spot along the road where Rialto had parked among the trees and bushes, running a hunch that he'd be following that red BMW once more before the night was over.

Rialto jerked awake as the BMW roared by and had to floor the Caddy for half a mile before he saw the taillights of the BMW shining red up ahead again.

Felitia was into her skirt, looking right and left on the seat as though expecting to find her blouse there.

"You know who the hell was in that house?" she asked. "You know who the hell hired my time through that one-eyed pimp sonofabitch Rialto, which—I leave there running for my life— he's nowheres around?"

"Twelvetrees," Spinneran said.

"That's right. The fucking gazoony who beat the shit out of Boots."

Spinneran glanced at her. "Is that what you call your mother?"

"What are you talking about, what do I call my mother? She was your mother, too. You used to call her Boots before you went to live with Uncle Benny."

"You know her other street name?"

"Sure I know her other street name. It was Felitia's Mother because everybody knew me, I was so cute. How come you went to stay with Uncle Benny?"

"I thought it was better than doing triples with the old lady."

"So look at you, now you're calling our mother 'old lady.' Is that any way to talk about her? So was it better living with Benny?"

"No, it wasn't better. Uncle Benny's dead."

"I didn't know that. When did it happen?"

"A long time ago. Maybe only a few months after I went to live with him."

"Too bad," Felitia said. "You don't happen to want to lend me that jacket you got on?"

Spinneran pulled over and set the hand brake.

Back half a mile, Rialto almost got caught napping. He slowed to a crawl and then turned into a driveway. If Spinneran looked back up the road he'd have seen what looked like somebody pulling into his garage.

Spinneran went into the trunk and came back with the thin black karate coat. When he drove on, Rialto backed out of the driveway and picked up the tail.

"What have you got back there, a store?" Felitia asked, getting into the jacket. She reached out and patted Spinneran on the chest. "How come you got your tits bound up? How come you're walking around looking like a faggot? Hey, you're not a bull dyker, are you?"

"I don't want to get into it."

"Hell, I don't care you want to do boys, you want to do girls, you want to do ponies, fachrissakes. There's nothing you do, I haven't done once or twice myself, Alice."

"I call myself Connor Spinneran."

"So, okay, I don't mind calling my sister by her last name. Connor I understand. But where did you get Spinneran? There any Spinnerans in our family? Hey, you know, you make a very good-looking man. I wasn't your sister, I could be interested. I'm mad at you."

It was like old times listening to her rattle on like she'd rattled on ever since she was two or three.

"Why are you mad at me?" Spinneran wanted to know.

"I'm mad at you because you didn't come be with me when Boots died. I was all on my own."

"I only heard about it a long time after it happened. I came looking for you, but you weren't around."

"Well, no, I was with Gertie, wasn't I?"

"Gertie?"

"Gertie Fallon who had the whorehouse over in Downey."

"Jesus Christ."

"You said it. I got the hell out of there as soon as I could, you can bet. I was in Hollywood after that."

"Back on the stroll?"

"No, in the fucking candy store, what do you think? I had my living to make. You could of asked around."

"I was living other places after Uncle Benny died."

"Yeah, like where?"

"Connecticut, New York, Illinois."

"I been around a little myself," Felitia said, boastfully. "So why did you come back to L.A.?"

"I came back to kill the sonofabitch that punched out our mother's lights."

Felitia looked at Spinneran with awe and admiration.

"Are you kidding me?"

"I promised myself I'd kill him, and I was going to kill him tonight, except you came running out of his house. Now I'm going to have to try tomorrow night maybe." She turned around and looked into the backseat. "Sonofabitch, it was on the goddamn roof."

"What was on the goddamn roof?"

"Never mind."

They were at Pacific Coast Highway and Sunset. Spinneran pulled into the gas station on the corner and parked alongside the telephone booth.

While her sister made a call, Felitia watched her, thinking how easy it was to think of Alice as "him" the way she was dressed, and the way she acted. "Remind me to tell this story on the corners," she said to herself out loud, marveling how from one day to the next you couldn't tell what was going to pop out of a crack and surprise the hell out of a person.

Rialto had continued down Sunset, turned into a restaurant parking lot down the road, and came right out again so that he was parked the other way on the highway looking toward the telephone booth Spinneran was in.

Spinneran wasn't long. When she got back behind the wheel she took Sunset, heading for Hollywood.

"Hey," Felitia said, as though she'd been thinking about it for some time. "You didn't get one of them operations where a girl thinks she's maybe a boy and some doctor makes her a pecker?"

"I've been thinking about it."

"I could never do that."

"Well, I guess you wouldn't. You like being a girl."

"I don't know if I *like* it. There's just not a hell of a lot I can do about it."

"Well, I've been thinking maybe there's something I can do about it."

"Because you really want to?"

"Yes, because I want to."

"Jesus Christ."

Felitia was quiet for a little while, chewing that over.

Finally she said, "You mind if I call you Alice when nobody else is around?"

"Why would you want to do that?"

"Because I've been missing my sister for a long time. And this is gonna take some getting used to."

Spinneran reached over and squeezed her hand.

"Where do you want me to drop you off?"

"Drop me off?"

"I've got to see a man."

"So you're gonna drop me off. I ain't seen you in years, I've just had a very upsetting experience—two, in fact. It seems to me the least you could do is come to my place, have a cup of coffee, and we could fill each other in."

"We'll do that."

"You mind if I took a little nap?" Felitia asked.

"Can you still fall asleep on a dime?"

"Sometimes I think I could fall asleep on the point of a pin."

She curled up in the corner by the door and closed her eyes. In seconds, it seemed, her breathing grew shallow and even.

Spinneran looked over and thought about how she'd watched her little sister sleep a hundred times when they were small.

Felitia was still asleep when Spinneran turned into the alley where the Club Armentières squatted.

THIRTY-TWO

RIALTO FOLLOWED THE BMW up Sunset, in and out of Beverly Hills, through the heavy traffic along the stretch by the nightclubs and the thinning traffic past the stroll at Fairfax. He kept a distance and saw Spinneran turn left into the alley. He drove on past and took his left at Gardner and another at Hawthorne, pulling into the curb beside a quiet apartment house. He killed his lights and motor, got out with soft grunts and groans, and hurried down to the mouth of the alley where the weeds grew tall.

Peeking around the corner, he could see the BMW sitting there, its parking lights still on, halfway up the alley in front of the Club Armentières. The neon sign above the nightclub's door washed the trash on the gravel road a sickly pink.

He moved back and looked at the windows in the apartment house. There were lights behind several windows. He kept standing there the way he was doing, some sleepless person could take a look out the window, see him hanging around, and mistake him for a mugger. They could call the cops, and then what?

Another car pulled into the alley without its lights on. A man dressed in a tank top and tight Levis got out. He walked past the BMW several paces. Spinneran left the BMW. The interior lights popped on and for a second, before he turned around, Danny Cortez was caught in the wash of light.

Rialto was ready to give an arm to hear what was being said.

He crouched as low as he could, considering the size of his gut, and crossed the mouth of the alley. He ran like hell down Hawthorne to Gardner, down Gardner to Sunset, and up Sunset to the other mouth of the alley, puffing like a winded hippo but making it with surprising speed. He eased himself around the edge of the building where some vines grew. The two cars, parked side by side, would block him from their view if he could only get down low enough.

It was an effort, but he managed to practically four-foot it close enough to catch some of what was being said. Cortez was facing Sunset, so almost all of what he said was audible. What Spinneran said was mostly mumble.

"So after your wise remarks about me pissing on my shoe, you don't get in and do the job," Cortez said.

"Couldn't . . . supposed to do? . . . came running. . . ."

"You could of done her, too. Blew her up with Twelvetrees and his fucking daughter."

". . . sister."

"Oh, fachrissakes. Your sister?"

". . . home . . . tonight . . . shot."

"You heard a gunshot? What else."

". . . else."

"All right. You hold on to the box. . . ."

Spinneran said something Rialto couldn't catch.

"On the fucking roof?" Cortez said loudly, then caught himself and brought his voice down low again, but not so low Rialto couldn't hear him call Spinneran an asshole and a faggot.

Spinneran started to turn away, but Cortez reached out and spun Spinneran around.

"Don't turn your back on me you fucking killer," Cortez said.

Spinneran spoke.

"You just better remember I can get you for three. I can still burn you for Harold Vyborg."

Spinneran spoke again.

"I can burn you right on the spot. I'll say I come down here and found you at the Armentières and shot you when you pulled a gun on me."

Spinneran said something else.

"I could do it now and shoot your fucking sister, too. Are you crazy bringing her here with you?"

". . . sleeping."

"She better goddamn well be sleeping or you'll have to do her. You hear what I'm telling you? Sister or no sister, you'll have to do her or I'll . . ." He turned his head and looked straight up the alley where Rialto huddled against the wall, behind the cars.

Rialto could just see a piece of Cortez's face through the windshield of the BMW. The cop stood there listening. Rialto didn't think he'd made a noise, but cops had antennae ordinary people didn't have.

Spinneran said something Rialto couldn't catch.

"I'll get another one rigged. You stay home. You hear me?" Cortez said. "You stay home until I find out what the hell went on down there. This ain't over yet."

Rialto started backing out of the alley as fast as he could go. Cortez said something else, but Rialto was already too far away to hear. He risked it and turned around, then crawled out of the alley until he hit the sidewalk. A motor turned over and roared. He got to his feet and ran like hell back to Gardner.

He turned the corner just about the time he heard one of the cars back out onto Sunset. He stood there trembling. He didn't hear the other car. It had probably driven straight on through to Hawthorne.

He waited a few long minutes, ready to put on a drunk act if the BMW came around the corner onto Gardner, but it never came. He walked back up to his car and got in behind the wheel.

He sat there, having a hell of a time getting his breath. Jesus Christ, he thought, I hope I ain't going to conk out from a heart attack crawling around like a fucking nut just so I can take the mickey out of Mocky Hush. He leaned his head over, hoping to get a little more air, but all he got was the hot wind.

He pulled at his collar, then leaned forward to put the key in the ignition. His antennae weren't so good. He didn't even feel the knife slip into his neck, but a second later he heard a muffled scream. Then he didn't feel or see or hear a thing anymore, except he had a passing thought. How come it was so cold all of a sudden?

THIRTY-THREE

WHISTLER HEARD ABOUT the death of Mr. Midnight America on the radio news as he drove north along the coast heading home to La-La Land.

The announcer made no mention of any murder, just that Twelvetrees had apparently been shot at his beach house in the Malibu Colony.

Whistler leaned on the hammer and the Chevy kicked ahead.

When he got to the Pacific Coast Highway and Sunset he stopped at the same gas station where Spinneran had stopped and stepped into the same telephone booth from which Spinneran had made his call.

Whistler called the Bel-Air Hotel.

When Marvin Dwyer answered, Whistler identified himself and asked if Mrs. Twelvetrees was all right.

"If she's all right, I wouldn't know it, Whistler. She's not here. She got a call about three A.M. Five minutes later she orders a cab; she leaves twenty minutes after that."

"For Christ's sake, you let her go?"

"Let me know are you crazy, or am I crazy?" Dwyer said. "You expected me to stop a guest from leaving the premises?"

"I'm crazy. It's the hour. I hardly ever stay up after four in the morning."

"Well, I should hope you're crazy."

"Is Patch in reach?"

"He's over in the corner having a nap."

"Stir him up and get him to the phone, will you?"

After a few minutes Patch got on the phone. "She left."

"Dwyer told me. Did you listen in on the call she got?"

"I was doing rounds. I walked into the lobby while she was on the phone."

"Dwyer let you listen in?"

"I got in on the end of the conversation. A fella says '. . . and we didn't have to have no part in it. We don't have to play the game out. You go home and wait for me. It'll maybe be a while. I want to stay on this and see nothing happens we don't know about.' 'How are you going to do that? It's not your jurisdiction,' Mrs. Twelvetrees says. 'Don't you worry about that,' he says. 'You just do like I say.' 'All right, Danny,' she says. Then she hangs up, and five minutes later calls for a cab. Whistler?"

"Yeah?"

"This gazoony she talked to. It sounds to me like he's a cop. Don't it sound that way to you?"

"Well, that's the way it is," Whistler said.

"So if I was you, Whistler, what with Twelvetrees getting shot in the small hours, in case you know anything you shouldn't know or got any ideas about finding out things you shouldn't find out, I'd forget 'em. I wouldn't have nothing more to do with this business. You know what I mean?"

"Thanks, Patch. You've been a friend. I owe you plenty."

"Don't worry," Patch said. "I won't forget."

Whistler called the number of the house where Mary Beth lived, and which Nell owned. He let it ring a long time, but there was no answer.

By the time he drove down the road toward the Colony gatehouse, the sun hadn't topped the hills, but there was a layer of dishwater in the sky and the sea was shining like dull silver.

There was a colony guard and a sheriff's deputy standing inside. The guard started coming out as Whistler pulled up, but the deputy half-shouldered him aside and got out first. Whistler looked past him and saw that the gateman was annoyed. Whistler caught his eye and put both hands over his face, with his fingers spread out so that even a fool could see there were ten, as though rubbing the sleep out of his eyes.

Before the officer could say anything, Hankus said, "Morning Mr. Chips. You been on the road all night?"

"Well, the Benz died on me up in San Francisco after the convention, and I had to borrow my friend's car. Actually it's his kid's car. What's going on?"

"There's been an accident," the deputy said.

"There's been a death, Mr. Chips," Hankus said, moving right up to the window and tossing a glance at the county cop as if he had no right to be eavesdropping on people who belonged there. "Your neighbor, Mr. Twelvetrees, got killed with a gun."

"Oh, dear God. Why the hell won't people learn not to fool with firearms?"

The deputy went back into the gatehouse.

Whistler put his hand on the window frame. The ten he'd plucked from his pocket and folded twice lay under his finger. "What do they call you?" he murmured.

Hankus took the ten. "The people here call me Hankus. Who are you?"

"What's the difference? Just say I'm an interested party."

"Well, depending on how interested a party you are, come back when the cops are gone and maybe we can do a little more business."

"You know something they don't know?"

"Oh, they know it, but you don't know it."

"Thank you, Hankus," Whistler said loudly. "You think I'm going to get any sleep?"

"I wouldn't count on it, Mr. Chips. The police are questioning everybody for six, seven houses either side of the Twelvetrees place."

Whistler drove down along the shorefront road. There were several cruisers with their lights flashing scattered out around a house with white pillars and a black door. There was also an unmarked city car. Several men and women, some in uniform, some not, were standing around in little clusters.

A television crew was packing up their van. They probably had been the first to get there. Before the week was out, there'd be plenty more of them filming the empty front of the house. Even in death, celebrities couldn't get away from the consequences of their fame.

Whistler parked four houses back. He got out and walked down toward the action. The air smelled very heavy with salt and rotting weed.

A heavyset man in a windbreaker and a baseball cap looked his way and said something. The man he was talking to turned around. It was Cortez. He tapped the other man on the elbow and walked toward Whistler.

"What brings you here, Whistler?" he asked.

"I could ask you the same."

"It came over the police band. They said Twelvetrees was shot and there was a woman in the house. Right away I thought of Nell."

"Nell?"

"Mrs. Twelvetrees. Why ain't you with her, watching out for her?"

"I put her someplace safe. But you already know that, don't you?"

"What are you talking about?"

"So if it wasn't Nell with Twelvetrees when he got shot, who was it?" Whistler asked, ignoring Cortez's reaction.

"It was the daughter, Jenny. She says she came home from a date, walked in the house, and got ready for bed."

"She don't know her old man's in the place?"

"She says not. She says there were only the lamps that go on automatically at dusk and off at dawn when nobody's here. She gets into bed and she's just falling asleep when this shadow attacks her. She pulls away and runs into her father's room, figuring it's closest to the beach and maybe she can get away through the sliding doors. This somebody grabs her again."

"She still don't know it's Twelvetrees?"

"She says not. In the struggle they knock over the night table by the bed. She's on her knees, and feels the gun under her hand. She turns around and pulls the trigger. The attacker calls her name. *Now* she knows it's her old man."

"You believe her story?"

"Why shouldn't I believe her story? The man's got a bad reputation. He'd fuck a snake if it'd stay still long enough. He's half in the bag. You should hear the medical examiner. He says the smell of booze on Twelvetrees could stun a mule. But who cares if I believe her story, anyway? This ain't my reservation. I was just interested because you were doing a job for Mrs. Twelvetrees and I met her once or twice."

"A lot more than once or twice, isn't it, Cortez?"

"That's two," Cortez said.

"You must be very happy, Jenny Twelvetrees icing her old man. It saved you the trouble."

"That's three," Cortez said. "That's three times you said something that I maybe don't understand, but which I could easily take the wrong way. What do you think you know?"

"I don't know much of anything. But I've got some surmises. I've got some uneducated guesses."

"So let me hear the story. I'll tell you if I know anybody who'll buy it."

"I don't know about the sequence of events. I don't know what comes first, what comes next. Number one—it doesn't matter which is the chicken, which is the egg—you catch the investigation when Twelvetrees beats up on a hooker named Boots or Felitia's Mother. I don't know, does he ask a favor? Probably not. I don't think you'd have done him a favor at the time. You were probably junior anyway, so what could you do? There probably wasn't enough to make a case against him. Besides, who cared about this whore who was known to let people use her for a punching bag?

"Number two, you arrest a hooker by the name of Eleanora Reinbeck . . ."

"I never worked vice."

"So you got introduced while she's in the cage," Whistler said harshly. "She probably had some other street name or more than one. You got friendly. Cops and whores make good sweethearts."

Something scary moved behind the black eyes that stared at Whistler without blinking from under Mongol lids.

"I don't like this story," Cortez said. "I think it stinks. Go home and try again."

"A cop and a hooker. Both of them right in there with the action. Right there with the cars that cost like houses, fur coats for taking out the garbage, champagne to rinse out your mouth after you brush your teeth. Except they only get to see the money, smell the money. Once in a while maybe they get to feel the money. But it isn't their money. All that goddamn money and all they get is a few rags of it now and then.

"Then Nell makes a connection with Twelvetrees, and she plays it so he marries her. I don't know how you figured in her life during the five years the marriage lasted. Maybe she tried to play it straight and cut you off. Maybe you kept it going on the side. Anyway, one day, Nell Twelvetrees decides she's had enough of Mr. Midnight America and she tells you she's going to get divorced."

"Twelvetrees paid off that second wife of his very big according to all I read," Cortez said. "Now he's worth a hundred times as much. He'd be paying Nell off even bigger."

"You'd think that would be enough, wouldn't you? I mean five, six million should be enough for anybody. Even a cop and a hooker. But with some people enough is never enough. Look at these millionaires, even billionaires, staying up nights and cutting throats just to make another two, three million."

"It boggles the mind," Cortez said.

"I'll never understand it. Maybe they're very scared. Maybe they got an addiction. Maybe they think if they got enough money when death comes calling they can buy him off. Anyway, you and Nell figured why settle for such a small piece of such a big pie? Why not get it all. Why not kill the sonofabitch?"

"So I seduce the daughter and get her to pull the trigger on her old man?"

"No. You get Nell to hire a private license you don't think much of. Then you find a killer, the one who knifed Harold Vyborg in the belly, and who was probably in your pocket even before that. You had murders hanging over him. He'd do what you told him to do. Why the hell not? It was what he did for a living anyway."

"I get it, so it's this hired killer, not the daughter, who murdered Twelvetrees," Cortez said like he was very amused, but getting impatient, with the story Whistler was telling.

Whistler shook his head. "No. He was supposed to. First he took some pictures of Nell and me bare-assed. I walked right into that. She drugged her dogs and let the man with the camera in and got me into her bedroom."

"What for? So she could have a look at your cock?"

"So she could give Twelvetrees reason to get pissed off enough to tell her whatever she got out of him she'd have to get over his dead body. She pushed him to say that in front of me, your handy witness, standing by for two hundred fifty a day and gas money. Oh, there were two other witnesses to what he said that time, his lawyer and her lawyer, but I'm the only one who was there for the next couple of performances. Once at the daughter's birthday party when Nell handed Twelvetrees something, a tape, I think, that put him into a rage all over again.

"And I'm the only one there when this killer in your pocket takes a couple of shots in our direction down on the beach at Venice."

"By way of what?"

"By way of making it look like Twelvetrees had put out a contract on Nell."

"And?"

Whistler had run out of story.

"Where's your big finish for Christ's sake?" Cortez taunted. "All that fuckin' around for what?"

"The reel broke in the middle of the picture," Whistler said. "Twelvetrees came down here without his bodyguards for some reason. His daughter came down here after a date instead of going to the big house on Skyline for some reason. Twelvetrees is drunk and went after his daughter and she shot him. So you don't need to go through with whatever . . ."

"For some reason." Cortez said it sarcastically. "You're a joke, Whistler. You couldn't find your fucking shoe if it was on your foot. With you, two and two makes a hundred and fifty million. You're an asshole, and I don't want anything to do with you anymore. Not because you make up this story about me, but because you're such an asshole."

He turned and started to walk away. The door opened and a woman in uniform came out with Jenny, who was wrapped in a man's overcoat.

The flesh around her eyes was stained with shock and exhaustion. Her eyes were like glass. She raised them and looked directly at Whistler. He walked toward her, and she started to cry.

"I need a friend," she said.

He nodded as one of the deputies moved to block him, and the uniformed woman helped Jenny into the back of a cruiser.

"Go home, asshole," Cortez said into his ear. "Nobody needs you anymore."

THIRTY-FOUR

WHISTLER WATCHED CORTEZ saunter over to his car and pull out with a last disdainful glance his way. He watched a man from the sheriff's office put a crime scene seal on the door. One officer was left to stand guard in case souvenir hunters found ways to get past colony security and loot the house for mementos of Mr. Midnight America. They'd been known to do worse. He hung around as the official cars and the cruisers pulled out one by one.

After a while, as the beach beyond the barrier of houses started to come to life with the shouts of children and the rattle of rigging as catamarans were hauled down to the water, he went back to his Chevy and drove down to the gatehouse.

Hankus was still there, lounging against the shelf of the Dutch door, his replacement standing inside going over some paper-work.

When Whistler braked, Hankus pushed off and came strolling over.

"I thought you were moving in," he said.

"I hung around while they put a lock on it," Whistler said. "It's the end of a fucking era, ain't it?"

"What's this business the police know that I might want to know, and what gives you the idea I'd pay to know it?"

Hankus stared at Whistler flat-eyed, not even giving him a nickel grin. "You're here, ain't you?"

"Well, I've got a curiosity, just like anybody else."

"How much is it worth to you to satisfy your curiosity?"

Whistler placed a folded ten on the edge of the window frame. Hankus stared at it. Whistler added another. When there were three, Hankus started to reach.

Whistler pressed his fingers down on the bills. "Don't be silly. You might think it's worth three cents. But I don't know if it's worth three cents."

"Well, first this pimp by the name of Rialto—"

"Mike Rialto?"

"You know this pimp?"

"I know him."

"Well, first he comes through the gate with some little school-girl hooker flashing her ass."

"What does that mean exactly?"

"It means exactly what I said. A hooker that dresses up in a short pleated skirt, and what they call a middy blouse, and short white socks, and them little shoes with the straps."

Whistler nodded and, separating one of the tens, handed it to Hankus to give him encouragement.

"He's making a delivery to Twelvetrees," Hankus went on. "It's not unusual, though it hasn't been happening as much the last few years as it happened before that. Next I see the Twelve-trees girl drive through in a red BMW with some skinny blond-haired queer behind the wheel." He grinned broadly, showing missing back teeth, which suddenly gave his face the look of a horse. "I expect—"

"Wait a second. Where's Rialto at this time?"

"He's just going out. He stops and talks to me for a minute, and I say how I expect there's going to be some things happening."

"What things?"

"Well, I don't know what things, but something. Fachrissakes, her old man's got this whore in there doing him, and his daughter comes trotting in. Something's got to fucking happen. So I ain't surprised when the blond guy in the BMW comes roaring the hell out of here. I am surprised when I see it ain't the Twelvetrees girl in the car, but the schoolgirl hooker. Now, how does a person figure a thing like that?"

Whistler handed over another ten.

"I'm doing good, ain't I?" Hankus said. "Well, it gets better."

"I'm all ears."

"I think how very funny it is that this skinny fuck should come here with one broad and leave with another. So I take a little walk down there, and I find Miss Twelvetrees standing in the road outside her house with blood all over her front and her dress half off. Some of the neighbors are already out. It seems she's been screaming and got some dogs to raising hell. Now she's in shock. I go inside and I find Twelvetrees in his bedroom with his chest a bloody mess. He's staring at the ceiling, but he ain't seeing nothing. I put in a call right away," he finished proudly. Then his expression changed. "I wasn't the first, though. Somebody else had already dialed nine one one."

He stared off for a second. Whistler could read his thoughts like captions over a foreign movie closeup. Hankus was wondering if not being the first to put in the call to the cops would ruin his chances of getting interviewed or even being asked to appear on some of the talk shows. Then his look changed and Whistler knew he'd decided that being the officer—sort of an officer—on the scene would probably get him some invitations anyhow.

"That's not the 'better' you mentioned, is it?" Whistler said, bringing him back.

"The better is, I see something glinting over in the brush by the side of the road. I go over and have a look. It's some pieces of a clock. There's also some wire and some sticks of dynamite all taped together with friction tape. It was a cigar box bomb, just like you see in the movies."

Whistler gave up the last sawbuck.

THIRTY-FIVE

WHISTLER HAD BEEN in Cortez's apartment a few times to little stags that had been lame attempts to make friendships out of poker, beer, and dirty stories.

Cortez had never mentioned Nell. But in light of what Whistler now thought he knew that was no more than was to be expected.

The garage apartment on Laurel off Fountain was reached by a wooden staircase that ended at the front door. There was a knee-high wooden gate that once kept a turtle Cortez had acquired God-knew-where confined to a small side porch. A hand-lettered sign still hung on the latch. "Warning—Attack Turtle." Whistler hadn't thought it very funny the first time he'd seen it, and couldn't understand what it was still doing there. The turtle was long since dead. Cortez had cleaned it out, filled it with sand and stoppered it with wax.

Whistler knocked on the door and watched the lens of the spyhole. It got dark. Someone was looking him over. But nothing happened. The door stayed closed.

He thumped down the stairs, then raced back up on his toes, keeping very low. He stepped over the gate and went around to the french doors that opened on to the porch. The drapes were drawn.

He hesitated, remembering a night when Cortez had proved just how tough and mean he was.

There was an actor, about six feet six, who advertised himself as the second or third most decorated marine to come out of the Korean police action. He had a very bad reputation for hurting people and liked to carry a gun.

He hung around Gentry's and joined Whistler at the table whenever there was room.

One night he started flashing a huge automatic.

Cortez was at the table across the aisle. He reached over and tapped the actor on the arm. "Hey," he said, "if I was you, I wouldn't wave that gun around. Guns are very dangerous things."

"Not if I'm holding it. I know about guns."

"But do you know *everything* about guns?" Cortez asked, slipping over and shoving his hip against the actor so he had to slide across and give him room, looking at Cortez as though wondering what the crazy Mex thought he was doing.

"I know plenty," the actor said.

"Do you know a gun that size shoved up your asshole could have you shitting bricks for the rest of your life? You don't put that goddamn pistola away, sucker, that's just where I'm going to put it."

"For Christ's sake, Danny," the actor said.

"No! Goddamn it, no! Do like I say. Don't fucking make conversation with me."

Cortez had grabbed the actor's arm and slammed it down on the edge of the table, breaking the bone.

Whistler took a deep breath. He could get very badly hurt doing what he was about to do.

He took his handkerchief out of his pocket and punched out the small pane of glass closest to the door handle. It fell on the rug inside and didn't make much noise. He snapped the lock and opened the door. He almost tripped over an ottoman sitting there.

The living room smelled of beer and dust. A clock ticked loudly on top of a portable TV on a stand that could be wheeled around. The faucet in the kitchen sink dripped on the other side of a curtained doorway. The place was syncopating, rocking to a soft rhythm, about to break out and scream.

He went into the bedroom. The bedclothes were kicked all around. He walked across the rug to the bathroom door and shoved it open with his fingertips.

It was like he remembered it, just big enough for a shower over tub, a toilet and a sink with a medicine cabinet above it. The mirror had lost part of the silvering and gave back only a piece of his face.

Back in the bedroom he went down on one knee and looked under the bed. He looked in the closet and slid the clothes back and forth on their hangers.

There was a big pine wardrobe against one wall. He hammered the side of his fist hard against it. The door popped open. Nell was huddled in there, her mouth open, ready to scream.

"Thank God, it's you, Whistler," she said.

"Who were you expecting?"

She stepped out of the wardrobe, trying to gather up the ruffled feathers of her dignity, and walked out into the living room where she reached for a bottle of bourbon and a glass standing on the TV.

"You want a drink?" she asked, as she poured herself three fingers.

"I don't use it. You should know that by now."

"Oh, sure, I forgot."

"What are you doing here, Nell?"

She went to sit down on a green tweed chair, crossing her legs and looking at the toe of her high-heeled slipper. She was wearing a bathrobe a size too big for her. It probably belonged to Cortez, but was gaudy enough to belong to a hooker.

"Well, when you left me alone in the hotel after somebody tried to kill me like they did, I started getting very scared," she said.

"I had somebody watching out over you."

"I know that," she almost yelled, her voice rising sharply as if she was warning him that she had no patience with explanations, reasonable or otherwise. "I was frightened out of my wits. Can't you understand that?"

"I can understand that. So you came to . . ."

"One of your friends who I thought could protect me if anyone could protect me."

"You were scared, there was Bosco."

"He's not a cop."

"There was Canaan."

"I didn't know where Canaan lived."

"But you knew where Cortez lived?"

She stared at him and he stared back. Her foot was kicking. The robe split along the side and one half fell away revealing her leg all the way to the top of her thigh. She swiped at it automatically, managing to reveal more of herself.

"All right, I knew Danny from years back."

"Why didn't you say?"

"I hired you to protect me from Roger. I wasn't obligated to give you my life history."

She altered her position in the chair and uncrossed her legs. She sat there nude all the way to where the sash tied the robe around her waist. The light seemed to strike off her small triangular shield as though it were burnished copper.

Whistler took his eyes away. He looked all around the room. He saw the weighted turtle shell holding down a bunch of magazines. He went over and picked it up, then sat down on the ottoman so that his view of her body was less provocative.

She closed the front of the robe, arranging it so it covered her legs all the way down to her ankles. "Look, if you think this is anything more than . . ." she started to say, but stopped when Whistler lifted his head a little. It was as though he'd spoken and told her not to go on lying, not to go on trying to work him as though it mattered.

"I just got back from Malibu," he said.

"You saw Jenny?"

"They were just taking her away."

"She'll be all right."

"What makes you say that? She killed her father. How is she going to be all right?"

"Any lawyer worth a dime'll plead self-defense. She'll say the sonofabitch tried to rape her."

"So she'll inherit. She'll inherit and you'll inherit. But it won't change things. She'll always remember she killed her father. You ought to give her something for that. In a way, she did it for you. She fixed it so you wouldn't have to remember that you killed a man who was your husband for five years."

"He was rotten."

"So. Rotten. What's that? I'm talking about killing a man. You could've just taken the five, ten million Hindy Reno would've squeezed out of Twelvetrees for you. But no, you wanted the whole goddamn enchilada."

"I don't know what you're talking about, me killing—"

"Not you by yourself. You and Cortez. Maybe that's why you were so greedy. There's two of you and two can't really live as cheap as one, can they?"

"I'm trying to tell you—"

"Give it up. I told Cortez a story about how a cop and hooker set out to murder this celebrity, this Mr. Midnight America. He didn't shake his head no to what I told him. I just didn't tell him all the story, because I didn't know all the story."

"Now you know all of it?" There was a thin edge of derision in her voice.

"I know how it was supposed to look. Like Twelvetrees hired you killed, and when the shooter couldn't make it happen, he decided to use what he learned about blowing off balls and things back when he was in the army, and do it himself. But something goes wrong and he blows himself and his innocent daughter up along with it. And after, when the questions start— plenty of questions when a man as famous as Twelvetrees dies like that—I'd be there to swear how he'd tried to do you."

Whistler stood up.

"You've got to understand—"

"I don't have to understand anything," Whistler interrupted. "And you don't have to try and make me understand. You don't have to bother. There's nothing—"

"I just wanted to say, if things had been different, give or take fifteen, twenty years, we could've had a dance," Nell said softly.

"—I can do to you," he went on as if she hadn't said a word. "I can't prove a thing. And even if I could, what could they do to you? You didn't actually kill anybody, did you?"

A key turned in the lock and Cortez walked in. He half smiled and took a step, his hands coming up ready to lash out. Then he stopped flat-footed and shook his head.

"Goddamn it, Whistler, you take chances," he said.

Whistler ignored him as though Cortez wasn't even there. He just kept staring at Nell.

"You didn't kill anybody, did you?" he said again. "Unless you paid to have young Roger's throat slit up there in Seattle."

"All right. Get the fuck out of here," Cortez said.

Whistler tossed the turtle shell across the room. Cortez caught it.

"You stuff all your pets?" Whistler asked and left them together.

THIRTY-SIX

WHISTLER SAT IN Gentry's looking out the window at the street freaks, soiled saints and perfumed sinners, the children of Sodom walking up and down in constant agitation, sweating in their skins as the Santa Anas blew and swept the gutters.

He was alone with his thoughts, with nothing to soothe his nerves, the only medication being Bosco's black coffee and the only consulting physician Bosco, the one-armed searcher through a thousand books.

He was feeling very bad and said so when Bosco came to listen. "Read me something that'll heal my heart," he said with more than a touch of irony.

"Don't make yourself a mountain or a tree," Bosco told him.

"What the hell is that supposed to mean?"

"One tremor don't make an earthquake. One lay don't make a love affair."

Anger marked Whistler's face as though a hand had slapped his mouth crooked. "That's not what it's about, fachrissakes. I never did."

"So maybe that raised your hopes even higher," Bosco said, leaning across the table as if inviting Whistler to take a punch at him, if that's what it would take to knock his head back on straight.

"You met the queen of greedy ladies, and you ain't learned enough about the world to take it in your stride."

"A poor man doesn't know much about greed," Whistler said,

thinking about the millions Nell and Cortez were going to cop, and staring out the window at the street action, wondering what a crumb of it would mean to the whore wearing the baby doll or the bum cupping the match from the hot blow of the wind.

". . . but he sure does know a lot about hunger," Bosco said, completing Whistler's thoughts, moving with the tide.

"On the other hand, no man, rich or poor, knows a hell of a lot about women," Whistler said.

"Except it's a seller's market. The ladies own most of the merchandise. Nell just decided to get top dollar for her goods."

"Easy money," Whistler said.

"Not so easy. She must have paid a lot to get her head in the place it's at."

"You're a goddamn city sage," Whistler said.

Bosco grinned and pulled down the lower lid of one eye with a finger like a spike. "I read tea leaves, mud spatters, and chicken shit."

Canaan walked in and ordered a hamburger and coffee. He waited for Bosco to slip out of the booth and go place the order, then took the seat opposite Whistler, pushing his hat half an inch back off his brow with his thumb.

"Isn't that hat hot on your head? You'll cook your brains."

"My hat's the only thing I can depend on," Canaan said.

"Maybe I should get a hat."

"You're feeling bad," Canaan said.

"They were going to murder somebody, Isaac."

"Well, we can't prove that, can we?"

"They killed the boy up in Seattle or had him killed."

"We can't prove that either."

"So Cortez and Nell walk off into the sunset hand in hand?"

"Well, maybe it's not the happy ending you wanted when the lights went up, but it's the happy ending they wanted."

"And that's it?"

"For the minute, that's it."

Bosco brought the hamburger and coffee, then sat down next to Whistler. Canaan took a bite and chewed like an old cow, staring off into space.

Whistler waited. He knew Canaan was going to say something more.

"Along with everything else last night, Mike Rialto—you know Mike Rialto?"

"I know Mike Rialto."

"He got it in the neck."

"What do you mean?"

"I mean he got a knife in the neck down in the alley by the Club Armentières. He's over to Central Receiving. He put out the word. He wants to see you."

"What for?"

"Gimme a break, fagod's sake. I'm not your appointment secretary."

It was odd. Rialto's real eye was dry and his glass eye was weeping. He was laying flat on his back, his stomach rising up like the stomach of a pregnant woman beneath the sheet. He started to turn his head when Whistler bent across the bed, but the pain stopped him, and he shuddered.

"How's it going, Mike?"

"Hurts like hell, you know? I can't stand pain of any sort," he said, as though God should have remembered that and not visited this trial on him.

"You're alive," Whistler said.

"Don't get me wrong, I ain't ungrateful."

"You wanted to see me, Mike?"

"I ask around, here and there, I find out you was guarding Mrs. Twelvetrees's body."

"In a manner of speaking."

"Well, in a manner of speaking you almost got your ass shot off."

"You know about that?"

"I was sitting on the bench down there in Venice and watched the shooter do it from the roof."

"You could have yelled."

"Well, look, if I would've yelled, you would've turned around and made a better target."

"You thought about that, did you?"

"Oh, sure."

"So that's what you wanted to tell me? You were there when somebody took a shot?"

"That was just to get your interest."

"You got my interest."

"Ain't you going to get my interest, now?"

"Jesus Christ, Mike, you could be on your deathbed, and you're trying to do business?"

"I ain't on no deathbed, Whistler. That little whore gave a yell and scared the sonofabitch away from me before he had a chance to see if he did the job."

"What little whore, Felitia?"

"How do you know that?"

"Somebody told me about a schoolgirl trickster."

"I know something a lot better than that."

"I'm listening."

"Hospitals are expensive nowadays."

Whistler sighed and counted fifty dollars in small bills off his money clip. He rolled them up and tucked them into Rialto's hand.

"I won't argue," he said. "There's fifty. I can't do better."

"I ain't trying to gouge you, but a man who don't get paid for his work loses his pride."

"I'll give you that."

"The shooter down in Venice is a private license by the name of Connor Spinneran. He's a skinny little fella about five six, a hundred ten pounds, brassy hair combed flat on his head. Dresses fashionable. Looks like a pansy."

"I haven't heard that word in years."

"Me neither, but it fits. He reminds you of a person out of the twenties. You know what I mean?"

Whistler nodded.

"Also, this Spinneran was hanging around a lot with Twelve-trees's daughter," Rialto said.

"Jenny."

"It was Spinneran what drove her down to Malibu last night. He drives in with Jenny and out with Felitia. I follow them all the way back into town. He parks that red BMW of his in the alley by the Armentières. It looks to me like Felitia went to sleep. After a few minutes, guess who comes driving up to have a chat?"

Whistler could have said, but he didn't. Rialto didn't expect an answer anyhow. He was just building suspense.

Everybody's a goddamn screenwriter in this lunatic town, Whistler thought.

"Danny Cortez the vice cop is who."

THIRTY-SEVEN

FELITIA HAD DISAPPEARED from the stroll at Hollywood and Vine.

In the magical ways of a closed and secret society, the whores, pimps, gonifs, street clowns, and magimpers knew all or nearly all about what had gone down at the beach house in Malibu. The undercover cops, johns, marks, and unmade beds did not.

A few Angelinos and some early winter geese drifted out of Canaan's way like dry leaves in a hot wind. He walked right out into the street against the light, not even hearing the horns and squeal of brakes, with the single-mindedness of a hunter following his prey. Whistler brought up the rear.

The three whores, known as the Hard-Metal Fates (there are scholars among the lowlifes populating the strolls of La-La Land), didn't move, having long since learned that if Canaan wanted you, he would get you, sooner or later. Bitchie-Boo, in her trademark silver wig of chromium threads, wore a crotch-high skirt. She had also changed her ankle-length boots for ones that climbed almost to her knee. Miami Magic was in lace with her body showing through. Dee-Dee was in a middy blouse and short pleated skirt, apparently filling the gap left by the absence of Felitia, the schoolgirl trickster. They waited for Canaan, making a good job of looking unafraid and unconcerned.

"I want to talk a minute with Felitia."

"She ain' at home?" Bitchie-Boo asked, wide-eyed.

"Do you know what these other two know?" Canaan asked.

"I don' know what they know, but whatever it is I prob'ly know it."

"So okay, Dee-Dee, you and Magic take a walk."

"What for they got to take a walk?" Bitchie-Boo asked.

"Because I want to concentrate on you, Bitchie-Boo."

"Like in the song?"

"Like in I'm going to threaten you a lot if you try to jerk me around, and I don't want any witnesses."

"Ooof!" Bitchie-Boo said, as though he'd punched her in the belly.

Miami Magic and Dee-Dee drifted off with a smile and a wave.

"So you know where Felitia is nesting?"

"I truly don', Isaac. The stories about what happened with that Mr. Midnight America are wingin' around, but no sign of Felitia."

"What do the stories say?"

"Jus' that she was delivered by Mike Rialto—you know somebody stuck him?"

Canaan nodded.

"Okay, so Rialto delivered her to this Roger Twelvetrees. She recognized the sumbitch—"

"What's not to recognize?" Canaan said. "His kisser's on the tube, how could you not recognize him?"

"Well," said Bitchie-Boo, "in our profession we don't see as much late-night shows, you might imagine. Think about it. Anyways, who give's a rat's ass why she don't glom him right that first second. She don't. It ain't until she's down to her smalls and he's got his thing in his hand that she sees it's the sumbitch punched her old lady—you remember Boots?"

"I remember Boots."

"Well, so he was the one who hurt Boots so bad she died."

"So what did Felitia do?"

"What the fuck you think she did? She got the hell out of there. Rialto was supposed to be waitin' on Felitia to say was it going to be a quick trick or a dawner. But Rialto wasn't there."

"Twelvetrees chase her?"

"Started to but as Felitia scoots out the bedroom she almost bumps into this person what I read by the paper was the daughter. She done her old man with a gun?"

"That's what they say. So Rialto wasn't there?"

"He wasn't there, but Felitia's sister was there."

"Her what?" Whistler chimed in.

"Her sister. What's the matter with you, Whistler, can' you hear?"

"Is that what Felitia said, it was her sister?" Canaan asked.

"What do I know what Felitia said. What I'm sayin' to you was said to me by the street, not by any person. Not by Felitia in my face. You understan' what I mean?"

"That's all I can do," Canaan said when he and Whistler were back in a booth with Bosco. "If the Hard-Metal Fates don't know where Felitia is nesting, nobody knows. They know everything that goes down out there."

"But do they know it right?"

Canaan shrugged and bent to his coffee cup like one of those birds that dips its beak in a glass of water and drives you crazy, you're dumb enough to buy one and keep it on the shelf.

"Rialto tells me Felitia got out of Malibu with a gazoony works for Mocky Hush and Fink Torino by the name of Spinneran. A faggot, maybe, but nobody's sister."

"You don't know," Bosco said. "You never know. You got to keep in mind persons like Bobby Ducky."

"You think?" Whistler asked.

Canaan looked out at the street.

"I don't think, I know. On some strolls seventy, eighty percent of the hookers are faggot transvestites or homos in drag. Bobby Ducky is a rare bird only because he went under the knife."

"And you got to also keep in mind that Felitia had a sister."

"Who maybe . . ." Whistler started.

"Who maybe what?" Canaan and Bosco said at almost the same time. But Whistler was out of the booth and out the door, legging it back to the parking lot where his Chevy waited.

THIRTY-EIGHT

SPINNERAN WAS A true blond. She lay spread-eagled and naked in the middle of Jenny's whorehouse bed, her head propped up on a pillow. The late afternoon sun was red-gold. It turned her white skin saffron and turned her cap of hair to brass. Her pubic hair was so palé and thin she almost looked shaven.

In her preferred masculine identity and dress she'd gone down to the Hall of Justice, where Jenny, after being gently passed from hand to hand, had been questioned last by the commissioner, the chief of police, the commanding officer, Bureau of Special Investigations, and the chief of detectives.

Bernie Mandell, looking like a neighborhood storekeeper in rumpled clothes tossed on in haste, was in on the interrogations every step of the way from the moment a call was placed to him from the Hollywood Station.

The police doctor had looked Jenny over and treated her for shock. She'd been allowed to wash up and change her blood-stained dress for a cotton smock.

It had been late in the day when Mandell was permitted to take his client home. He'd wrapped his own jacket around Jenny's shoulders and said he'd call the family doctor the minute he got her back to his house.

"No. I want to go back to my own house," Jenny said.

"I don't think that would be a very good idea," Mandell told her. "You shouldn't be alone."

Spinneran approached them, looking calm and very capable. "She won't be alone," she said.

"Do I know you?" Mandell said.

"Connor was at my birthday party," Jenny said. "Maybe you didn' get introduced."

"Well, no, we didn't," Spinneran said, and stuck out her small, neat hand, which Mandell took with an air of hesitation and suspicion.

"I can drive Jenny home. I'll stay with her," Spinneran said.

"I don't know," Mandell protested. "I don't know if I should let my client walk off—"

"Your client?" Jenny said.

"Only if you want me," Mandell said quickly. "After all, I've been your father's attorney for many years and—"

"But I don' need a lawyer to take me home, Mr. Mandell."

"I feel that, in the absence of a guardian—"

"My twenty-first birthday party. I think I can be responsible for myself."

Spinneran moved closer to Jenny, and Jenny seemed to sag against her, Spinneran's light frame swaying until she spread her legs wider and steadied Jenny's weight. There was something in the act that reassured Mandell.

"If you need me, all you've got to do is call, day or night. Even if all you want is somebody to talk to."

Jenny handed Mandell his jacket. "Thank you for everything. I was very scared."

"I think the worst is mostly over."

"I'll see she isn't left alone," Spinneran had said.

She'd taken Jenny home to the empty house on Skyline, shut off all the phones, and finally revealed herself. Who she was. What she was. A man trapped inside a woman's body. A man with small breasts and a vagina, and a special knowledge of women. She'd been soft-spoken and tender, understanding of Jenny's anger against her father and her grief for having killed him in order to save herself from rape. The seduction had been very easy. Jenny's seduction of her and hers of Jenny.

Jenny Twelvetrees sat on the stool, legs crossed at the knee, hiding the dark patch between her legs, arms folded in an intricate way, one hand cocked, a cigarette between her fingers,

staring at Spinneran's body and dragging on the cigarette every
now and then.

"God, you know, I never would've believed. I mean, I should
have known. When I close my eyes now and hear you talk, I
know it's a girl's voice. And your hands. I should've known from
your hands," Jenny said.

She smashed the cigarette out, then got up from the stool,
padded over to the wall, and pushed against it. The magnetic
catch clicked and a section of a closet filled with her clothes
opened up. She took out a pair of high-heeled sandals and put
them on, stamping her feet lightly, settling the shoes, her body
quivering a little at each impact.

"Where are you going?" Spinneran asked, rolling off the bed
and landing all coiled up, as though ready to attack.

Jenny took a dressing gown from its hanger. She held it
dangling from one hand, arms angled out from her sides, and
upraised as though she were a high-tech mannequin showing it
off. She stared at Spinneran as though believing Spinneran was
part of some dream from which she would awaken.

Spinneran moved up behind her until they were barely touching back to front.

Spinneran turned her around. Jenny looked ready to cry.

"My God, my God," she said. "I killed my father last night and
here I am makin' love with a woman. I must be very sick or very
bad."

Spinneran put her arms around Jenny, bent her legs, and lifted
Jenny off the floor the way a man would do. "Oh, babe, what are
you saying?"

Whistler parked the Chevy around the corner on the first side
street nearest the top of Skyline and trudged up to the gates on
foot.

The house looked remote and unreal sitting on the crest of the
hill in the bright sunlight. There were no vehicles to be seen. No
people. It might have been an empty set on the back lot of a
studio. Tara waiting for Scarlett to come tripping down the
sweeping flight of stairs dressed in crinoline and lace.

Where were the guards? There should have been guards.
Thieves checked the news. Whenever there was a death they
knew that houses would be left empty as the bereaved went off

to make arrangements, often forgetting to secure doors and windows.

Where were the sensation seekers? The curious?

Down in Malibu. Keeping ten-minute deathwatches from the roads and beaches, half pleased that the man who'd enjoyed such fame and riches was no longer around to enjoy them.

The electric gates scarcely moved when he grabbed the bars and shook them. He walked along the perimeter of the wall, topped by three strands of razor wire, until it made the first turn and skirted around the bowl of the cul-de-sac. The land fell off steeply at the back. There was no razor wire on top of the wall that faced the long view out over the city.

The owner of the slope below Twelvetrees's estate had erected a long, ugly chain-link fence, securing his rights to land not yet built upon, declaring ownership all the same.

Whistler climbed the fence. By balancing on the top he was able to make the jump to the top of Twelvetrees's wall. He tore his jacket scrambling over and dropping into the brush.

He was in a neglected part of the garden. He pushed his way through the undergrowth and up the slope toward the wing of garages along the side of the house beyond the curved drive. A shed roof extended toward the swimming pool enclosure so that the cars of visitors would not be left standing in the hot sun.

The wine-red BMW 633CSi stood in the shadows. Whistler went over and placed his hand on the hood. It was cool and had been parked there for some time.

He took every bit of cover he could find getting to the main house, where he started looking for a way in.

Spinneran lay on her back again, feeling her body parts joining up like an army scattered in battle coming back to count its losses and its gains. She'd worked her tongue dry and sore. Jenny had demanded almost more than Spinneran had had to give.

The sun was moving down the sky, the shadows were turning purple.

"Where did you ever learn?" Jenny asked.

"I knew all there was to know by the time I was thirteen. I love you," Spinneran said, listening for whatever truth might jump out of the words and surprise her.

Jenny half turned and burrowed in underneath Spinneran's arm, against her side. "My California Golden Girl," she said.

It was such a stupid thing to say, Spinneran thought, so why did she feel like she was going to cry?

Another time, another place, another woman and she would have laughed out loud, but Jenny'd put the sign on her. She didn't altogether believe Jenny cared for her, but she *wanted* to believe. And that was as good as it usually gets in La-La Land. She sat bolt upright. "What was that?"

"What was what?"

"I heard a noise downstairs."

"This house is so big it's always talkin'," Jenny said.

"No, a noise made by somebody." Spinneran got off the bed and took another robe from the closet, tossing Jenny the one that had fallen on the floor. "Put it on."

"It's probably Walter or Stan, my father's bodyguards."

"You're not afraid to go and see?"

"No, I'm not afraid."

"I'll be close by. You're not to worry," Spinneran said.

Whistler was at the bottom of the grand staircase, not trying to hide himself, when Jenny came cautiously padding down in her slippers.

At first she smiled, as if relieved, and then she looked annoyed. "What do you think you're doin' here, I'd like to know."

"I got to worrying about you."

"That's all very well an' good, an' I expect you mean it kindly, but you got no right to come breakin' into a person's house."

"The doors to the garden were unlocked."

She swept past him, her hands agitated, fussing at the front of her robe, down the short flight of steps into the sunken living room. "I don' know what to do. I don' know if I should call the police."

"Don't you have servants for a place this size?"

"They don' live here. My daddy didn' like servants livin' in the house."

"Still, you've got servants coming in by the day."

"Well, the housekeeper, the garage man, the gardeners . . ."

"Where are they?"

"I sent them home. I didn' want them aroun'."

"You shouldn't be alone."

She found a cigarette in a silver box and lit it. "What the hell am I talkin' to you for? I hardly know you."

"You asked me once if I'd be your friend."

"Well, I don' exactly need a friend at the minute."

"You've got a friend?"

Her eyes flickered over his shoulder.

"Is somebody standing behind me?"

"Why don't you turn around and see?" Spinneran said.

Whistler turned around to face Spinneran. She was standing on the landing, just as she'd been standing at the party when Whistler's attention had been drawn to her, the pale, contemptuous man who'd accepted Jenny's kiss on his smooth cheek. Spinneran was as bare-footed as Jenny, a light robe loosely tied about her waist, her hands in the pockets.

Jenny passed him and went to stand beside Spinneran.

"I see," Whistler said.

"What do you think you see?" Spinneran challenged.

"I see Alice Connors's daughter."

"So you see a lot."

"How does this goddamn cat's cradle work?"

"Cat's cradle?" Jenny asked.

"This tangle of string."

Spinneran smiled. "You see a lot, but you don't see that?"

"You killed a phony biker over at the Armentières. Cortez got on to you or was on to you from before. He made you a deal. He wanted you to make it look like Twelvetrees had hired somebody to do Nell. Then you were to kill Twelvetrees and Jenny . . ."

Jenny looked at Spinneran and took a step away.

". . . for him. After which you'd plant a bomb to make it look like Twelvetrees'd fumbled it. Cortez and Nell wanted everything. You just wanted Twelvetrees dead. You got Twelvetrees to hire you to kill Nell. It gave you the way of getting Twelvetrees alone without his bodyguards. What you wanted and what Nell and Cortez wanted turned out to be the same thing. Cortez didn't know you were looking for a way to kill Twelvetrees. He didn't know you had old reasons."

"What do you think you're going to do with this fairy tale?"

The door to the library on the other side of the entry hall opened up like a moving shadow. Cortez stood there with a gun in his hand. He took a half dozen slow steps across the carpet.

"What difference does it make? You don't think Cortez is going to let you walk away? He'll kill you one time and say you resisted arrest."

Spinneran removed her hand from the pocket of the robe. The movement loosened the belt and the ends fell free. She didn't try to retie it because she'd need two hands to do it, and one of her hands was occupied with a flat knife that lay in her open palm.

"You should've stayed in Gentry's watching the parade go by, Whistler," Cortez said.

Spinneran turned around, the robe falling open and her hand with the knife swinging back.

Whistler saw Cortez's eyes widen slightly as he saw Spinneran's body. The naked pubic mound and the small breasts. His surprise made him hesitate just that little bit. The knife caught him in the throat. His hand convulsed and pulled the trigger.

Whistler could have stopped the two half-naked girls from running out of the room, but he just stood there watching their bare legs flash as they took off. Didn't even move when he heard the BMW engine roar down the driveway, stop while one of them worked the gate, and then start up again, whining like a diesel as it raced down from Skyline into the guts of the city.

After a while he called the cops.

THIRTY-NINE

NIGHT WAS ON the city and the lights were bright all around Gentry's on the corner of Hollywood and Vine.

The faulty air-conditioning had finally given up the ghost altogether. The heat inside was greater than the heat outside, but no wetter. The humidity was up and rising all over La-La Land. The lights of the cars streaming by were dimmed by a kind of mist that hung suspended above the boulevard; the electric lights along the street haloed through a kind of fog.

Out on the stroll the whores kept pulling at the scraps of clothing that stuck to perspiring skin.

But Bitchie-Boo still wore her knee-high boots, knowing something nobody else seemed to know.

Gentry's was full of night types. Gargoyles, imps, and monsters painted a rainbow of colors. Hunchbacks, one-legged whores, and throat-cutters taking a break from the prowl that never ended.

The night manager, a tall, pale ghost of a man some people called Yondro, came in late as usual. Bosco finished counting his cash, turned over the drawer, picked up his copy of *Through the Looking Glass*, and came over to sit facing Whistler.

"You must have a home," Bosco said. "I know you must have a home because I never see you sleeping in the gutters."

"What good's a home with an empty bed on a night like this? What good's a home without a color TV where a man can watch tales of love, honor, and landlords that never ask for the rent?"

"You can come home with me and watch my television."

"This is the show I like best," Whistler said, nodding toward the street scene outside the plate-glass storefront. "Look, here comes a commercial."

A late model Ferrari pulled up to the curb. Three whores lined up at the window fighting for tit space on the sill, bent over in a line, asses like hot cross buns in a bakery window. Whistler and Bosco couldn't see the customer but they could imagine the dicker. The girls laughed and cursed and carried on, working out the price.

"Something exotic is wanted," Bosco said.

"A threesome, a foursome, a holiday party?" Whistler guessed.

No bargain was struck, the Ferrari roared away.

They stared in silence for a time.

"La-La Land's a land of losers," Whistler said. "We're all just a bunch of dreamers with a nickel in our shoe. Why do we come out here chasing dreams that are so hard to catch? It takes your heart, your guts, and your liver just to find the lock, and then nine hundred ninety-nine times out of a grand you can't find the key. I ought to go down to the Greyhound, over to LAX, down to Union Station and tell all the pilgrims to turn around and go back to Pennsylvania, New Jersey, West Virginia. Even if they're working in the mines or selling hot dogs from a wagon. Ought to block the freeways. Keep the damn fools out. Do them a favor. Shoot them in the legs if they won't take warning."

"You do Jenny and Spinneran a favor and let them get away?" Bosco asked, never having been told how it happened but knowing anyway.

Whistler looked a little sad and a little surprised. "Hey, Bosco, they were lovers." Then he looked out the window again.

"You want some coffee?" Bosco offered. Whistler didn't answer.

He was eating despair and drinking melancholy, Bosco thought. If he kept it up, he'd go wandering around the streets and alleys all night long. And one night, Bosco feared, Whistler would meet death in some alley or all-night movie house and wouldn't take the trouble to run away.

"You know when I first suspected Nell was up to no good?" Whistler said, giving the true reason for his blues away.

"When was that?"

"When I saw her coming across that boulevard wearing a fur stole and a felt hat when the Santa Ana winds were blowing. She had to have been coming from an all-nighter, not making it out of some man's bed until long past noon. Classy broads don't wear the next day what they wore the night before."

Isaac Canaan came in with a rush of cool wind. All the night birds lifted their heads as though it carried with it the smell of home.

"We should keep all the poor sonsofbitches out of La-La Land," Whistler said by way of greeting.

"The harder you try to keep them out, the harder they'll try to get in," Canaan said as he slid in and settled down.

"This is the promised land," Bosco said.

"This is where the coconuts grow," Whistler said, looking out the window again. "I need a miracle. It doesn't have to be a big miracle. A little miracle will do."

"Like what?"

"Like everybody in the world finds what they want at home, so La-La Land can close up and turn out the lights."

"That would be a very large miracle. A very large miracle, indeed."

There was a sudden rise in the wind that made the big plate-glass window buckle and sway. Then the cooling rain poured down.

"By God," Whistler said, looking at the drops running down the pane, "there's a miracle if I ever saw one."

"Predictable," Bosco said. "Bitchie-Boo changed her boots."

Bestselling Crime

☐ Moonspender	Jonathan Gash	£2.50
☐ Shake Hands For Ever	Ruth Rendell	£2.50
☐ A Guilty Thing Surprised	Ruth Rendell	£2.50
☐ The Tree of Hands	Ruth Rendell	£2.50
☐ Wexford: An Omnibus	Ruth Rendell	£5.95
☐ Evidence to Destroy	Margaret Yorke	£2.50
☐ No One Rides For Free	Larry Beinhart	£2.95
☐ In La La Land We Trust	Robert Campbell	£2.50
☐ Suspects	William J. Caunitz	£2.95
☐ Blood on the Moon	James Ellroy	£2.50
☐ Roses Are Dead	Loren D. Estleman	£2.50
☐ The Body in the Billiard Room	H.R.F. Keating	£2.50
☐ Rough Cider	Peter Lovesey	£2.50

Prices and other details are liable to change

ARROW BOOKS, BOOKSERVICE BY POST, PO BOX 29, DOUGLAS, ISLE OF MAN, BRITISH ISLES

NAME. . . . .

ADDRESS. . . . .

. . . .

. . . .

Please enclose a cheque or postal order made out to Arrow Books Ltd. for the amount due and allow the following for postage and packing.

U.K. CUSTOMERS: Please allow 22p per book to a maximum of £3.00.

B.F.P.O. & EIRE: Please allow 22p per book to a maximum of £3.00

OVERSEAS CUSTOMERS: Please allow 22p per book.

Whilst every effort is made to keep prices low it is sometimes necessary to increase cover prices at short notice. Arrow Books reserve the right to show new retail prices on covers which may differ from those previously advertised in the text or elsewhere.